MEGAN WHALEN TURNER

THICK AS THIEVES

A QUEEN'S THIEF NOVEL

GREENWILLOW BOOKS

An Imprint of HarperCollins *Publishers*

Thick as Thieves
Copyright © 2017 by Megan Whalen Turner
Map illustrations copyright © 2017 by Maxime Plasse

The text of this book is set in 12-point ITC Galliard.
Book design by Paul Zakris

Library of Congress Cataloging-in-Publication Data

Names: Turner, Megan Whalen, author.
Title: Thick as thieves : a Queen's thief novel / Megan Whalen Turner.
Description: New York, NY : Greenwillow Books, an imprint of HarperCollins Publishers, [2017] | Series: Queen's thief; 5 | Summary: "Kamet, a secretary and slave to his Mede master, has the ambition and the means to become one of the most powerful people in the Empire. But with a whispered warning the future he envisioned is wrenched away, and he is forced onto a very different path" — Provided by publisher.
Identifiers: LCCN 2016047028 | ISBN 9780062568243 (hardcover)
Subjects: | CYAC: Adventure and adventurers—Fiction. | Slavery—Fiction. | Secretaries—Fiction. | Kings, queens, rulers, etc.—Fiction. | Fantasy.
Classification: LCC PZ7.T85565 Tg 2017 | DDC [Fic]—dc23
LC record available at https://lccn.loc.gov/2016047028

17 18 19 20 21 PC/LSCH 10 9 8 7 6 5 4 3 2 1
First Edition

GREENWILLOW BOOKS
An Imprint of HarperCollins Publishers

For my editor, Virginia Duncan,
one of those guiding stars
whose influence is all the more
profound for being so often unseen

If a man who claims to see the future is a fool,

how much more so, the man who believes he can control it?

We think we steer the ship of fate,

but all of us are guided by unseen stars.

—Enoclitus

CHAPTER ONE

*I*t was midday and the passageway quiet and cool. The stone walls kept out the heat while the openings near the high ceilings admitted some of the sun's fierce light. Midday, and the houseboy was gone on an errand, probably stealing a nap somewhere, so I was alone at the door to my master's apartments, holding my head in my hand and cursing myself for an idiot. I was not prone to stupidity, but I'd made a foolish mistake and was paying the price. My knees shook and I would have leaned against the wall for support, but it had recently been whitewashed and the blood would stain—I did not want to be reminded of this moment every time I passed until the stones were whitened again.

Sighing, I tried to think through the fire in my head and my shoulder. I wanted a place where I could withdraw until the pain had eased, but my usual retreat was an alcove off the main room of my master's apartments—on the other side of the door in front of me. I was absolutely not going through that door until summoned. I'd invited disaster already that day by offering my master an evidently entirely inappropriate glass of remchik. The bottle of remchik was smashed, the glasses were smashed, and, judging by the pain in my shoulder and my side, the small statuette of Kamia Shesmegah formerly resting on his writing desk was smashed as well—from which I gathered that the emperor had not, in fact, offered my master the governorship of Hemsha.

I rubbed my head and checked my hand to see if it was still bleeding. It was, but not much.

In my defense, it had not been unreasonable on my part to assume that my master would become governor. He was still the nephew of the emperor and the brother of the emperor's chosen heir, the prince Naheelid. The governorship of Hemsha, a minor coastal province with a single small harbor, was not outside his expectations. I am the first to admit that he has a habit of overreaching, and I had been very quietly relieved that he had set his sights so low.

After the debacle in Attolia, he'd taken us to rusticate on his family estate. We'd hidden there for more than a year while the laughter died down, my master fighting with his wife the entire time—she had been, unsurprisingly, unenthusiastic about his attempts to marry the Attolian queen. Finally, we had returned to the capital, where my master found that even his oldest friends had turned their backs on him. When he'd applied for the post of governor, I'd thought he was conceding defeat. I'd thought that if Hemsha was far away from the capital, at least it was equally far away from his wife. I would have sworn on my aching shoulder that there was no reason for him to be denied such a reasonable request. Which is why, when he returned with one of his cousins, I had been waiting for him with a tray of glasses and a newly opened bottle of remchik, ready for congratulations.

"I so hate presumption in a slave," I'd heard his cousin say, as I crept out of the room.

I sighed again. I hated being beaten. Nothing could make me feel so stupid and so angry at myself, and on top of everything else, I'd have to deal with the smirks and pitying remarks of other slaves. It did my authority no good to be seen with my face covered in blood, but I really couldn't go back into my master's apartments.

"Kamet?"

I had already bowed and begged pardon before I realized that it was Laela beside me. She reached to touch my shoulder and I flinched.

"Dear Kamet," she said. "Is it more than the face?"

I nodded. My shoulder wasn't going to heal for some time, I could tell.

Laela had been one of my master's dancing girls. When she fell out of favor, she'd asked if I could do anything for her—

afraid of where she might be sold to next. I had persuaded my master that she should stay with the household as a matron over the other girls, and she was one of the few slaves I could trust to do me a favor. "Come to my room," she suggested.

Shaking my head slowly, I said, "He will call me back." He always did, sooner or later. I needed to be closer than her rooms, which were deep in the slaves' dormitories.

"I'll make sure the houseboys know where you are," she said, and took me gently by the arm to lead me down the hall.

As matron, Laela had a narrow room much the same size as the alcove where I slept. With the curtain pulled across the doorway, it was almost dark inside. She watched me lie down, then went to fetch a bowl with cool water and a cup to dip in it. After I'd had a drink, she soaked a cloth in the bowl and laid it on my face, wiping away the blood. It made her bedding wet, and I mumbled an apology.

"It will dry," she said. "Faster than your face will heal. Whatever did you do?"

"Offered him a glass of remchik."

She made a puzzled sound, though she and I both knew that slaves were beaten for all sorts of reasons and sometimes for no reason at all.

"He didn't get the governorship of Hemsha."

"Ah," said Laela. She wasn't a dancing girl anymore; she

was as experienced as I was in listening to rumor and sorting out its meanings. "Well, you couldn't have known," she told me, but I didn't agree.

"I'm a fool," I said.

"You handle him well," Laela reminded me. "Don't blame yourself."

Her words helped as much as the cool cloth on my face. My expertise had been painfully acquired over the years, but it was mostly reliable. I did usually handle my master better than I had that day, and I was proud of my skill.

"I should see to the girls. They'll need to know he's in a mood," Laela said. "I'll come back if he sends for you." And she went away, leaving me to rest while I could.

When Laela came to fetch me, it was already dark. She lifted a lamp to my face and winced.

"You look like a pomegranate," she told me.

"Thank you so much," I said. My voice was mocking, but she knew I was grateful. I was stiff as well as sore, and she had to steady me while I got to my feet. She walked me as far as the entrance to the dormitory, then left me to make my own way.

"Kamet, you look like a pomegranate," my master said.

I said nothing.

"Get your clothes off so I can see the rest of the damage."

Slowly, I peeled my tunic off, in order to allow him to inspect his handiwork. He always did, after a beating, partly to be sure that any serious injury was seen to, and partly just to admire the bruises. When he was done with me, I was shaking and sick, my skin prickled with a cold sweat, but he had wrapped my chest and shoulder in bandages and given me a dose of lethium to put me to sleep. He helped me over to the cot in my office, then gently covered me with a blanket, checking to see that I was as comfortable as possible before he went back to his own sleeping room.

I moved very gingerly for the next few weeks, in part because of my healing body and in part because my master was still in a dangerous mood. It was best to stay out of his sight as much as possible until his temper evened out. I kept the curtain pulled across my alcove, though it was stifling in the small space, with no movement of the air.

The quarterly accounts had come in, and they kept me busy. The allowance for household costs was delivered to me four times a year, mostly on the basis of these accounts, and they had to be examined thoroughly. I oversaw all of my master's finances, not just for the palace household but for his outlying estates as well. His slaves and servants answered to me, and I in turn to him. Reading between the lines, I suspected that the steward at the family estate was at his wit's end trying to keep my master's wife's expenses in check. I might have had some sympathy for him—she was very strong-minded—but I'd been unimpressed by what I had seen of his management. I decided to cover the added expense for the quarter, but I thought that I would replace him soon. I could move a man I had in mind from one of my master's smaller estates. The incompetent steward was a free man—he could be turned out without the trouble of selling him.

When I heard the houseboy open the apartment door, I twitched the curtain on my alcove aside. My master was out and Kep, the houseboy, could only be coming in to speak to me.

"It's Rakra, Kamet, about his pay."

I nodded and the houseboy showed Rakra in. A burly man in his thirties, he'd been a houseman on the family estate and had returned with us to the capital. In the palace, he had little to do to earn his pay and had perhaps too much free time to sample the pleasures of the city.

Rakra looked me over, his eyes lingering on my bruised face, and I felt my own eyes narrow. Pomegranate? I wondered, but he didn't say it, just snorted. Honestly, I looked a little more like an overripe melon at that point— purple and green.

"I'll need more money," Rakra said. "Same amount as before."

Quite a few of my master's palace servants came to me for advances on their pay. I made loans out of the discretionary funds in my budget and charged them a fee, deducted from their pay at the end of the quarter—in this way making a bit of money for myself. There was an embroidered bag holding all my savings sitting in my master's cashbox under my desk. Unlike Rakra, most of the people in need of a loan arrived at my threshold with some embarrassment, not with bold demands.

"Better our master doesn't know about our business, eh?" Rakra suggested.

"Ah," I said.

This was exactly the sort of loss of discipline I hated to deal with after a beating. Rakra assumed my loan-making was a secret. He'd heard a rumor that I was in disfavor and thought he could threaten me with its revelation. In my experience, crooked men assume others are crooked as well, and I was reconsidering Rakra's character. He opened his mouth to say something even more unpleasant, I was sure, but I held up a hand to stop him.

"Very well," I said. "I will take what you owe from next quarter's pay and charge you no fee." I bent under the desk to lift the cashbox, and opened it with the key on a tie around my waist. I counted three coins into his meaty palm while Rakra looked pleased with himself.

"I'm sure my master is well aware of the payday loans," I told him. This voided the power of his threat, and was also true. There was no reason my master should not know of my loans, and I had always assumed he did. Rakra's eyes narrowed, belatedly wary, but I dismissed him with a wave of my hand toward the door and looked back down at my work. Rakra hesitated, but I went on ignoring him until he left. I could have discharged him from my master's service—I had that kind of authority—but Rakra had been hired by the steward at the family estate, the very one whose accounts were out of order. I resolved to check the expenses more thoroughly, and I did not want Rakra returning in disgrace to the estates too quickly, as it might alert the steward to my suspicions. I would soon know if there was a larger problem to address. If there was, I would bring it to my master's attention and possibly he would be pleased with me.

Once the accounts had been attended to and the money disbursed, there were housekeeping arrangements to be made. My master's rooms were growing shabby, and if we were not to be displaced to Hemsha, he would expect them to be updated. The lingering ache in my shoulder reminded me that I needed to find him another statue of Shesmegah. I called in various merchants to discuss new rugs and furnishings, doing as much as I could from my little office. The tradespeople had representatives in the palace and they were wise enough to show no sign they noticed my bruises. Unlike Rakra, they knew the authority I wielded over their purses.

Laela stopped by to fill me in on some of the stories

circulating among the lower echelons of the palace—the laborers and slaves. They knew little and made up more. She told me that Abashad had been named general and admitted to the Imperial Council of War. She said she thought the poor little country of Attolia was doomed, but that was not news. Our emperor continued to pretend he did not mean to invade the Little Peninsula and had browbeaten the Attolians into exchanging ambassadors, but all of the city-states there, Eddis and Sounis as well as Attolia, were doomed. We all knew it. I think Laela had a friend among the servants set aside for the Attolian ambassador. She told me that Ornon was a pleasant enough man who didn't harass the slaves or otherwise increase their labors.

"Little countries get eaten up by larger ones," I said with a shrug. "It is the nature of the world. They will be better off once they are integrated into the empire."

I used some of my funds to purchase a bracelet for Laela to thank her for her good turn for me, because people like Laela and me cannot leave debts outstanding.

After my bruises faded, I resumed my other business for my master. Not everything could be arranged from my office, and anyway, I liked to exercise my privilege to go in and out of the palace at my own discretion. My master's previous secretary, who had trained me as a child, had warned me that I must not spend every day looking into ledgers by the

light of a smoking lamp or my eyesight would suffer. My
eyesight is poor, but probably would have been worse had I
not taken his advice to go out of doors as often as possible.

In fact, if my eyesight had been better, the whole course
of this narrative might have been different. I would have seen
the Attolian waiting ahead of me in an empty hallway of the
palace in time to dodge into one of the side passages used
by the menial slaves and servants. Instead, I approached,
unaware that he was an Attolian until it was too late to
change direction without drawing his attention. Thinking
that we had met by chance, I kept my eyes down and moved
a little faster.

He was a very large Attolian, by size and dress a soldier.
When I saw him casting glances up and down the passage to
see who was nearby, my stomach sank. My master had tried
to usurp the Attolian throne. His failure had endeared him
neither to his wife nor to the emperor. He may have been
a laughingstock in the emperor's palace, but I doubted that
anyone in Attolia was laughing.

"Kamet," said the Attolian with a firm nod of greeting.
This was growing worse and worse. I didn't think anyone in
Attolia knew my name, and if this soldier did, he probably
also knew that I was the one who had set fire to our rooms to
create the distraction that would allow my master to escape
the fortress at Ephrata. Our meeting in this hallway was not
an accident.

The soldier stooped to bring his lips close enough to my ear to say very quietly, "My king blames your master for the loss of his hand."

That, too, was an issue—and a perfectly reasonable sentiment on the part of the Attolian king. The Thief of Eddis had been arrested in Attolia's capital city, and my master told me he had deliberately stoked the queen of Attolia's rage, hoping to prompt war between the two countries. Attolia had exercised an old-fashioned option for dealing with thieves, and my master had been quite pleased. Only now, that same Eddisian thief was the king of Attolia— the queen had married him to save her throne, choosing him over my master. Oh, my poor face, I thought, and oh, my poor ribs—they'd just recently stopped hurting every time I tried to stand up or bend over to tighten my sandal. I could only assume the Attolian meant to exact a petty revenge on my person. It wasn't my fault that my master was an enemy of his king, but I doubted that mattered.

At least the Attolian was still talking. The longer he talked, the better my chances that someone might come along. Thank the eternal gods he was a chatty Attolian, or so I thought at the time.

"My king wants your master to suffer the loss of *his* right hand," the Attolian was saying, and I admit I was distracted as he grabbed my wrist and it took me a minute to realize that he was speaking metaphorically. He meant me—I was my master's right hand. It dawned on me that I might be facing something far, far worse than a casual beating in one of the back passages of the emperor's palace. I tried to pry his fingers apart as I looked desperately up and down the corridor for help. There was no one, not even a blurry sign of movement in the distance that would indicate a witness was coming.

Surely the Attolians understood it was uncivil for a guest to beat to death someone else's property in a deserted hallway of his host's palace? Maybe not. They weren't very civilized, and it would be a significant revenge, petty, but intensely disruptive. I was an expensive slave and my master relied on me—his entire estate was going to fall into chaos until he found a replacement secretary—but when all was said and done, I was still just a slave. Maybe the Attolians would pay some small percentage of my worth to my master as an apology and in so doing add a little more insult to injury. Given my master's uncertain position at the emperor's court, they might get away with it. The Attolian king obviously had a deep well of spite and I would have appreciated his low cunning more if I hadn't thought the Attolian was about to wring my neck.

"Meet me at the Rethru docks after sunset," he said.

That sentence made so little sense that I stopped picking at his fingers to stare up at his face. I was close enough, as he had me by the wrist, to see him quite clearly. He was a typical

Attolian: sandy-brown hair, a broad face, light-colored eyes. Altogether he had a simple, straightforward look to him, and he seemed perfectly serious. He put his hands to my shoulders and stared back down at me, as if he thought I was stupid or didn't understand his heavily accented Mede. He could have just spoken in Attolian, but instead, he used very simple sentences. "I will help you escape your master. Come to the Rethru docks. Be there after sunset. And I will take you to Attolia. You will be free in Attolia. Do you understand?"

It was like being lectured by an earnest, oversized child.

I realized my mouth was open and shut it. I nodded. "Rethru docks," I repeated after him.

"After dark. Can you be there?"

I nodded again. Certainly I could get to the Rethru docks after dark. The Attolian nodded back, then checked the corridor again and hurried away.

I watched him go, my knees weak with relief. I staggered to the nearest alcove and slipped behind the large urn standing in the center of it. I wrapped my arms around myself and had a long, if quiet, laugh. My ribs hurt, but it was worth it. It had been a difficult few weeks, and it was good to laugh again.

I could be free in Attolia. If only I could have shared the joke with my master, but he wouldn't have seen the humor just then. Another time, I would have told him and he and

I would have laughed until we fell down. I could be free in Attolia—a place more backward than anywhere I have ever known, with its stinking sewers and its smoking furnaces and its preening idiot aristocrats. Gods support me, they were still memorizing all their poetry because none of them knew how to read. The only beautiful thing in the whole country was the queen, and she had sold herself into a marriage with the Eddisian Thief, the very one whose hand she had cut off. There was a match made in hell.

As a slave in the emperor's palace I had authority over all of my master's other slaves and most of his free men. I had my own money in my master's cashbox. I had a library of my own, a collection of texts in my alcove that I carefully packed into their own case whenever my master moved households. I not only could read and write, I could read and write in most of the significant languages of the empire. My master had paid good money for it to be so. Someday he meant to make a gift of me to his brother, and then, as the next emperor's personal slave, I would be one of the wealthiest and most powerful men in all the empire. I wouldn't have taken the Attolians' offer even if I'd believed it was sincere— and I didn't. They meant to slice my throat and toss me in a sewer, I was sure.

When my amusement passed, leaving my ribs aching, I shook my head at the self-aggrandizement of the Attolians, and headed back to my master's apartments. There is freedom in this life and there is power, and I was ambitious for the latter. I looked forward to the day I would be in my master's confidence again—I would tell him about the Attolian, and he and I would laugh together. In the meantime, I thought, I would be anywhere that evening but out on the Rethru docks.

I was still smiling when I saw Laela ahead of me. I knew her first by her robe. It had been a gift from our master and was dyed a deep blue that was expensive and unusual. I made out her face only as she drew nearer. Normally as warm toned as myself, she was sickly pale. She raised a hand to her lips as she approached, and silently she turned me around to pull me through a curtained entrance into the nearby serviceway. We stood in that narrower connecting passage, the slatted roof just above our heads admitting sunlight that striped Laela's face and clothes. When she'd checked to be sure we were alone, she leaned close. I could smell the cosmetics on her skin, and when she spoke, I was reminded of the Attolian's warm breath on my ear.

"Nahuseresh is dead," she whispered.

For the second time that day a statement was too nonsensical to understand.

"Poison," Laela said, looking at my face for some comprehension.

Dead. She meant, murdered.

"His meeting was cut short. He came back to the apartments and called for the doctor but when the doctor came, he was already gone." She turned my unresisting body away from her. "Go," she said, putting her hands to my shoulders and pushing me down the serviceway. "Go."

I turned back, reaching for her hand, but she pulled it free. Her face was in shadow and she put both hands to her cheeks, as if to hide her tears. "Save yourself, Kamet," she whispered.

I nodded as tears pricked my own eyes and started moving, one stumbling foot in front of the other.

"When?" I asked, over my shoulder.

"Just after the noon bell," she said as she, too, turned away, pulling the scarf at her shoulder to hood her face as she passed back through the curtain.

I needed to make a plan, but my thoughts ran in all directions at once, like rats in a grain store when the door is thrown open. I considered the Attolians—I'd already guessed they meant to kill me, not set me free. Had they meant to use my disappearance to implicate me in the murder of my master? It made no sense. They'd wanted me to leave that night and while they might have wanted to murder Nahuseresh, they couldn't have carried it out. I had been free to run errands in the city only because my master had meant to spend the entire morning with his brother. When his powerful friends had failed him, he had staked everything on the support of Naheelid, and he had been absolutely certain his brother would help him. If what Laela had said was true—if my master had returned directly from that meeting—then he had been fatally mistaken.

My master's brother was served by the emperor's own servants, his food provided from the emperor's own kitchens. The slaves who oversaw this process had served the emperor for years, and as most, if not all, would die with him— sacrificed at his funeral and buried in his tomb—they were fanatically loyal. There were only two men who could have poisoned my master—his brother, or the emperor himself.

The reversal of my master's plans in Attolia—that had not just been a personal humiliation. My master had showered the Attolian queen in gold, the emperor's gold, and then had nothing to show for it. The emperor had committed troops on my master's recommendation, troops that had been overwhelmed by the combined forces of Eddis and Attolia. Afterward there had been painfully expensive goodwill gestures to placate the Greater Powers of the Continent, alarmed as they were to find the emperor encroaching on what they thought of as their territory. It had been in every way a disaster, and every bit of it laid at my master's door. He had since schemed tirelessly to restore his position and he'd failed. Failed utterly.

I cast about for any possible alternative. My master could

have been poisoned earlier, but he would have died more slowly. I had eaten dinner with him the night before, and I was fine. Neither of us had eaten in the morning—my master had ignored his breakfast tray, as he often did, and I couldn't touch his leftovers if he hadn't eaten first. He would hardly have taken anything on his way to meet with his brother. I retraced what I knew, reordering my knowledge, trying to deny my conclusions, but they were too clear. It was not as if the emperor hadn't poisoned people before. There had been a number of imperial dinners that were the stuff of nightmares.

Trying to move more quickly, but not so quickly as to attract attention, I was still turning at random, distancing myself from my master's apartments.

And from Laela.

When a man is murdered, his slaves are tortured. If any confess, then all are executed whether they share in the guilt or not. No one will buy them and they can hardly be freed—what a temptation that would put before the enslaved population. In the case of a poisoning, where the administration of the poison is unclear, the slaves are put to death on principle. The Medes fear little in quite the way they fear their own slaves.

The torture begins with the most intimate servants, the valet, the secretary. If a slave implicates another in his confession, the rest of the slaves will be fiercely interrogated as well, but if not, there may be no torture for the others, just death. After the recent beating, I would be doubly suspect, and if anyone had seen Laela warning me, she would be in greater danger as well. That it was the emperor who was guilty, that everyone would know it, changed nothing. We would be arrested and tortured not just into confessing, but also into implicating our fellow slaves—all of us judged an infection in the body of the empire, to be cut out at any cost. The houseboys, eight and twelve years old. Hormud, my master's cook, and Mirad, his valet. The men in the stables, the dancing girls. None of them could leave the emperor's palace. Of all my master's slaves, only I had that privilege.

The only thing I could do for them was go. If I escaped, blame might fall on me alone. I might be a loose end that the emperor would tolerate—my successful flight bolstering an official story that I was involved in a conspiracy to murder my master, that the emperor had nothing to do with his death. A chance to die quickly instead of slowly was all I could give them.

So I walked on.

I hadn't known my master was in such danger. I blamed myself for that. A man like my master is not eliminated without hints and foretellings running through the palace first, like a fracture through glass before it breaks, but I had been cooped up in my little alcove hiding my bruises. Had my master's brother ordered his death, or had the emperor? Eternal gods, I thought, what if the emperor had turned against his heir and both he and my master had been killed? I shuddered at the chaos that could be coming to the entire empire and stumbled over my own feet.

Laela had said that my master had died not long after noon. I'd heard the great bell ring just after I spoke to the Attolian—while I was laughing at him from the alcove. Who was laughing now? I thought, before I wrenched my attention back to the matter at hand. The wheels of the palace turn slowly, but they would be turning. I had some time, but not much, before the doctor would call Nahuseresh's death poisoning and officially inform the emperor, and then the guard would be sent to arrest all of my master's slaves. I needed to leave the palace before all the gates were closed to keep me in.

I touched the pocket on my belt. I'd visited the tailor in the city that morning to order a robe for my master, one he would now never wear, and I had the money left over from that. My own savings, in the little bag inside my master's cashbox, were out of reach. My scrolls, my own small damaged statue of Shesmegah, goddess of mercy . . . I dared not return to the apartments to collect any of my things, and I knew it, but my thoughts kept circling back to my little office alcove. I wanted so much to be seated at my slanted desktop, with my cot behind me and my account books in front of me, my only problem in life my master's temporary dissatisfaction. My treacherous feet kept slowing down and I understood the impulse of small animals that hold themselves motionless until they are eaten. I felt a kinship for the rabbit sitting perfectly still, hoping that the lion would somehow pass him by.

I lifted my chin, forced myself to move faster. I didn't want to draw attention, and it was not like me to creep. I needed to move more briskly about my business. I passed a few other slaves without any acknowledgment, and they deferentially dropped their eyes.

The serviceways, narrow and only partially covered, lay between the walls of various apartments and ran throughout the palace in an endless warren, their sand floors silencing the footsteps of slaves and servants who carried out the work of the palace out of sight of its privileged inhabitants. This was where the slop jars were carried, where the laundry went on its way from the beautiful apartments to the washhouses and back again. It was an easy place to get lost, with as many twists and turns as there were dead ends, but I had known this labyrinth since I was a child newly brought to the palace by my master. I was only an apprentice to his secretary then and had had plenty of time to learn every path through it.

I passed into darkness where the passage was roofed over and then back into the sun as I turned this way and that, choosing the narrowest, darkest, and least-used route that would carry me toward one of the work gates where the wagons came in and out, carrying all that was needed for the inhabitants of the city inside a city that was the emperor's palace. There were several such gates, but I wanted the one nearest the stables and the emperor's zoo, with its cages of lions and wild dogs and other animals. I'd visited it often over the years, feeling sorry for the sad-eyed gazelles tapping nervously about, so near to their predators. There was a giraffe and several zebras, as well as lions and cheetahs. There had been a white bear once, a gift from the Braelings in the north, but it had died in the heat. My mind was wandering again, and I forced it back to the present.

The narrow passages grew wider and became alleys between separate buildings. Where there had been apartments and gardens on the other side of the high walls around me, there were now storage sheds and dormitories. I came to open ground near the enclosure where a placid giraffe stood chewing as he gazed off into space. Between the animals in the zoo and the working animals in the stables, wagon after wagon of dung had to be hauled out every day, usually at about noon when the morning cleanout was completed. I didn't use this gate often, but I would be allowed to pass through without question and probably without any notice so long as there had been no news of my master's death yet, no call for my arrest.

Taking a deep breath, I stepped out toward the open gate.

"Kamet," one of the guards called like a curse out of a clear blue sky.

Even before I recognized him, I smiled politely. Well trained, I would have smiled so at my executioner.

"On your way out again already?" he asked. He'd been at the main east gate earlier that morning and we'd said hello to each other as I'd left to see the tailor. I brought up the story I'd prepared, just in case.

"More orders for the feast my master plans for the emperor's birthday," I said.

"Is it going to be as big as the one he sponsored before you went abroad?"

"Bigger," I said.

"Will you get me onto the guard duty for it? We ate like kings at the last one."

I promised that I would, the lie easy on my lips, and waved a good-bye to him as I passed through the gate.

I crossed the wide boulevard that surrounded the palace and headed directly into the narrow streets on the other side. In a few steps I knew I was out of his sight. I still hurried around several corners and deeper into side streets before I breathed a sigh of relief. Then I made my way to the tailor's.

CHAPTER TWO

"Gessiret," I explained apologetically, "my master says that one set of robes is insufficient. He will want two."

Gessiret looked at me suspiciously, but I was used to that and so was he. Tradesmen have few means to force their powerful clients to pay their debts, and no one was more mistreated financially than the tailors. They are so dependent on their trade with the wealthy they can't afford to offend even the most delinquent clients.

"Two?" Gessiret asked.

"Indeed, he will give you twice the sum we agreed upon."

"Very well," said Gessiret. "He is good to bring us his business." He was still waiting for the bad news.

"It is a large sum, and my master will pay for the robes when they are completed."

Gessiret nodded fatalistically. "And he would like returned

the money that you paid me this morning?"

I nodded back at him, trying to look sympathetic. Gessiret knew I was lying but assumed it was on my master's behalf. He thought my master had decided to put his cash to better use. Gessiret could refuse to return the coins, but he would offend Nahuseresh—and Nahuseresh was the rare client who paid his bills more often than not. Two robes was a substantial commission. Sighing, he reached into his cashbox. Together we nodded our heads and rolled our eyes at the ways of our betters—me knowing exactly how he felt, him thinking he knew how I did.

I agreed upon a meaningless date for the robes to be completed and left. I had crossed the city to get to Gessiret's little shop, focused on nothing but retrieving the money I'd paid him earlier that morning. Now that I had it, I had no reason not to face the truth I had been hiding from: I had nowhere to go.

I needed to leave the city, but I could think of no way out.

The imperial city of Ianna-Ir sits on the flat plain of the wide, slow-moving river Ianna. The city itself is surrounded by its famous copper-topped walls, many times the height of a man and wide enough at the top to allow two chariots to pass in opposite directions. Except for the riverfront and a smaller, unfortified area on the opposite bank, outside the walls of Ianna-Ir, there are only open fields, irrigated by the river to provide food. There is nothing else for miles.

As a slave, I could hardly ask a farmer with a cart for a ride out to the wilderness or downriver to the Ianna's delta to board a ship. I was entrusted by my master with the freedom to move around the city, but not to leave it. The guards at the walls of the palace were used to seeing me come and go, but the guards at the gates of the city were not. I might cover the chain at my neck, but in my straight shift, with my legs bare, I was obviously a slave, allowed to pass through those outer walls only in the company of my master. If I approached the gate alone, I would be stopped and then returned to the palace to be tortured.

I thought again about where I might hide inside the city walls. I had very little time and no one to turn to. I had done business with many of the merchants of Ianna-Ir, but no honest man would break the emperor's law to hide me. I knew dishonest men as well, quite a few, in fact, but they wouldn't risk the emperor's wrath except for sums of money I didn't have. The money from the tailor wasn't enough to buy me any safety. It probably wasn't good for anything except a last meal if I bought it quickly.

My mind began to fill with visions of the rack and spikes, of instruments heated until they were red hot, of the barbed lash. These were the thoughts I'd tried to bury with memories of the Braelings' white bear, and imaginary plans for a feast, and concern for my master's *other* slaves, but all my other thoughts were retreating in the face of this remorseless horror. The sweat on my skin stung—I tried to breathe and heard myself gasping instead. I had to get out. I told myself I was too well dressed, much too respectable to be taken for an escaping slave—I had an embroidered shift and a gold chain on my neck, after all. I decided to go to the Iannis-Sa gate and try to brazen my way through. I would attach myself to the party of a wealthy man and hope to pass unquestioned. I started toward the south side of the city.

"Kamet of Nahuseresh!" bellowed a voice behind me.

I should have gone to the Attolians to get my throat cut. At least it would have been faster.

I took one step, but it was too late to run. I faced around, expecting to see the palace guard and instead found a single burly older man in a handsome robe, imposing and obviously wealthy. He was also obviously a former soldier. He still had the bearing and the scars—he was missing his right eye— but he was certainly not the palace guard, nor one of the city's Enforcers of the Imperial Peace.

"You *are* Kamet of Nahuseresh?" the man asked, looking me up and down.

I admitted it, bowing as I did so. I had no idea who he was.

He hesitated, almost as if he were the one making up a story. "I am a—a wine merchant," he said. He didn't look like a wine merchant. "And—and your master says I should arrange some deliveries with you."

Mystified, I looked around. There was no wineshop near.

"My warehouse is at the dock," the man said, as if daring me to contradict him. The sweeping black terror that had flooded my heart a moment before was receding, leaving me weak in the knees, with darkness crowding at the edge of my vision. The merchant almost glowed in contrast, and the noise of the street faded to nothing. "Come along with me and inspect the casks," he said. Dazed but obedient, I followed.

He hired a chair. I do remember thinking that no one would expect to find a fugitive slave traveling beside a chair, head down and well behaved—that the merchant would take me through the city walls to the riverfront, and then I must devise a way past the secondary walls upriver and downriver of the city limits. But then my thoughts scattered and did not return. They churned against one another like waves in a storm and the darkness at the edge of my vision didn't fade. Meanwhile, the merchant gave conflicting directions to the chair men, and we wandered through the back alleys of the warehouse district by the river until, just as we reached an open boulevard, he called a halt. With his hands on the elaborately carved armrests of the chair, he twisted to look down at me and said, "Never mind. I've forgotten another appointment. I will contact you later." And he left me standing in the street, at a loss.

I kept moving only because it was dangerous to draw attention by standing still. I continued down the boulevard and found myself at the Rethru docks, of all places. If only I could believe the Attolians might be there to help me when the sun went down. It was busy, with the smaller riverboats tied two and three deep to the stone quays along the water. There were ferrymen in even smaller boats plying their trade, carrying people and packages across the water to the unfortified part of the city on the far side. Not a few slaves had escaped the city by waiting until dark and slipping into the water, but I couldn't swim. When my master and I had fled Attolia, he had come up with the plan to swim out to a boat offshore. I'd begged him to leave me behind, but he'd insisted on pulling me through the water, determined to leave nothing that belonged to him behind for the Attolian queen. I'd swallowed half the sea that night, and after the crew lifted us on board the larger ship waiting for us, I'd vomited it out on the deck until I was too weak to stand. Even thinking of going in the water made my stomach heave.

The ferries wouldn't take me in daylight, not without permission from my master. They might take me at night, when they had less chance of being seen breaking the law, but by nightfall I would be notorious. Ten times the money I had in my pocket wouldn't get me across the river. And the sun was lower in the sky than I expected. Somehow the first part of the afternoon was already gone. I couldn't afford to stand there in the open like I'd been turned to stone. If I didn't find somewhere out of sight, I wouldn't make it until dark. I would try to slip into one of the warehouses to hide among the bales and barrels. When it was dark, I could . . . sneak into one of the ships? Steal one of the rowing boats? Drown myself? I'd have to think of something while I waited.

Turning away from the water, I found myself nose to chest with the Attolian.

Again, well trained, I stepped back with a bow and an immediate apology.

The Attolian leaned in over me. "I told you after sunset," he said quietly. "After dark." Then, after a hesitation—"I did say after dark?"

After noon, after dark, the phrases are almost identical, and it was an easy mistake for a foreigner to have made. He hadn't heard of my master's death, that was clear. I seized my opportunity and stared at him helplessly, begging him with my eyes to save me. Should I have said, "Yes, you did say after dark, but my master has been poisoned, and it will be more convenient for me to run away right now?" I still thought he meant to murder me, not free me, but I didn't care. If this man meant to take me out of the city before disposing of me, I had a much better chance of escaping one Attolian soldier than of escaping the combined forces of the palace guard and the city's enforcers. If he could be fooled into helping me for even a little while, Gessiret's money might see me to a chance at least of escaping the emperor's torture chambers.

I cleared my throat. "You said, 'after noon,'" I whispered, the first of my many lies.

"Oh," he said, and then, may gods bless him forever, he rose to the occasion. He slid his hand into his purse and tossed me a coin, like any man offering a charity to a slave. I bowed over it as he moved by me.

"Follow me," he said quietly. "Pay the fee for the cheapest entrance." He smiled as if he were accepting my apology for bumping him, then passed on. I waited until he was a little ways ahead, and then, heart in mouth, I went after him, drawing on all my years of practice to give an appearance of calm that I didn't feel.

We went to the theater.

If it hadn't been a matter of life and death—mine—I would have been amused. Alone, the Attolian wouldn't have drawn attention in the cosmopolitan mix of the city, and were I not being hunted, I could have disappeared into a number of places where slaves are welcome so long as they have at least a little coin in their pockets. An Attolian soldier and a high-status slave could go nowhere together without arousing interest—except the theater. In the open ground just below the stage, free men and slaves frequently mixed. I bought my ticket and followed the Attolian in, finding a space to stand with a few other slaves not far from him.

It was a cheap production. The amphitheater near the docks didn't cater to a discerning crowd. It hosted comedies and variety shows for those whose taste matched their finances. It had the usual stone benches of a more prestigious theater, but the semicircular space below the stage was unusually large. The least expensive tickets would let anyone stand there, and slaves and the poorest of the free people in the city packed themselves in. It made it almost impossible to hear the actors if you were seated on the benches up the back of the amphitheater, but the performances were always formulaic and the people in the seats weren't interested in the play. They were there to conduct business.

A series of comedy skits, with the wily slave Senabid outwitting his foolish master, were acted out for the jeering audience, and then the long performance followed—the story of Immakuk and Ennikar stealing Anet's Chariot. I paid little attention to the actors—I was too busy scanning the crowd around me for any sign that I had been recognized. I watched the Attolian, seemingly enthralled by the play, wishing I had his apparent equanimity. By the time the two main actors were lifted off the stage in a giant chariot with wings painted on the side in cheap yellow paint, I could have puked my fear into a bucket if someone had offered me one. My master had been dead for hours. The city gates would already be closed. All the places a runaway slave might hide were being turned over while I stood there, listening to the epilogue.

The performance over, I followed the Attolian on shaking legs as he made his way out of the amphitheater. The sun had some time before dipped below the horizon, and only the last of its light was glimmering in the clouds overhead, making them smudges of gray against the darker sky. As he walked, the Attolian pulled the hood of his cloak up over his head, and it was much harder to pick him out of the crowd. I worried that I would lose him in the deep twilight, but he went straight back to the docks and waited there for me to catch up.

"Ornon, our ambassador, has arranged for passage on a riverboat called the *Anet's Dream*. Our bags have been sent ahead," he told me. "You must get us aboard without revealing that I am Attolian. You are a slave with your master, and you do the talking."

I nodded. With the cloak over his breastplate and his hood up, he could pass for a Mede merchant, so long as he didn't speak.

"Can you do this?" the Attolian asked. He seemed entirely sincere. I am a good judge of men, and if he meant to slit my throat and drop me in a sewer, he was a far better actor than any of those I had just seen on the stage.

"Of course, master," I said. I might have been like a headless chicken crisscrossing the city that day, but on my own behalf, let me point out that I was not, in fact, dead. I had escaped the palace, and retrieved the money from Gessiret. I had survived that long, and I knew I could get onto the riverboat. I just didn't know—couldn't know—if the ambassador who had arranged for our flight had already sent a message to the *Anet's Dream* that would put an end to it. The whole palace would know of my master's death, but the gates that would have shut me in might have trapped any messenger as well. If there had been any alternative, I would have taken it, but I could see none, and there was no time for hesitation.

I walked up the docks looking for a ship named the *Anet's Dream*. If only it would leave the city before the Attolian learned that my master was dead, I might be free. I could evade the Attolian far more easily than the palace guard.

I found the ship quickly. There was no sign of anything amiss on the deck—the crew seemed to be preparing to leave the wharf. It was an unremarkable riverboat with a shallow draft and an outrigger. Designed to travel up and down the river under sail, it had only a small galley for rowers. The crew probably did the rowing when necessary. Most of its profit would be in its cargo, but there were a few cabins for passengers on the deck at the bow and stern.

I took a breath and walked confidently up the plank. I spoke to a deckhand, explained that my master and I had arrived and would require dinner. When he directed us to one of the cabins at the bow, I led the way, the Attolian silent behind me. Unfortunately, the captain came to join us before we were halfway to the cabin. I smiled and bowed. The Attolian bowed. The captain bowed. The awkward moment lengthened. It had been entirely appropriate for me to speak to the crew member on my master's behalf. The captain of the ship, even a shabby riverboat like the *Anet's Dream,* was a different matter.

Bowing again, I said, "My master has taken a vow of silence while the star of Mes Reia is in retrograde." I'd never heard of anyone taking a vow of silence for such a reason, but the retrograde of Mes Reia is supposed to be a time of confusion when communication can be broken and misunderstandings are more likely, and I hoped the excuse would carry water. The Attolian bowed again, a little more deeply, as if apologetically. The captain returned the gesture, deferring to his piety.

"Journey in your god's favor," he said, and waved a hand to a ship's boy who was hanging about nearby. "Xem, light the way to the cabin. Our deck is too crowded to have gentlefolk wandering in the dark."

So Xem lit a torch from the one at the top of the gangplank and carried it ahead of us. The deck was piled with cargo, though I couldn't make out what kind. The bright flame ruined my ability to see our unlit surroundings, and I probably would have been safer walking the cluttered deck in the dark, but there you have the disadvantages of courtesy. We followed Xem to the cabin and ducked through its curtain to find it lit by a much smaller and more useful oil lamp.

I stood blinking while my eyes adjusted. When they did, I realized that the Attolian was looking me over, and I dropped my gaze to the decking under my feet—I didn't need to be so bold as to return the favor. I'd had ample time to watch him in the amphitheater as he had looked up at Immakuk and Ennikar pounding back and forth across the stage.

In our first meeting at the palace and again at the docks, I'd been close enough to see his face, and there were none of the signs there that made slaves anxious. If there was not much intelligence in his features, there was no sign of cruelty, either. He was large, as I already knew, and a soldier. He had the scars on his hands and forearms and the unmistakable muscles that developed from swinging a sword day in and day out. I had no doubt he was good at what he did—he rather reminded one of an ox, very strong, not terribly quick—but I thought killing was his work, not his pleasure.

He was well dressed, but not wealthy, his clothes no doubt provided by his king. He had a gold ring in his ear, dangling a polished cylinder of stone—the stone was solid black, semiprecious at best. That and a ring on his right hand were his only jewelry. The ring was finely worked, with the emblem of his god, probably Miras, the Attolian god of light and arrows, the one most Attolian soldiers prayed to, but it wasn't heavy, so not very valuable. He moved easily, so he was no veteran crippled in his country's service, but he was too young to have done his twenty years—my own age, or perhaps younger. He was almost certainly not educated. He spoke Mede, but with a heavy accent, so he hadn't been trained as a child. His king trusted him at a long distance, but stealing someone else's slave was not what I would call a prestigious task. I guessed that he was probably not a favorite in the court, nor a very highly ranked officer, although I couldn't be certain—the king himself was a thief, so what did I know about what he valued? Still, it did not seem to me that the king of Attolia was investing one of his best men in this petty revenge of his.

He told me his name, as if he expected me to use it. He slowly circled, looking closely at the heavy gold chain around my neck, fixed with my master's seal. I knew he saw the flogging scars on my back, where they were visible above my collar, but he said nothing.

I looked around at the tiny cabin, trying to think of a polite way to ask when we might leave the dock. There was no polite way to ask if he meant to wring my neck and throw me in the river during the night.

"We leave within the hour," he said. I thought the

ambassador must have paid a fortune to send a riverboat downstream at night. The ships that went down the Ianna usually left in the morning. I had traveled often enough with my master to know.

"We aren't going downriver," said the Attolian, to my surprise. "We will go north instead, to Menle, and then follow the emperor's road to Zabrisa, on the coast. An Attolian ship will carry us across the Middle Sea from there."

It would take longer to leave the empire than if we went down the Ianna and boarded a ship across the Southern Ocean, but perhaps we would throw off any pursuit. There would be a bounty posted for me, but by the time bounty hunters realized we weren't on our way south, we would be halfway to Menle. Or anyway, the *Anet's Dream* would be halfway to Menle. If the Attolian truly meant to carry out this journey, he probably meant to do it alone, but I began to hope he might let me go without killing me. I couldn't think why the ambassador would have planned such a complicated and expensive trip for the Attolian only to have me knifed while still at the dock. And if I was to be carried alive out of the city, why bother to kill me then? In an alley in the city, I would have died without fuss. On the riverboat, it would be messier.

"Here, Kamet, take a seat," said the Attolian, gesturing to the stools facing each other across the narrow table. I was glad to perch on one, bitterly amused that it had taken him so long to realize that I wouldn't sit until he told me I could. What I failed to understand was that in his mind I was a free man, had been since the moment he met me, and as my host he wouldn't sit until I did.

We remained there, without another word, until Xem, the ship's boy, came back and knocked at the doorframe. He stayed only long enough to set his tray of nuts and cheese on the table between us. The Attolian scrupulously divided it in half and, when Xem left, motioned to me to eat at the same time that he did, aping the manners of a free man to a free man. He still didn't speak, though, having no more to say to me than I to him. We continued on in silence.

I looked around the tiny cabin, unable to believe that I had come to this when I had woken that morning on my cot in my office so certain of my place in the world. I could hear the faint slap of water against the boat. The commonplace sounds of the dock. I was listening for the sound of running feet, my death coming by way of a fleet-footed messenger or the tramping feet of the palace guard or the Ianna-Ir's enforcers of the peace. I knew from long experience how tiring fear is, and was not surprised to be suddenly exhausted. Let the Attolian kill me if he would, I didn't care. I just wanted to lie down.

The Attolian nodded then, as if I'd said something and he was merely agreeing. He stood and divested himself of his shirt and sandals. He unrolled the bedding set out for us and gave me one of the blankets, then rolled himself up in the other and lay down on the single bunk. I was glad we hadn't had to go through any pantomime of his offering the bunk to a lowly slave and my declining. I pulled the blanket over my shoulders and, without taking off my sandals, lay down on the floor. I'd thought the Attolian was a talker, but I'd been mistaken.

The floor was hard, the blanket unpleasant in both smell and texture. There was a lump under my hip, the key to my master's cashbox, which I would never use again. I lay there awake as the boat was warped away from the quay and we began to make our way upriver. I hadn't gotten around to sorting out Rakra and the steward who had hired him. Gessiret would never get the money for the two robes he was making for my master. No one would need the rugs and furnishings I'd ordered from the palace's tradesmen. I missed my far more comfortable bed, but I knew what circumstances my master's other slaves faced that night. I thought of them as we slowly left the city of Ianna-Ir behind. If there was any unease on my conscience about the Attolian's potential punishment for being deceived by a slave, I wasn't much worried about it. All the slaves of my master would soon be dead, and they might not die easily. Whatever happened to the Attolian would be mild in comparison.

Shifting on the unyielding floorboards, I thought of Laela and prayed for her. I would light candles on the altar of

Shesmegah and I would leave honey cakes, I swore, for her to feast on in the afterlife. Keeping my tears silent, I wept.

I woke to find I had not been murdered in my sleep. Perhaps the Attolian did indeed mean to take me to his king to be paraded around the court as a trophy. I lay looking at the wooden plank ceiling above my head for a moment and then sat up. The Attolian immediately did so as well, and I assumed that some noise outside the cabin had woken us both.

"I'll get you something to eat," I said, and scrambled to my feet.

"You don't have to do that," he protested.

"Indeed, master," I said, but he held up a hand—no need for the "master." "They know me as a slave," I explained. A dead giveaway if I stopped saying "master" now.

He grimaced, but conceded.

"And you as a Mede," I added.

That problem he dismissed at first. "There is no one they can tell when they see otherwise."

Treading carefully, I pointed out that the boat would make many stops. "We are not yet very far from the city," I said, "and the crew may mention an Attolian on board to those on the shore." At any stop, the crew might hear a rumor about a slave who had murdered his master, which was why, even if the Attolian did intend to take me back to his king, I needed to abandon the *Anet's Dream* as soon as I could. Once the crew realized that the Attolian was pretending to be something he was not, they would become suspicious of me as well. When they heard the rumor, they would put two and two together quickly. And of course, if the rumor came to the Attolian's ears, I'd be dead.

Twice I had corrected him. Nothing so hateful as presumption in a slave, as my master's cousin had only recently reminded me. I waited, on edge, to see how he would react, but the Attolian was amiable. He agreed to stay in the cabin for the time being, and I went out to get him some food.

Dawn was breaking. The ship was still moving north, pushed up the river by the light breeze catching in its oversized sails. If the breeze dropped entirely, the crew would row, probably tying up in the middle of the day and then moving on in the evening. The indeterminate banks were empty of everything but rushes. In the distance there were mud houses, built up on whatever ground would be above water during the yearly flood. The wealthy had homes in the hills on the far side of the plains or farther up the river where the banks were higher and more defined. Here, where the banks were low, the boat would anchor midstream and I would be trapped on board.

I went to the midship, where I had seen a rudimentary

galley area, to arrange for food and to make the acquaintance of the others on board. Xem, it turned out, was the captain's youngest son. In charge of the galley, he told me that a merchant was traveling alone in one cabin and the other two were empty. I made it a point to avoid any interaction with the merchant. Slaves too easily become beholden to any free man in need of a servant. I would be fetching and carrying for the Attolian, and I didn't want to give some nobody merchant any ideas. The only others on board were the captain and his crew, most of them his sons or other relatives.

I carried the tray back to the Attolian, and again he divided the food scrupulously in half, and again we ate together. Rather than giving me a more elevated sense of myself, I'm afraid his behavior lowered my opinion of the Attolian. I had lost everything, I suppose, but my pride. I should have had more respect for his quick thinking when he had come upon me at the docks, but I credited myself instead with our safe arrival on board the *Anet's Dream*, focusing on our meeting with the captain. Like a sailor clinging to the wheel of a sinking ship, I wanted to believe I steered the course of my life.

When the food was gone, I carried the tray back to the galley and then wandered the ship. It had a hold, but a fair amount of cargo seemed to be ceramic cooking stoves stacked on the deck and tied down with mismatched lines. I moved between the cargo and the cabins, identifying places I might like to sit out of the sun and out of sight of the other paying passenger in the front cabin. At the stern, I found a rowboat trailing behind on a long line. I could climb down into it if necessary, and I thought I could navigate it to shore if I had to, though I hoped I wouldn't. I looked over at the rush-lined bank of the river—too shallow for the *Anet's Dream* to come near. Farther upriver, that would change. The ship would tie up at the shore and it would be easier for me to slip away.

It was three days to Sherguz, the first town of any significance north of Ianna-Ir. So long as there was no news from someone on shore before then, I had that long to make a plan. I would watch for times when the crew might be distracted or asleep, and if an opportunity arose, I would decide whether or not to take the little boat. It would be risky to climb over the side of the *Anet's Dream*, but if I wanted to live, I might have to, and I very much wanted to live.

I'd been gone some time from the cabin. It wouldn't do to anger the Attolian, so I returned to see if he wanted anything.

The cabin was narrow, only about twice the width of the Attolian's bunk. Entered from the center of the boat, it stretched almost to the outer rail with only a narrow strip of deck to allow the sailors to pass by. The outer wall was mostly open to admit light and air. Across the opening were the table and stools where the Attolian sat looking at the water.

"Did you need me, master?" I asked.

He smiled and shook his head, offered me the other seat with a gracious wave that the rickety cane-seated excuse for a stool didn't deserve. I gingerly sat. The riverbank slid by. We said nothing. I was both anxious and bored, but the Attolian seemed neither. I am used to hiding my feelings, and I sat with my hands folded in my lap. In time, the captain decided we had made enough progress and the ship anchored in mid-river. The ship's boy came around with water and fruit.

In response to no stimulus that I could see, the Attolian said, "You needn't stay cooped up with me," and I gratefully abandoned him to stretch my legs again on deck.

I came back after what I guessed was a respectful time, and as I sat, he asked about the play we had seen the day before.

"The bigger man was king? And all of those people were coming to him to say that something bad had happened?" He had followed most of the story, but not all of it.

"Yes. Immakuk was the king of Ianna-Ir. When the spring floods came and didn't recede, the people were suffering. They thought the king was too old to help them. They all say his hero days are past. His friend Ennikar convinces him that he is not too old and that he should try to save his city. So, together they steal the chariot of the sun god, Anet, and fly off to shut the gates of heaven and stop the floodwaters from drowning Ianna-Ir."

"That yellow thing was supposed to be a chariot?" the Attolian asked.

"It was not a very good production."

"I see."

"Immakuk and Ennikar are never seen again, but the floods recede and are never again so severe, so they must still be working the gates of heaven and protecting the city."

"I've never heard of Immakuk and Ennikar," he said, and I wasn't surprised. The Attolians are for the most part uneducated.

"I could tell you more about them if you like. There is a translation of the first tablet into Attolian."

"Thank you," he said. "I'd like that."

It was my own translation, but I didn't tell him. He might have thought I was bragging, and he would have been right. I tapped my hand to my lower lip, bidding the gods to speak through me, and I began.

Greatly wise cloaked in wisdom was Immakuk
 greatly strong clothed in strength was his true friend
 Ennikar
 great was their love and greatly did it sustain them in
 their journeys together

greatly did Immakuk rule with his friend

when he came home to Ianna-Ir

Before their journeys began was Immakuk prince and keeper

of the water gates in the temple of Nuri

bound to open the gates to allow the god to enter with

the water

to fill the reservoirs and bring life to the city

Immakuk

bound but not bound well

bound but not committed

bound but not performing

the gates not open the water wasted the god offended

Immakuk left the city in shame

in shame sent out to wander the world

to learn the ways of welcome and unwelcome

Immakuk went into the world and learned about gates closed

against him and gates opened

Learned about blessings

accepted and blessings deserved

Wandered lonely

until Shesmegah took pity turned Immakuk's path

turned it to Ennikar

led him to Ennikar

Strong Ennikar

great in strength greatly admired

in the city from whence he came

bound to attend the gates of Nuri

but not attending attending instead

a pretty maid

left the gates open let the blessings of the god

flow out of the temple flow into the world

uncontained

Wasted said the priests

Left his city in shame

   sent by the priests out to wander

   to learn waste not and want not

In the world Ennikar learned about blessings

   denied and blessings shared

Met the witch of Urkull met the daughter of Ninur

   stayed with her until his path led him on

Followed the herds of the god Prokip and helped

   himself at the honeyed hives of Cassa

Fled angry Cassa and met Immakuk

   who had wandered

   met and shared his takings from the hives

Asked Ennikar of Immakuk what have you learned?

   Learned about welcome and unwelcome said Immakuk

Wise Immakuk asked Proud Ennikar what he had learned

   Learned I like to wander said Ennikar

"Bit of a freethinker, Ennikar," said the Attolian. I smiled, but kept going, pleased I had conveyed Ennikar's untamed nature.

Wander with me then friend Immakuk of
    friend Ennikar asked together they went
    seeking the day of their return to Immakuk's city
    where in his Wise Years
    he would build the stalls of animals
    found streets and houses and cities
    where he would build the great temple of Nuri
    invite the god in
Immakuk ruled with his friend Ennikar at his side
    saw the walls of the city built by the gods
    many chariots wide the walls
    topped in copper strong in glass-faced stone
    unbreakable walls to make the city strong
    keep its blessings in
    its gates open
    to send the blessings flowing out
    into the world

The Attolian thanked me politely when I was done and asked about some of the words he didn't understand. Then he asked, "Yesterday, who were the others? With the, you know . . ." He gestured to indicate the outsize accoutrements of Senabid and his master.

"Oh," I said, ducking my head, "they aren't part of the story. That's Senabid, the slave. It's a sort of a—crowd-pleaser, a chance to laugh as a slave outwits his master." I hated the Senabid skits, though. I knew other slaves who found them funny, but I thought they were stupid, as if any man would let his slave get away with that kind of trickery. I could only imagine what my master would have done with Senabid, and the thought made me sick. I couldn't be amused.

"I see," said the Attolian, nodding. "We have something similar in our theater. Only not a slave, just a lazy workman." He fell silent again, staring out over the river. By this time I was fairly sure I had his measure, and as the churning sense of terror and dislocation faded, my sense of superiority was slowly reasserting itself.

The breeze held, and we continued upriver all day. The crew took turns resting in the shade under the low awnings. In the evening we stopped to unload a single cookstove at a tiny dock. I went to lurk near the captain and his men as they worked—to catch any hint of a rumor about my master's death—but there was none. It seemed the news was still too fresh to have traveled north from the city.

That night I debated with myself whether or not to try to slip away. Once I thought the Attolian asleep, I left the cabin and made my way to the stern to look at the rowboat bobbing along at the length of its rope. I would have to pull it close, climb over the rail, and then lower myself into it without anyone seeing me. If I fell, I'd drown. I'd like to think that I stayed on the *Anet's Dream* because it was prudent, not because I was afraid. I told myself I was still too close to Ianna-Ir. I planned to wait for our first stop at a real town where I could slip from the boat directly to a dock and hide more easily among the buildings than out where there was nothing but rushes.

The next day was as quiet as the first. We sat, mostly in silence, watching the riverbank slowly slide by.

"You said you were reciting from the first tablet," said the Attolian.

"There are more than a hundred in the temple of Anet alone," I said. "No one knows how many there are altogether. Scholars argue about it. Some of the tablets are retellings of other tablets, only differing in style. Sometimes parts of the story change. In some versions Ennikar takes the honey from Cassa's hives because he does not know that they aren't wild hives . . ."

Handsome Ennikar helped himself
    knew not cultivated from uncultivated
    blessed from unblessed
Furious Cassa drove him off

sent her warriors against him stinging

until he fled honey smeared

"In other versions, he is about to help himself when he meets Cassa and she gives him the honey. Later he shares it with Immakuk when they meet on the road."

I was nattering. I bit my tongue, and it was quiet again.

In the dark at the end of the next day, we arrived at the bridge just below Sherguz. The caravan sites on either side of the river loomed—black backdrops to the burning lights of the town, like truncated versions of the ziggurats in Ianna-Ir—but these were not temples, unless they were for the worship of trade. The sloping walls protected the warehouses and meeting grounds of the merchant caravans that moved along the emperor's roads.

I was alarmed when the crew moored us, as usual, mid-river. When I asked why, the captain said we would move into the dock in the morning to avoid a fee from the town for the overnight docking. I went to look again at the rowboat floating on the black water and decided it was still wisest to wait until the next day and see what happened. If I could not get to shore, I would take the little boat the next night.

I wrapped myself in my smelly blanket and fell asleep only to wake to shouting. The Attolian stood over me, buckling his armor. There was a crashing roar and the shouting became screaming. I could smell smoke as the deck underneath me shivered.

"Up!" shouted the Attolian. "The ship is on fire!"

Before I could move, the ceiling overhead exploded and I threw myself under the sleeping bench. With my back pressed against the wall of the ship, I looked out from under the bench at a smoking spear that had buried itself in the deck where I had been lying.

I was still staring at it when the Attolian grabbed me by the ankle and ruthlessly dragged me out. He hauled me out onto the deck, where men were running past. The captain and his sons had given up saving the ship and were snatching at possessions before they leapt over the side. The rigging above us was all on fire, the sail a rippling sheet of flames flaring over our heads. The ropes holding a spar had burned through, and that was what had dropped to pierce the flimsy roof of the cabin, almost impaling me.

The Attolian pulled me to the side of the ship. Unlike the sailors, I couldn't go into the river. "I can't, I can't—" I shouted as we got closer to the railing, but I didn't have any choice. The Attolian jumped up onto the railing and pulled me up as well, in spite of my desperate struggle to get free. I felt my shift tear and I almost slipped away, but the Attolian adjusted his grip, cursing, and threw me into the water. I was screaming as it closed over me and directly inhaled an entire lungful.

Sprawled underneath the surface, I didn't know at first

which way was up. I clawed my way toward the moonlight, coughing out water and gasping for air before I sank again. I felt the pressure wave as the Attolian landed with a huge splash nearby. I was still flailing when his hand caught me under the arm and lifted me up. Clutching at him, I gasped, "I can't swim! I can't swim!"—first in Mede and then in Attolian. I would be more proud of my ability to translate during such a crisis if the Attolian hadn't calmly suggested I stand up.

The water came only to my chin, not even to his shoulder. When I'd stretched for a footing and found it, I glared at him from the corner of my eye.

"Good thing it isn't deeper," he observed.

If he had previously displayed any sense of humor, I would have suspected him of laughing at me, but what he said was no more than the truth. In his armor he would have sunk like a stone, swimmer or not.

"I'm sorry about the captain's ship," he said, watching the burning boat, and if he didn't sound very sorry, it was the only sign of how much he'd hated being cooped up in the tiny cabin.

Each time I bobbed up to make it a little easier to catch a breath, the current of the river gently moved me downstream. The Attolian, impervious to the current because of his greater weight, finally took me by the arm and towed me toward the shore.

We made an uncomfortable progress to the riverbank. My feet trailed behind me, and my head went down into the water. In order to breathe, I hung around his neck until we reached a spot where we could scramble out of the water. I had an easier time than the Attolian, who made several attempts on the muddy slope before he gave up and stood in the waist-deep water to unbuckle his armor and sword and pass them up to me on the bank.

Once he'd pulled himself up, we both turned again to watch the *Anet's Dream*. Having burned through its anchor lines, it had begun to float downstream. All around it, smaller boats were swarming, their boatmen striving to keep the burning wreck from drifting down onto any other ship. Already another boat was on fire and its crew was abandoning it, too. Some of them could be seen, black figures against the flames, as they climbed down into smaller boats. Some were jumping directly into the water. As we watched, another boat's rigging was suddenly engulfed.

"Well," said the Attolian, "that is all of my king's money gone."

My pride was still stinging, and I asked him, "You didn't get your purse?" He'd certainly made haste to get his armor out of our bags.

"It fell off in the river," he said.

I sighed to myself. What sort of idiot can't keep his purse tied to his belt? I declined to consider the obvious answer—

one with a man clinging to him like a monkey in the water.

"Our clothes, too," he said morosely.

He'd had a bundle of clothes suitable for me to change into once we were away from prying eyes—anyone who would have noticed a slave walking aboard the ship and a free man walking off. If the clothes weren't burned, they were on their way to the bottom of the river with the Attolian's purse.

I reached for my own purse and found it just where it should be—stupidly revealing its existence to the Attolian.

"Do you have enough for a night at an inn?" he asked.

Concealing my reluctance, I untied the purse and gave it to him. "There's not much there," I said.

"We have your chain," said the Attolian, pointing to the gold around my neck.

My slave chain was solid gold, with heavy links in the distinctive double-cuff pattern that distinguished it from any free man's jewelry. Not quite long enough to pull over my head, it had a plate hanging from it, also gold, stamped with my master's seal to identify me. Of course I had known I would take it off at some point, but I was suddenly, perversely, unwilling to give it up.

"Only my master may remove it," I said.

"He isn't going to know. I thought you would want to be rid of it."

I'd thought I would, too, but now that the moment had

arrived, I didn't want to hand it over to the Attolian as I had handed over my purse. I suppose I felt that it belonged to me just as much as I had ever belonged to my master. I hesitated, searching for some justification to keep the chain, and said, "No one will give you money for the chain unless you can prove with your own copy of the seal on it that you are my owner. Removing the chain from another man's slave is a crime."

"More so than stealing him?" the Attolian asked, incredulously.

"Yes," I said curtly, dangerously close to being rude. Other shipwrecked sailors, from our own ship and from the others that were burning, were now nearby on the bank. The Attolian needed to stop talking. This was not the place or time to explain that stealing a man's property was one crime and freeing his slave was another, only the second punishable by death. The first was theft, while the other was disturbing the order of the empire. Slaves are slaves until freed by their masters. I was a runaway slave, not a free man.

Under my breath, I said, "If the chain is found in your possession—if you try to sell the links—you'll be arrested."

"Then we should pitch it in the river," said the Attolian, shifting his bulk until he blocked me from the view of the nearest group of men. He was not completely thickheaded, but he still didn't understand. I was clearly dressed as a slave, and until I found a change of clothes, whoever saw me would wonder where my chain was. Also, I still hoped to keep some part of the chain's value if I could.

"That would be a waste of good gold," I said.

I thought he might pull the chain off, and I braced myself, but he just shook his head, bemused.

"Well, perhaps we have enough to secure a room for the night." He hefted my small purse in his hand. "Let's go get dry and see what we think of next."

He bent to pick up his armor, but I stopped him. "Better leave it for me."

"It's only the breast and backplate and the sword," he said. "I left the rest aboard ship."

"No matter," I said. "Better I carry it."

CHAPTER THREE

Again I played the part of a trusted slave making arrangements for my master. I found a pleasant-looking inn and left the Attolian out in the street while I went in to present my still-soaking person to the innkeeper and spin him a story of our woebegone state. We'd lost our traveling companions—all that was left of our guards was the armor I was carrying. Did he have room for myself and my master, the wealthy son of a foreign merchant family? I regretted that my master's purse was lost, but he would apply for funds in the morning, trading on his good name with men who knew his father. And if our lost guards appeared, undrowned, we would need accommodations for them as well.

The innkeeper, impressed by the gold around my neck and more than happy to believe my story, agreed to open up his finest room, upstairs where the breeze blew in from the doorway overlooking a private courtyard.

I think the Attolian was surprised by the warmth of our reception.

"They know I am Attolian?" he asked.

"Yes," I said. "I didn't think . . ." I didn't think he could carry off an impersonation of a Mede for very long.

"They are very hospitable," he said.

"Hospitality is much the same in many countries—and they think you are rich."

"Ah." That made sense to him. Money is the same from country to country, too.

When we had dried off and changed into the clean clothes the innkeeper had loaned us, the Attolian wanted to go out. He was eager to exercise his unexpected freedom. I didn't dare try to dissuade him, very aware that I had been disobedient over the matter of the chain at the river, so I followed him back downstairs, where he wanted me to ask the innkeeper for directions to the part of town where he might find an open wineshop that would serve a late supper.

There was no way to avoid relaying the question, but I added a request for something in our room. The innkeeper, thank the gods, waved toward the people sitting at tables and chairs in the open courtyard behind him. The implication was too obvious for even the Attolian to miss. Not only could we eat there, it would be impolite to refuse.

Bowing to good sense, the Attolian picked a table while

the innkeeper bustled away, and gestured to me to sit. I shook my head, hoping he would realize how odd it would look to the other patrons. He looked back at me, puzzled, and opened his mouth. It would draw more attention if we stood talking about it, so I quickly took the stool across from him. A servant brought out two bowls of stewed lamb and a wine bottle with two cups, raising his eyebrows as he served me.

I ate quickly. The Attolian didn't. He looked idly around at the other occupants of the inn enjoying the night air. I'd made up the story I had and chosen the inn with care in order to avoid anyone from the *Anet's Dream*. They would be seeking shelter in a poorer part of town, but several men nearby were off boats that had been damaged and were complaining about the irresponsibility of the captain, blaming him for the fire.

Two more men came, asking the innkeeper for wine before sitting at a nearby table. They, too, were talking about the fire on the river. It was only a matter of time, though, before they started discussing other events. The story of my master's murder at the hand of his secretary had to have preceded us. That sort of news travels faster than horses, faster than boats. The messengers of the gods carry rumors through the sky the way bees carry pollen and drop them from their wings onto the earth below.

I wasn't sure that the Attolian could understand the

conversations around us, but I wasn't sure he couldn't, either. I debated excusing myself—he'd let me go if I said I was returning to our room—and then fleeing the inn, but there was every chance someone would notice me leaving and alert my "master." In addition, the Attolian had all my money. If I waited until he was asleep, I would have my purse back and the coin in it would buy a set of clothes suitable for a free man. I could leave in the very early morning, telling the innkeeper I was running errands. Unlike trying to sneak away in the night, leaving in the morning would be unexceptional. No one had any cause to doubt my good conduct, and the boat fire would offer me a perfect excuse to be buying more clothes for my master.

The town was at an intersection of one of the emperor's trade roads and the river, which is why it had been a planned stop on our captain's route. It offered a much better chance for my escape than any of the sad collections of mud houses I'd seen from our boat over the last few days. I could thank the gods that the boat hadn't caught fire next to one of those. Once I was dressed as a free man, I could break the links of the slave chain and go to one of the caravan sites on either side of the river to offer my services as a scribe and record keeper. Invisible in the crowd of a caravan, I could make my way out of the empire and only then convert the gold in my chain to coin to live very comfortably. I just wished the Attolian would leave the men talking in the courtyard and go to bed. He didn't seem tired at all.

Just as I was at my wit's end, a man entered the courtyard, none other than the wine merchant I had followed around Ianna-Ir. His trade must have brought him upriver.

"Master," I said in a whisper.

"You don't—"

Gods, I asked, how stupid was he?

"Master," I repeated more firmly, and he remembered where we were and the story I had given the innkeeper.

I leaned close to him and whispered, "There is a man here who will know me if he sees me. He has done business with Nahuseresh."

He began to turn his head to look, and I hastily cleared my throat to stop him.

"You are certain?"

"I am certain," I said. "We should go up to the room."

He nodded and hastily finished the last bites of his stewed lamb. When the wine merchant's back was turned, I signaled the Attolian. Then he stood and walked to the stairs while I kept his bulk between me and the wine merchant, should he look our way.

Once safely in our room, I waited, hiding my impatience, for the Attolian to lie down. It seemed like hours that he sat on the small stool by the bed, lost in his thoughts—or whatever he had in his head that approximated thoughts.

Finally, he did lie down, but each time I checked, his eyes were still open. The third time I checked, he looked back at me, curious, and I hastily closed my own eyes.

I woke with a start to find the room full of sunlight. It was not only morning, it was *late* morning, and the Attolian was gone. I leapt up and looked all around me while berating myself. I'd thought the Attolian was thickheaded the night before, but I was so much more stupid. I couldn't imagine what had come over me, not just to oversleep, but to oversleep when the Attolian was up and moving around. I had already grown spoiled and blamed the Attolian for it. I could very clearly imagine what my master would have done if such a thing had happened while I was with him.

Wherever the Attolian had gone, he'd taken my purse, and gods alone knew what he might be doing to give us away to the local population. I combed my fingers through my hair and straightened my shift, then hastily headed downstairs to speak to the innkeeper. My stomach sank when I saw his expression; we were no longer honored guests, that much was clear.

"The *guard*," he said, emphasizing the word, "has gone to the caravan site on the west side of the river to see about a job that will carry both of you back to your master in Zabrisa," he said in a stony voice. "Now that the goods whose transport you were overseeing have been lost." He sounded quite vengeful. He was probably pleased to think of me facing a disappointed master with my invented failure to explain.

I bowed and thanked him. I would need to leave immediately, even without my money. We had been memorable, the Attolian and I, and the Attolian had offended the innkeeper by making him feel a fool for believing my story about a rich merchant. The innkeeper would jump at the chance to describe us to any slave catchers who looked for me here, and for all I knew, they *would* look for me here when they had no success finding me downriver. I sent up a quick prayer that the emperor would be satisfied to have me just disappear and turned to go back up to the room. I hadn't thought to look to see if the Attolian had left his armor. If he had, I intended to sell it.

"Ahem," said the innkeeper, and I turned back. The innkeeper pointedly presented me with my clothing, washed and dried after my immersion in the river. He wanted back the shift he'd generously offered me the day before. I smiled obsequiously, taking the bundle, and hurried upstairs to change. The armor was gone.

Once dressed in my own clothes, I went right back down to find the innkeeper standing with his arms crossed and a sour look on his face, speaking to the Attolian. The Attolian, dressed in his armor, had a pack at his feet and a self-satisfied expression on his face.

"Our innkeeper is our long-lost brother no more," he

whispered to me in Attolian.

"It has come to him that you are not the son of a wealthy merchant," I answered in the same language.

"Well, so long as he doesn't tell anyone that I have signed on as a guard for a caravan headed toward Zabrisa, I don't care if he is my dear brother or not."

I didn't wince. The innkeeper—who didn't need to speak Attolian to understand what he'd just heard—already knew we were headed to Zabrisa, after all. I nodded serenely instead. At least the Attolian was going to Zabrisa, not I.

"I've paid our bills," said the Attolian. He bowed to the innkeeper, who bowed stiffly back. The worked-gold ring of Miras was gone from the Attolian's finger. If he had used it to pay our fee, he had been cheated, and no clearer trail could have been left of our presence here. The Medes do not worship Miras, and anyone who saw the ring would know it came from an Attolian. Outside, we headed toward the river, but after only a short distance, the Attolian pulled me aside into a narrower street and led the way between houses until we were alone.

"Take off your shift," he said as he lifted the pack I'd been carrying from my back. He opened the pack to pull out a smaller bundle and handed it to me. Inside were a free man's clothes. "Quickly," he said.

I kicked off my sandals and pulled on the loose trousers, the fabric against my legs making me shiver. Then I removed my shift and pulled on the sleeved shirt he'd given me—anyone observing this moment would know my secret—and then the moment passed. I was dressed. My hair was a little short, but no matter. So long as I had the clothes and the bearing of a free man, no one would give me a second look. I still had no money, though, and I laced the shirt tightly closed over the slave chain before the Attolian could suggest again that we get rid of it. He, meanwhile, had folded my shift around a rock and tucked it somewhat awkwardly under his breastplate. When he saw I was ready, he gestured to me to walk at his side, and we proceeded to the bridge over the Ianna.

The bridge was provided by the emperor to carry his road across the river, north toward Menle and then west to Zabrisa. It was built of white stone in arches that grew higher toward the center, but they were not high enough to let through the masts of the larger riverboats. The center part of the bridge was wooden and could be raised to allow those boats to pass through. The drawbridge was down when we arrived, but the Attolian dawdled, looking at the blankets spread with cheap merchandise in the shadow of the bridge railing. Trinket sellers with no money for a stall in a marketplace displayed their wares there. The Attolian looked at various armbands as we moved across the bridge, and by the time we'd gotten to the center, the wooden deck had been raised to let a boat through. As we stood waiting, the Attolian smoothly pulled the shift out from under his armor and dropped it into the river without anyone around us the wiser—the thumping of the gearing of the drawbridge and the noise of the riverboat working its way through the narrow opening covered the much smaller splash of the rock covered in cloth hitting the water.

Once on the far side of the river, we went about halfway to the caravan site and then again turned off the imperial road into the side alleys. I followed, curious but not alarmed, until it seemed that the Attolian had lost his way and was turning back on his path. The Attolian showed no hesitation, only checking the sun before he chose another wrong turn, but I grew more and more anxious. We were heading back east toward the river, and I was afraid that by the time we reached the caravan site, the Attolian would have lost his position as guard. I was counting on that distraction, as well as the crowds at the caravan site, to give me a chance to slip away from him.

"Master, the West Caravan site is in that direction," I finally said.

"We aren't going to the West Caravan site," the Attolian replied, and his words were knife-edged. "We aren't going to Zabrisa, either," he added, and I swallowed, my mouth suddenly dry. I had been indiscreet. He had seen what I had been thinking.

"Don't call me master again," he warned, and walked on.

✦ ✦ ✦

Chastened, I followed him back over the bridge to the east side of the river as he carefully joined a crowd to hide us as well as possible from the watching eyes of the trinket sellers. We threaded our way through the narrow side streets, circling around the inn where we had stayed the night before, lest anyone see us and note our change of direction. The Attolian waved an arm to indicate that I should walk beside him in accordance with my new identity as a free man—and so that he could keep an eye on me. The town of Sherguz had grown more slowly on this side of the river, so there was still empty ground to cross before we reached the high walls of the East Caravan site. Its only gate faced away from us, and its blank walls made it look even more like one of the ziggurats of the capital surrounded by their open plazas.

The emperor provided the enclosed site to keep trade safe and regulated. Those who used it paid taxes on the goods they moved or paid a small fee to enter and seek employment from the merchants within. The Attolian showed the keeper at the gate the dye on his finger, proving that he'd paid a fee once already to enter the site. Then he paid the fee for me, and I dipped a finger in the dye pot. It was the first time I'd done so, though I'd often passed through sites such as this one with my master. My master didn't dip his finger because he was above such things. I didn't because as a slave I was beneath them. Unused to the sensation of the slick dye, I rubbed at it and managed to smudge it all over my hand. I only barely stopped myself from trying to wipe it off on my new clothes.

Some caravan sites are just walled courtyards with a well in the middle, but Sherguz was a large trading center where goods were shifted from caravans to boats and sent down or up the river. Its walls were three or more stories high, lined with stables and warehouses. One wall had a covered terrace with an arcade where a row of entryways were pitch-black holes in contrast to the bright sun shining down in the open yard. Inside each would be a business office rented by the day or week or year. Above the arcade, and on the roofs of the warehouses, was another level—rooms for housing and more storage. Above that was a wooden gallery where guards would have walked around the tops of the walls if they'd been needed. In Sherguz, it provided a space for people not afraid of heights to loiter and conduct their business above the stink below.

The Attolian had started across the teeming courtyard filled with animals and men but was looking over his shoulder to see why I lagged. I stepped quickly to catch up. He seemed quite comfortable ducking around the back ends of horses, but I noticed he gave the camels wider berth. Either they were unfamiliar to him and he gave them more room, or they *were* familiar to him and he gave them more room. He approached several people and asked in his heavily accented Mede for a particular caravan master by the name of Roamanj. He worked his way around the edge of the courtyard, never stepping more than a pace ahead of me, keeping me in the corner of his eye. If I slowed, he lifted an arm around my shoulder, as if in friendship.

We eventually found the man he was seeking, an enormous shaggy-haired Ferrian. Like many of their traders, he had probably spent most of his life in the empire. He was directing the packaging of some bales of fine cloth—each length of worked fabric wrapped in less-fine material that in turn was being wrapped in a larger and coarser cloth, in a meticulous order meant to keep it from the dust and dirt.

"Careful with that, you've got it too close to the edge of the baling cloth, move it in and don't step on the baling cloth, you fool—and who by the gods eternal is this?" the caravan master asked, looking me over with suspicion. "He had better be a paying passenger."

"Extra guard," said the Attolian.

The caravan master was unimpressed.

"Good with a sword," said the Attolian, and I squared my shoulders.

Roamanj snorted. "I don't need one more guard. He pays passage." And turning his back he bellowed, "Queen of the Night devour you, off the cloth!" at a poor unfortunate who wasn't even on the cloth, just too close to it for comfort.

Seeing the Attolian still standing beside him, Roamanj raised his bushy eyebrows, as if surprised. The Attolian looked pointedly at the other caravans mustering around us. He could find work with any of them, but there was no way to know how long that might take and no way to know if there were bounty hunters coming up the river after me. I didn't want to dawdle for a day or two in Sherguz to find out.

Roamanj crossed his arms. "I'm not paying him. He's paying me."

The Attolian lifted one shoulder and let it drop.

"All right, he can travel with us half passage, as he is a friend of yours."

The Attolian waited, far and away the most eloquent nonspeaker I think I have ever known.

"By gods, I have no time for this!" shouted Roamanj.

The Attolian took a half step away.

"Fine," said Roamanj, throwing up a hand in defeat, "he comes with us, but I am not giving him a single hennat, you understand?" He shook his finger in the Attolian's face.

The Attolian waited until Roamanj turned again to his cloth before he said, "Needs a sword."

"May the Queen of the Night take you!" Roamanj turned back to him. "I should provide a freeloader with a sword, and you are asking this because I look like your generous old uncle, maybe?"

I shuffled farther away, but the Attolian only nodded. "Just like," he said with a straight face.

The caravan master chuckled. "Fine, fine," he said. "Go to the quartermaster. So long as you stop wasting my time." He waved toward a man counting cooking pots not far away—and that's how I became a caravan guard heading toward the city of Perf.

The Attolian led the way over to the quartermaster. In a few minutes I was holding the sword he'd selected for me from the limited armory. I buckled it around my hips with a sense of unreality. I'd never touched a knife longer than my finger. Even when I dressed my master, I did not touch his weapons, nor did any of his other slaves. He racked and unracked his sword himself and a free man sharpened it and cared for its leathers.

I looked up at the Attolian, who nodded approvingly and clapped me on the shoulder. The chill in his demeanor had thawed a little. Following directions from the quartermaster, we circled the courtyard looking for an entryway with a green-striped curtain. As we walked, the Attolian explained that earlier in the morning he'd gone to pick up a job as a guard at the West Caravan site. With his qualifications obvious, it had been easily done, more easily than if I had been with him. Once he'd secured a position with a large caravan, where he would have been only one new face among many, he'd gone looking for other mercenaries in the job market. When he'd found a likely prospect, another foreigner from the southern coast of the Continent, the

Attolian had offered him his job for the westbound caravan, explaining that he'd made a mistake and would earn more money heading east. The mercenary wasn't stupid, and in exchange for a little palm grease he had agreed to the swap and to tell people he was Attolian if asked.

"Will he not reveal your plans if slave hunters catch up with him?" I asked, but the Attolian shook his head.

"He was happy to fool whoever was pursuing me in exchange for most of the coin I got for my ring, but he didn't know a slave was involved. I understand that imperial law takes a very dim view of people who aid escaping slaves, even unwittingly." So he had taken my warning seriously. "If that guard finds out he's helped a slave escape, he is most likely to lay very low and pretend he never met me at all."

"Perf is the wrong direction, though." I almost didn't say anything, still unsettled to have misjudged him, wary of seeming to doubt him, but he answered without any sign of offense.

"We can go northwest on the road from Perf to Koadester, then cross the Taymet Mountains into Zaboar. There's an Attolian trade house there, and Attolian ships often trade in the Shallow Sea. Any of them will take us at least to the Narrows, where we can get another ship to carry us home."

He had an open face and an honest one, and I'd mistaken that for stupidity. He was not a liar by nature, certainly, but he was not the fool I had taken him for.

"Not the fool you took me for, Kamet?" he asked.

Wrong-footed, I could only wring my hands. I'd not only underestimated him, I'd let my opinion show. "It seems to be me who is all kinds of fool lately," I said. I almost added "master" but bit it back in time.

The Attolian snorted. "Look up, Kamet, you're a free man."

I raised my eyes to his face.

He shrugged. "We all spend our time under the sign of the idiot," he said, and the matter seemed settled, at least as far as he was concerned.

We found the entryway with the striped curtain and made our way up the steps that led to it. Inside, on bales and boxes, were the other guards for the caravan, sitting at their ease with cups of tea. The Attolian nodded to the men. I did not miss their measuring glances—I don't think I looked "good with a sword." Once the Attolian picked a bale for himself, I settled on a box nearby. Raising the height of the floor above the courtyard to keep the dust and dirt out seemed to have been a futile effort. Everything was coated in a fine grit. One of the guards shouted through another doorway that led deeper into the warren of windowless rooms, and a skinny boy appeared with a tea tray and poured from a large pot into the men's cups. Silently he handed two more cups to us, filled them, and then slipped back into the darkness.

My cup was cracked and mended with staples, ugly but serviceable. The crack was a ragged black line like a road on a map, surrounded by stains that might mark deserts or seas, if only I could read them. I ran my finger along the rim to make sure there was no rough edge before I put my lip to it. Then I sipped the hot tea and listened as the guards talked. Most of them were longtime retainers of Roamanj. One of them looked like a westerner. I thought he might be from the Greater Peninsula, but he greeted us in the round vowels of a Southern Gant and said his name was Benno. Another guard, new like us, was a Braeling, with fair hair and the bright blue eyes of the north. He had loosened his shirt, and his fair skin was a motley of red where the sun had burned it and white where the sun hadn't touched.

He had been in the midst of introducing himself to the others when we arrived, and he backtracked to tell us that he had come down the inland waterways from Mûr to the Shallow Sea with a company of mercenaries. It was a common story. Men set out in companies, and one by one, the companies were whittled down either by death or by disagreements. The Braeling, whose name was Skell, or Skerrell, I was never certain which, had parted ways with his friends when they had decided to return to the north. He was working his way to Perf and meant to press on farther to the empire's eastern frontier. In the mountains there, he thought his experience of winter would make him valuable.

He said that he would have to regrow his heavy beard when he reached cold weather again.

"And you?" he asked the Attolian.

"Aris," he answered, pointing to himself. "Metit," he said, pointing to me. There was a moment when the other guards waited for more, but it passed quickly. One by one, the men offered their own names. They answered questions about Roamanj, saying that he orchestrated his caravans well and that there were rarely problems from bandits on the road to Perf. There might be more trouble heading south from there, but the caravan would join another, and more of Roamanj's regulars were waiting in Perf to sign on. They were all old hands, and it appeared that the caravan was going to be safe even if I was one of the people responsible for protecting it.

We whiled away the afternoon, the guards exchanging stories about the merchants and the caravan masters and the various jobs they had worked up and down the emperor's roads. The Attolian nodded along at the appropriate moments, his Mede evidently good enough to follow the conversation. The boy from the back room eventually brought us food, and after some reshuffling we slept there on thin mattresses rolled out on the floor. Long before the first light of day had dawned, we would be up and on the road.

I woke to the sound of the animal keepers leading out the

horses and the camels and loading them with their burdens. The guards around me yawned and stretched themselves and called for more tea and cakes for breakfast. One by one, the boxes and bales we were sitting on were carried away until we were sitting cross-legged on the filthy stone floor. In several more hours all was prepared outside and Roamanj put his head through the curtain to call us to our work.

The other guards had bundles that they dropped into an assigned wagon. The single bundle that the Attolian and I had shared was much smaller, just a change of clothes. Again, we drew measuring looks, but no one commented. As guards we took turns on horseback, moving up and down the caravan. When not riding, we sat on one of the wagons or walked beside them. They went slowly enough and rattled so much that walking was almost a relief. There were sixteen wagons altogether, with about three times as many beasts of burden interspersed between them. When I had nothing else to do, I tried to count them, but never came to a number I could trust. The merchants traveled with their goods, and many, also, with their families. Wives, children, livestock roamed in every direction. It was part of the guards' job to make sure none wandered too far. As the caravan traveled, its components would slowly spread out, and then at Roamanj's direction those at the front would stop and wait until it had been collected back together before moving on.

No one seemed able to speak in anything but a shout.

By the end of the first, very long day we were still climbing out of the fertile valley of the Ianna and I was surprised anyone still had a voice, but evidently some did. There was a great deal of loud swearing as the animals were staked for the night and the camp set up. There were arguments about everything, from where tents would be pitched to who would water what animals in what order. Roamanj was the universal arbiter and walked the camp with a guard at either shoulder.

There was no caravan site to protect us that night or for the next several nights; none seemed to be needed this close to Sherguz. (I felt we had traveled halfway to Perf and was dismayed when I learned the actual distance we'd covered.) With no bandits to fear, our responsibility was to prevent petty theft. Cook fires were started, and food made, if you could call it that, and the guards arranged among themselves to take the night shifts in turn.

As the camp quieted down, I regretted not breaking my slave chain in the town behind us and dropping it quietly into the river with my shift. I'd kept it because its heavy gold links were my only asset, but I'd underappreciated its danger. If anyone else in the caravan saw it, it meant certain betrayal, yet I couldn't risk being seen trying to pull it off, and even if I could, it was less safe in a pocket than it was around my neck. I could keep my shirt pulled tightly shut, but couldn't keep my pockets so private. I'd felt the little fingers of the children in the caravan dipping in and out of them already.

I could leave the camp for my private business and yank the chain loose in the dark, but if I went far enough away to be out of sight, it would be noted. If I tried to bury something out there in the hard dirt, everyone would be curious. If I dropped the chain without burying it, it might be found, and suspicion would fall on me instantly. Already I had drawn inquisitive looks—I was so obviously not a guard—and it would be foolish to draw even more attention. I resolved to sleep lightly and with the blanket the Attolian had purchased drawn close around my shoulders.

The next day I left the horseback riding to the real guards. The men had taken their measure of me and seemed content to pretend I was one of them, but no one wanted to rely on me for defense. That evening the food was even worse than it had been the night before. The Attolian silently laughed at me when he caught me looking at my meal in consternation, and I tried to be good-humored about it. It would be two weeks or more to Perf. I thought I might starve on the way.

The Attolian ate the swill, slept heavily, and woke alert. He got on well with the guards, and if he listened far more than he spoke, he had his broken Mede as an excuse. He sparred with them in the evenings, or wrestled in the dirt, testing himself against their skill and strength. They had invited me to join them the first time, and I had refused—with some haughtiness so that they would not ask me again—and so they were friendly with the Attolian but eyed me sideways. I knew my anxiety had made me appear arrogant, and I tried to be more ingratiating, but that seemed to draw even more questioning looks. I longed to be in Perf already, but even more I longed to be back in my alcove, just off my master's main room with the curtain to give me a pretense of privacy and my daily tasks before me and my master living and breathing in the outer room. Then I remembered Laela and told myself not to be so stupid.

The Attolian frequently volunteered the two of us for the least attractive shifts of guard duty, though he always glanced at me first to see if I was amenable. We worked as one man, he and I, so that no resentment built up over my inabilities.

Late at night, as we sat alone at a watch fire, the Attolian voiced my thoughts for me. "We could have made it to Perf on our own much faster."

He scratched at a row of bug bites on his arm and explained. "I would have needed to buy supplies, and that would have taken time we didn't have. I didn't have money for a horse, maybe for a mule or a donkey once I'd sold my ring, but it's hard to buy a decent mount from strangers. And people notice who buys their animals."

I hadn't thought of that. I was coming to understand how narrow my world had been and how little I knew of others' experiences. "I am not familiar with this kind of traveling," I admitted, after clearing my throat. I didn't want the Attolian to think that I felt he was under any obligation to justify his actions to me.

I had been many places with my master, and I may have slept on the floor next to his bed, but I had slept wrapped in fine linen with a soft cushion for a pillow. Here I slept on the dirt. I had never walked so far in my life and never been so bone weary. I considered the journey still ahead in this new light and wondered if the Attolian had any idea how challenging the Taymet Mountains were. If they weren't so formidable, the tiny nation of Zaboar would be part of the Mede empire instead of its own little city-state on the Shallow Sea. It was too dangerous to discuss our plans, though, even if we believed all those around us were asleep. There was nothing else we had to speak of, so we fell silent, sitting together by the fire.

Every evening the guards not on duty ate together before their shifts started, so there was a group around the fire as the Braeling told us his plans. He meant to make enough money fighting for the emperor that he could go back home and buy land. The other guards were pessimistic. Tikir and Simkit, who I'd learned were brothers, exchanged a look and then dropped their eyes, but no one said anything.

"The money is good," insisted the Braeling. "Two years,

and I'll have the stake for a small farm. Four, and I'll have a stake for a large one."

I thought it was a sensible plan, but even the Attolian was shaking his head.

"Bah!" said the Braeling, dismissing all of them. "You are old women, afraid of sweat and blood. And you," he said to me, "don't have any meat in your dish."

It was true—I didn't dive into the common pot to claim my share. I wasn't going to try to chisel a piece of meat away from a man twice my size, especially not when that man was eating with his knife. I made myself content with whatever was left once they'd served themselves.

The Braeling generously filled up my bowl and castigated the Attolian. "You should take better care of your little friend," he said, and the other guards joined in agreement, happier to give the Attolian a good-natured ribbing than to talk about the Braeling's future.

Later, when we were alone, I asked the Attolian why he and the other guards had seemed so doubtful about the Braeling's plans. "He'll overstay his luck," said the Attolian. "He'll take a wound that kills or cripples him, and he'll live out his life among strangers. He knows he'll never see his home again."

"Why not turn back, then?"

The Attolian shrugged. "Maybe he left debts behind. Maybe he killed the wrong man." The other guards had asked us no questions about our past. No one would ask the Braeling about his. He would go east and fight the emperor's wars, carrying out the bloody business of larger countries eating up the littler ones. It wasn't a matter of theory in a tiny office in the emperor's palace. It was the work of their lives and the end of many of them.

CHAPTER FOUR

We were more than halfway to Perf. Everything around us was rocks and chalky red dirt. We had spent the previous day climbing up to a rocky and narrow passage that twisted through the range of hills that lay across our path. The guards had been particularly alert—this was where a few daring bandits might have swept out of a narrow side canyon to pluck up a sheep or a goat or a child and disappear back into the rocky terrain—but the pass was behind us without incident. On our right, the hills still rose, and on our left, the ground fell away to a rolling, mostly barren plain. Presumably there was life growing out there, but I couldn't see it. Ahead of us, we had a long and gradual descent and the fading possibility of bandits. Two of the guards, as well as the Attolian and myself, were relaxing on the back end of the last wagon of the caravan.

I was counting the hours left in the day when we heard hoofbeats echoing in the pass behind us. We all looked up at the sound, alert but not particularly concerned. It was only when two horsemen came into view behind us, riding hard, that the guards stiffened. The Attolian suddenly dropped off the back of the wagon, pulling me with him.

"Ride on," he said. "We will take care of this and catch up."

He didn't need to say it twice. I heard the driver shout, passing an alarm toward the front of the caravan, and the wagon began to rumble faster down the road. Not so fast that I didn't have time to see the shocked faces of the guards staring back at us as they rolled farther and farther away. I looked toward the approaching riders. Even with my poor eyes, I could see that there were only two of them, and the guards' alarm seemed outsized. For them, I mean. My alarm was perfectly reasonable, as the horsemen appeared to be waving at us, and I was certain that what they were waving was swords. The Attolian, meanwhile, was striding confidently back uphill. Awkwardly I pulled my sword out of its sheath and followed him.

The first horseman, well ahead of his companion, tried to ride the Attolian down, but the Attolian stepped abruptly to the side at the last possible moment and swung his sword up toward the head of the horse. It reared and fell backward with its rider still on its back. The Attolian began to run then toward the second rider, who was more careful in his approach, swinging his horse away from the Attolian at the last moment and striking as he passed. They were too far away for me to see anything except that the second rider's caution did him little good. He was unseated a moment later and fell to the ground. I didn't see whether he got up. I had a more pressing concern. The first rider had struggled out from under his rolling horse and was limping toward me.

I clutched the sword in both hands and tried to imitate the stance I'd seen the guards take as they practiced together. As my attacker got close enough to see clearly, I realized with horror that he was no bandit. He was one of the Namreen, the emperor's handpicked bodyguard. No wonder the wagons had rumbled away and no wonder the other guards had been shocked at the blithe way the Attolian had hopped off the cart.

I considered dropping the sword and running, but the Namreen was already too close. Even limping, he moved too fast for me to be sure I could escape him. I backed up a few shuffling steps as he shifted his sword to his left hand and reached for me with his right.

"Gut him!" screamed the Attolian from up the road, and I lifted my wobbling sword. The Namreen rolled his eyes, and without even switching his sword back to his right hand, he swung it at my head. As if it would help, I tried to duck. I felt the blow like a searing light followed by darkness, probably because I had closed my eyes, and I stumbled back as the Namreen knocked the sword from my hand. Putting both hands to my head, I continued backward off the road, the rough ground dropping away under my feet. I avoided the Namreen's next grab by virtue of falling over. The Attolian bellowed from somewhere close by, and the Namreen must have turned to face him.

He didn't reach for me again, and a moment later he was dead. His body dropped beside me, the Attolian's sword straight through his head.

Jerking the sword back out and wiping it on the dead man's clothes, the Attolian said, sounding puzzled but not angry, "Why didn't you gut him? He had no guard up at all."

Sitting up, I stared at the dead man lying in front of me while trying to blink the wetness from my eyes. It was my blood, I realized. I held my hands away from my head and looked at them. They were scarlet, the blood covering them an impossibly bright red. I would have screamed, but my throat was so tightly closed that only an airy whistling sound came out.

"Do you know," I said in a strangled whisper, "do you know what happens to a slave who arms himself in the empire? Do you have any idea what they do to slaves who even look for too long at a sword, or a dagger, or anything more dangerous than a penknife? Do you have any idea, you imbecile, what they do, what they do . . ." My voice seemed to be getting higher and higher as I repeated myself.

The Attolian dropped his sword in the dirt beside the dead Namreen and without another word grabbed me in his arms. I'd just called him an imbecile. I was sure he was going to kill me with his bare hands. I struggled but couldn't get free. He only squeezed tighter until I stopped thinking of anything but drawing my next sobbing breath.

"Kamet," the Attolian said quietly in my ear, "it's a flesh wound. It will be all right. It's messy, but it will be all right, I promise. Don't be frightened."

There was blood *everywhere*. All over me, all over the Attolian. It was not going to be all right. I was going to die out in the dirt in the hot sun on the road to Perf, and my whole life would have amounted to nothing. Nothing. I would not direct the empire, or be a great patron of the arts, or collect my own library of manuscripts. I would die. I conjugated it. Will die, would die. Present tense, dying. I was dying. *I was dying.*

But the Attolian just kept repeating over and over that all would be well. "Head wounds bleed, but we can stitch it up, I've done it before, don't be afraid. Kamet, I wouldn't tell you this if it weren't true. I swear to you, I am not going to leave your dead body beside the road to Perf. I didn't come all the way to this godsforsaken cesspit so that I could go home and tell my king I failed him."

Suddenly so chatty, I thought, and what was he calling a cesspit? Attolia, that was a cesspit. A backward, savage, stinking hole in the ground. I knew because I'd been there. They couldn't read there. They lived like animals. They were still counting on their fingers, for gods' sakes.

My feet stopped kicking and my breathing slowed down. He loosened his grip and sat supporting me with an arm behind my back.

"It really will be all right, Kamet," he said.

"They are *Namreen*," I wailed hopelessly, my tongue almost too numb to form words, doubting that the Attolian would even knew what I meant. The dead men were the elite of the emperor's guard. Loyal and deadly and supported by the bottomless funding of the emperor's purse, they were unstoppable. Obviously the emperor was *not* content that I might disappear carrying with me the guilt for my master's death. He meant to bring me back, no matter where I might run.

The Attolian grunted and swiveled to look over his shoulder at the body behind him. He clearly did know who the Namreen were. "I suppose we won't be catching up with the wagons after all," he said.

A little later, he got to his feet and helped me to mine, then led me across the road where the ground rose into the hills we'd been winding our way through for the last few days.

He found a place where a rocky outcrop provided a sliver of shade and sat me down. It only took a slight pressure on my shoulders and my knees folded up underneath me. He handed me a piece of fabric; he must have pulled the Namreen's headcloth off as we passed.

"Hold this to your head. Press down on it." He moved my hands into the correct position. "Just sit here while I take care of a few things."

One of the horses was still nearby. The Attolian caught it and rode away, coming back later with the other horse. He stripped the bodies of anything useful and then loaded them onto the backs of the horses, tying them in place. He reined the horses together and sent them, with a few well-placed rocks, down the road toward Perf. Distressed by their grisly cargo, the horses would keep moving until they caught up with the caravan ahead.

"Why not keep the horses?" I asked, not seeing the point in advertising the death of the Namreen. I didn't care if they rotted by the side of the road, but the Attolian shook his head.

"We can't rejoin the caravan, and we can't ride by it on the road. We can't go back toward Sherguz—there may be more Namreen behind us, and if there are, we can't outrun them on the open ground." He waved out at the undulating plains below us. He meant *I* couldn't outrun them on open ground. "We'll find a place to hide and see what happens.

We don't want the bodies lying out here like road markers."

He used his shirt to elide the telltale marks in the dust of the roadway and then looked ruefully at it before tucking it into his belt. Slinging his armor on over his bare chest, he shouldered the saddlebags and supplies from the Namreen and climbed back up to where I was sitting. Then we walked into the hills.

From a rise, the Attolian looked back down at the roadway.

"Why Namreen?" he wondered aloud. "Why send the emperor's bodyguard after an escaped slave?"

I knew why. I also knew that the Attolian wouldn't live to see his king again. I'd thought the worst he would suffer was pointless travel and some embarrassment when he returned to his king, but I'd failed to evade him in Sherguz and now he was much too closely tied to me to escape my fate. The innkeeper would have told the Namreen whom they were pursuing.

"I'm sorry," I said. I could apologize to him even if I couldn't tell him the truth.

"It makes no sense," said the Attolian, slowly shaking his head. He wasn't as stupid as I'd thought back on the riverboat. If he put too many things together, it would lead to more than the hostile look he'd given me in the trading city's back alleyways. If he knew I'd deceived him, if he knew what he and his king had been entangled in by my hand, he might march me right back to the city of Ianna-Ir and turn me over to the emperor. It was his only hope at this point—and my only hope was to continue to deceive him.

"It's because I'm so valuable. I was to be a gift to the new emperor, so my disappearance was an insult to him as well. Do you know what I'm worth?" I asked. At my price, the Attolian's eyebrows went up. I'd thought that would distract him.

"Perhaps your king did not know?"

The Attolian shrugged. "No one knows what my king knows," he said. Without saying more, he led the way to the next hill. Though the sun was still high in the sky, dark shadows filled more and more of my vision. The Attolian gave me his arm, and I leaned heavily on him. I knew I was moving slowly and struggled on, mumbling apologies. Finally, the Attolian left me sitting again and went to scout ahead. He came back saying he'd found a good spot and led me to a cave under a rocky overhang, with a small entrance. He helped me slide in and then left me again while he went to find water.

I woke lying on my back, the ceiling just above me as if I were in a very high bunk, but I was puzzled by the sense of hard ground directly underneath me. I thought I was back in the emperor's palace, waking after a beating. I turned my head to see the sandy floor of the cave and remembered the Namreen. My head throbbed as I tried to make sense of my surroundings. The cave was low, but deep, the back of it filled with darkness. It smelled strongly and very badly of whatever animal had lived in it before, probably a cat, possibly a herd of cats. The Attolian was squatting beside me, a dripping cloth in his hand.

"It stinks," I said.

The Attolian nodded. "It's all right, though. We'll be safe here. I'm going to have to stitch your head."

My panic had passed, replaced with a fatalism that was far more familiar. Hoping it would carry me graciously through to my demise, I nodded. Gently the Attolian began to wash my head until he could part my hair and see the wound clearly. I don't know where the needle and thread came from; perhaps the Namreen had it in their supplies, or perhaps the Attolian had bought it along with his other purchases back in the river town. He'd gotten a leather wallet that he wore strapped to his belt and may have carried the needle and thread in it. Anywhere else and it would have been on its way with the rest of our possessions to Perf.

As he threaded the needle, the light dimmed, and there was a scrabbling sound from the entrance to the cave. Keeping my head still, I rolled my eyes to see a lion cub poking its head through the opening. The Attolian hissed and threw a pebble. The cub hissed in return and retreated and it dawned on me that the cave stank not because it had been a lair in the past, but because it still was one. Twisting to look around, I found myself surrounded by gnawed bones.

I gaped at the Attolian, who was now clearly revealed as a madman.

"No one will look for us here," he said defensively.

"The lion will!" I said, my short-lived fatalism shattered.

"She'll care about the cubs more than the den," the Attolian said soothingly. He nodded to the relatively small opening and assured me we could keep out a full-grown cat. "It was just luck that I saw the cubs playing outside the den as I passed and that the lioness was away." He seemed so unconcerned I almost believed him.

"Put your head back down," he said. "Do you know any long prayers?"

"What? Ones to keep lions away?" I asked. I was thoroughly bewildered, and winced as the Attolian used both hands to adjust his work surface, my head.

"No, just something that will distract you while I stitch. I need you to hold still. Can you recite a poem?"

"I don't think so," I said. I find it hard to think clearly when I am in pain. It has always been a wonderment to me that people beat their slaves and ask them questions at the same time. Surely it is counterproductive to expect sense from someone you are beating senseless. "I can't remember any poems."

"No prayers?"

The Attolians recited long prayers in their temple rituals.

"We don't pray that way," I said. I couldn't think of any texts except the instructional ones from my homeland, taught to very small children.

Ine brings the rain
Ire starts the grain
Rae brings the dust
Harvest first we must

I remembered sitting in the dark temple chanting it with other children my age as the rains pattered down outside. I thought the Attolian's stitching would take longer than my reciting, though.

"You understand my language pretty well," he said.

"Yes," I answered. My Attolian was probably better than his. He had a farmer's accent and didn't always conjugate his verbs correctly.

"Good. I'll recite the chant we use. It's called the surgery song. I'll say it one time through first so you will know how long it is." He looked at my head speculatively, turning it back and forth in his hands. "I'll probably have to say it several times through," he warned me, "but this way you'll have an idea how long it will be until I am done."

This was not a technique I'd ever encountered in my experience with Mede healers, but then, I was not a soldier.

"It goes like this," the Attolian said, and recited very slowly:

There was a girl in Attolia town

Could knit and stitch with the best of them.

Wish she were here with my legion,

Wish she were here instead of the surgeon.

She'd take care of this painful lesion

With tiny little stitches

And without any reason

For me to suffer the dull needle poison

That comes from a point

Pushed through hides

Tougher than mine.

"Ready?" he asked, and I nodded. He stuck the needle in, and I shrieked.

"Shh," he said. "I don't want mama lion coming back just yet."

So I was quiet and held very still as he stitched and recited. He paused after each line to pull the thread through, tightening his stitch, then set the next as he moved to the next line. There were only a few longer pauses in his steady pace when he was biting off the thread. I focused on his words and on my breath, exhaling in the pauses, holding it during the stitching, wondering how many times the song had been recited in scenes similar to this one, only probably absent the lion cubs I could still hear meeping outside.

When he neared the end of his second recitation, he lifted

his head up from where he'd been hunched over my scalp in order to look me in the face. "I'm not finished," he said apologetically. "Just a little more. Can you recite it from the beginning?" So I did, fumbling for the words at his prompting until, at last, he was done.

He recited one last couplet like a benediction: "Stitched is the seam, whole is the skin, let it hold bad vapors out and blood in." Then he said, "I'll get you a drink."

He brought a blanket as well and draped it over me. I was glad, as I was shivering—more from distress than cold. I pinched it curiously between my fingers.

"A gift from the Namreen. Our bags must be nearly to Perf by now."

Once again, we had the clothes we wore and little else. At least he'd kept his wallet this time.

"Hungry?"

"No," I said.

"Rest, then," said the Attolian. He pulled his blade out of its sheath and put it with his dagger close to the entrance and then lay down beside them. I wasn't sure I could sleep, but at least the blanket was comforting. The pain in my head throbbed, but it grew no worse. I closed my eyes and tried to imagine that all was well.

I woke with my heart in my mouth. It was dark, and the lioness was screaming. Scrambling toward the back of the cave, I had only a sense of shapes and hasty movements as the Attolian frantically stabbed again and again. I could make out no more, until the lioness pulled her head back and allowed a little of the moonlight into the cave. She reached in, one paw at a time, and the Attolian struck at it with his dagger. I could hear her low, rumbling snarl just outside the cave.

Inside, I could hear the Attolian panting.

"Are you hurt?" I whispered.

"I'm fine," he said curtly. The lioness had obviously been more than he had expected.

We crouched, listening, as the lioness paced back and forth outside, still snarling. Twice more she tried to enter, but halfheartedly. The Attolian slashed at her face, and eventually she retreated, complaining, down the hillside.

"Try to get some more sleep," said the Attolian, as if that were a perfectly reasonable suggestion. I reached for the blanket I had abandoned. Pulling it toward me, I pushed myself up against the back wall of the cave as far as I could get from the entrance.

I was surprised when I opened my eyes to find that enough time had passed that it was light enough for me to see the Attolian curled up asleep. When I stirred, his eyes opened. Crouching over, he crossed to my side and bent over my head, sucking his teeth in concern. I reached a hand up to touch the sticky mess in my hair. I must have hit my head against the ceiling without realizing.

"Leave it," said the Attolian. "Only one or two of the stitches have gone."

He rifled through the Namreen's saddlebag and produced some dried meat and another waterskin, which we shared. I was tired and still rattled by the midnight arrival of the rightful owner of our lodgings, and the meat seemed more effort than it was worth. Still, the Attolian insisted, so I ate. I saw that he had two lines harrowed into his forearm, sticking out either end of an awkwardly tied bandage. I should have offered to stitch it for him, as he had stitched for me. I didn't have his experience and would only have made a mess of it, but I still felt guilty.

After I ate, the Attolian lay down to sleep again. "We'll hear the kittens if she comes back," he reassured me, before closing his eyes.

So I sat up, careful not to bump my head this time, and listened like a mouse in a mousehole for any scrabbling sound that might be the lioness and her offspring returning. I realized that I was hot, still tightly wrapped in my blanket, and threw it off. The day stretched long and painfully ahead.

It must have been after noon when we heard voices and a dog barking. The Attolian was instantly alert, and we both leaned close to the opening of the cave as they came nearer. I knew one of the voices—it belonged to a shepherd from the caravan. He kept the dog to help him manage his flock.

I didn't recognize the voice of the other man, but it wasn't one of Roamanj's guards, I was sure. I wondered if Roamanj had stopped the caravan to organize a hunt, but these two men seemed to be on their own. The shepherd was insisting his dog would find us, but the other man thought they were on the wrong trail.

"We haven't seen a single track in more than a mile; the dog is hunting caggi."

"Look at him. He's on a trail or he wouldn't be this eager." Indeed, we could hear the rising excitement of the dog. I looked to the Attolian, but he only put a finger to his lips.

The dog was barking now, louder and more frantic by the moment.

"Yeah, but trail of what? I'm telling you, he's hunting caggi. He's wasting our time following the trail of some—"

The man had been raising his voice to be heard over the dog until he broke off. I was afraid of what he had seen to stop so abruptly. Our footprints? Some other sign of our presence? We were trapped in the cave—escape would be impossible were we discovered. Then we heard the snarl directly over our heads and saw the lioness's shadow flick across the ground outside. The Attolian and I nearly knocked our heads together trying to see more. The men screamed, the dog barked, the lioness howled. The dog must have held her off for a moment because we could hear the men's shouts continuing as they ran downhill, followed by the yelping dog, perhaps followed by the lioness as well, we had no way to know. The noise they made diminished in the distance while I stared accusingly at the Attolian.

"They won't come back," he pointed out. "They'll assume the dog was following the scent of the lion, not us, and if they do think we were up here, they'll assume she has done for us and they can give up." He actually looked pleased with himself.

I longed to point out to him that there'd been a lion sitting *right above us* and we hadn't known it, but I was much too well behaved. I curled up on the blanket with my back to him and pretended to sleep.

When evening came, I turned up my nose at the little bit of food left from the Namreen's packs. I drank some water and only realized when it was gone that I'd had all that was left. The Attolian waved away my apologies, and I was too sick to care if he was angry.

"It's just the wound fever," he said as he covered me in a blanket I didn't want. "You'll feel better tomorrow." I fell into a nightmare-filled sleep of lions sent by my master to drag me to an afterlife I knew would be even worse than life itself.

When I awoke in the morning, I did feel better, my fever had broken, and the waterskins were full. The insane Attolian had been out to refill them. I told myself that I was lucky not to have been awakened by the lioness eating me and fell asleep again. A little later the Attolian checked his work on my head and nodded, pleased. He brought me water to drink and asked if I could eat something.

I nodded, and he gave me what I thought was probably the last of the dried meat. I held it in my mouth to soften before I swallowed it in a painful lump.

The Attolian went to where the ceiling of the cave was highest and he could sit upright with his feet splayed in front of him. He had his knife in his lap, though there'd been no sign of the lioness since the day before.

"I think she's moved to another den," the Attolian said quietly. "I'll go out later in the day and see if I can get us more to eat, but for now, it's best to keep out of sight of lions and any slave trackers, too."

"Do you think Roamanj's guards are out there?"

The Attolian shook his head. "If they were hunting us, one of them would have been with the dog. Roamanj won't hold up his caravan. He'll press on to Perf and report this business to the authorities there and let them deal with it. I think those two Namreen were alone, so we have some time to get clear of here."

That left only the lioness to consider.

The Attolian sat. I lay on the ground. Time passed very slowly. The Attolian tapped his toes restlessly and said, "So, there was a scholar once who got sick and called the doctor. The doctor wanted a fee for his services, and the scholar promised him he'd pay when he got better. Later the scholar's wife wanted to know why he was drinking so much wine when he was still sick. He said, 'Do you want me to get better and have to pay the doctor?'"

I smiled politely.

He tried again. "There was a young scholar once at the school of Etitus who was ashamed of his beardless state. One day one of the older scholars told him, 'Your beard is coming in,' so the scholar ran to the front gate of the school to wait for it. Another scholar, walking by, asked what he was waiting for. 'My beard! I was told it was coming in!' 'What an idiot,' said the other scholar. 'This is why people think we are such fools. How do you know it isn't coming in the back gate?'"

That was funnier, but I still couldn't produce more than a smile.

"Maybe you know a joke?" the Attolian asked. "A funny story?"

"Only Senabid jokes," I said, dismissing those with a shake of my head.

At the hottest part of the day, when the lioness was most likely to be sleeping somewhere in a patch of shade, I watched how the Attolian managed his exit from the cave. He'd pulled a lace from one of the Namreen's packs and tied a scrap of fabric to the end of it. He flipped the fabric out into the dirt outside the cave and pulled the string, making the scrap dance across the ground. He did this for some time, waiting for any lurking cat to jump on the scrap, and only when there was no sign of the lioness or her cubs did he carefully exit the cave himself. He must have set snares when he was out earlier because he came back fairly quickly, and I heard him outside starting a fire and cooking his catch. He rolled a rock into the cave and crawled in himself, holding his knife at an angle so that the meat he had speared on it wouldn't fall off.

"What is this?" he asked.

"It looks like caggi," I said. "Like a large rat that lives in the desert."

"That's what I thought. It's edible?"

I shrugged. I'd never heard of anyone eating caggi.

"It's caggi or nothing," the Attolian said. He put it on the stone and cut it into small pieces, then fed me one piece at a time. Never had I been so carefully served. If there was a little sand in my meal, I wasn't going to complain.

The Attolian made a face, though, when his teeth crunched on the grit. "Attolians who don't like my king," he said, "put sand in his food. I don't know how he puts up with it." I couldn't imagine. I was surprised they hadn't put something worse than sand in what he ate.

The Attolian smiled down at his food, lost in his memories for a moment. "When he gets fed up, he climbs up on the roofs or the tops of the walls. Sometimes he gets drunk first." That made me think the Attolians might be rid of him soon enough and poisoning their unwanted king was unnecessary.

"That chain around your neck," said the Attolian, abandoning his happy thoughts of the interloper king falling to his death to focus on the present. "I thought we might pound the links between two stones."

We could do that, but it wasn't going to hide the source of our gold. I said, "The flattened pieces of gold would still be suspicious if we tried to trade them for anything."

"What if we claimed to have found it out here in the hills? On a body?"

I shook my head. "The only safe thing a man could do if he found such a thing would be to take it to his local imperial justicer to deliver it back to its rightful owner, who might, or might not, send a reward. A lot of trouble, maybe for nothing. To have it and not have returned it makes a man liable—not just for the gold but for the value of the slave he is judged to have stolen."

"There must be a black market," he said.

"Yes, but difficult to find," I said. "And very dangerous if you ask the wrong person."

The Attolian grunted in disappointment and said we

should plan to move on the next day. "It smells even worse in here than it did before."

I agreed, envying him his time outside—except for the lion.

When the sun was high, we left the den. I lay on my back with my arms reaching out of the cave, and the Attolian dragged me outside to a rocky patch where I could stand without leaving any prints. He'd already piled the Namreen's saddlebags there, and we shrugged them over our shoulders and then checked to see that the long scuff mark we'd left in the soft dirt had covered all of the Attolian's remaining footprints.

The Attolian said, "With luck, the lioness will come back and leave a few more prints on top. Anyone who sees this will think she dragged you in."

I looked away.

"So, so, so," he said, conceding that he had doubts as well. "We'll hope they'll never see this at all."

As carefully as possible, we walked down from the hills back toward the road, stepping from rock to rock and then wiping away any prints we could not avoid leaving. If they brought a dog, of course, it wouldn't matter, but we thought that the men from the caravan had probably lost faith in their tracking animal. By the time Roamanj made it to Perf to report what had happened and imperial authorities of some kind returned to this spot to look for us, our scent would have faded.

We reached the empty road and waited there in a sheltered spot until dark before crossing in case someone was watching. While the Attolian hadn't seen any signs of searchers, he was very cautious. The moon was nearly full and waxing, and we would walk through most of the night, navigating by the visible stars. We would hunker down out of sight just before the sun came up. We were headed overland toward Traba. The Attolian, who had demonstrated he could knock down a caggi from a surprising distance with a stone and a flick of his wrist, would feed us. In Traba, we could pick up the road again and follow it to Koadester.

"With luck," said the Attolian, "we will be well ahead of any pursuit. They will be slow to track us overland, and we will be moving fast once we are on the road."

For the time being, our waterskins were full and we each carried a set of the Namreen's saddlebags stuffed with their extra clothes and a blanket apiece. Their distinctive vests and our own blood-covered shirts we had left in the lion's den.

Even in my best health, I did not think I could have matched the Attolian for traveling strength, and I watched him closely for signs of impatience as I picked my way slowly behind him.

Encouraged when I saw none, I asked, "When we get to Traba, what then?"

"I have a little coin left from your purse and more from the Namreen," he said over his shoulder. "If I have not found a means to make the money to pay for lodging and better food than rodents, we are going to have to find a way to sell that necklace."

As the moonlight was disappearing, the Attolian picked a spot to rest. We couldn't afford a fire, so we just sat in awkward silence until the Attolian said, "So, you don't like Senabid jokes."

The jokes about Senabid and his master are not the sort of thing a slave tells to a free man, and I was an idiot for mentioning them in the first place. I blame it on the fever.

"What about a story from Attolia?" I asked.

"No, I'm no storyteller. Can you tell me more about Immakuk and Ennikar?"

"If you like. First, tell me—how did you come to Ianna-Ir?"

He misunderstood. With a tilt of his head and a wince, he said, "I punched the king in the face."

Aghast, I had no idea how to respond. That wasn't what I had been asking about at all. I'd only been trying to decide which story to tell him. I assumed this meant the Attolian was no favorite after all and the king had tasked him with my theft as punishment.

"He was more kind to me than I deserved and he forgave me," the Attolian said.

Gods above and below. People died—gruesomely—for even thinking of harm to the emperor. Certainly he would never forgive such an offense. I couldn't imagine why the Attolian king would do so.

But the Attolian hadn't finished. "Because he was so kind, people thought I was a favorite, and because of that, he thought it safer to send me here."

At this point, I should have chalked it all up to foreign customs I couldn't possibly understand, but I was intensely curious. If the king had forgiven him for assault, then he was a favorite, wasn't he? What greater favor could the king have shown him? Why was his life in danger?

"How safer?" I asked.

"Well, the Namreen aren't dropping roof tiles on my head or trying to stab me in the back."

That I understood. It was what came of having a weak king. If the Thief was going to let people get away with punching him in the face, it was no wonder he had no control of his court. He couldn't keep his favorite safe and had to send him away. I understood, but I wasn't sure if the Attolian did, because he seemed chagrined for himself, not his king.

I cleared my throat. "I—I was actually asking what route you took to Ianna-Ir. Did you come from Zabrisa to Menle and down the river?"

"Oh," he said. "No. We sailed to Hylas and went overland on the Three Cities trade road to the Southern Ocean. Then took a ship to the delta and another one upriver to the capital."

"So, you crossed the Isthmus," I said. "You know—the narrow stretch of land between the Southern Ocean and the Middle Sea where the Three Cities lie." This was everyday geography—any child in the empire would know it. His eyebrows dropped, and I was afraid I had offended him. Hastily I said, "I was going to tell you the story of Unse-Sek, the monster of the Isthmus." I tapped my lip and began.

Narrow is the bridge between the lands of grain
    and the lands of sand
    the Isthmus evil stalked it
Terrifying Unse-Sek son of the Queen of the Night
    tower tall
    sword clawed
    teeth blood red needle sharp
    bat head and great bat wings
    barbed at their joints
Unse-Sek stalked the Isthmus in the night
    eyes gleaming
    gleaming like the copper domes
    of Ianna-Ir in the sunlight
In the dark gleamed Unse-Sek's eyes
    as he hunted men
    waited until they slept
    lurked and leapt
Then he devoured them greedy Unse-Sek

slurped their marrow

left their bones and gobbets of their flesh

scattered on the land

for their friends to find and grieve over

for their friends to weep over

So was the prince of Hylas lost

So did his father and mother grieve

and cry out for deliverance from

the demon saying who will slay the savage Unse-Sek

and make his name greatest

in the lands of grain and the lands of sand?

Glorified before the gods and potent will be his name

if he slays the savage Unse-Sek!

Came the news to Noble Immakuk and Brave Ennikar

Wise Immakuk Strong Ennikar

answered the grieving friends of the prince

the grieving mother grieving father

swore death to Unse-Sek

They went out across the Isthmus

wandered there stalking

the stalker

Lay in wait as he lay in wait

lurked as the demon lurked until he pounced

Foolish Unse-Sek seizing Ennikar

every hand with three talons

every talon a sword he seized Ennikar

was stung

stung by Immakuk's blade

Snapped with his needle teeth at Immakuk

and missed

Strong Ennikar broke free

swung his sword and lopped Unse-Sek's sword claws

lopped one hand and its sword claws

Howling for his mother Unse-Sek fled

chased

by Immakuk

and by Ennikar

He flew they followed

He turned and fought and was stung

fought for days

First Immakuk

Then Ennikar

drove the monster

wearied him until Unse-Sek turned

seized Immakuk in his teeth

his bloodred teeth knife sharp

shook him as a cat shakes

a mouse a mouse was Immakuk

Unse-Sek howled with victory snapped again

savage Unse-Sek seized again with sword claws

battered Immakuk with his wings

His barbed wings
    pierced Immakuk's eye with his claws
    opened his eye bled out its life
    dimmed its light forever
Immakuk raged
    could not escape Unse-Sek
Ennikar Strong Ennikar rescued Immakuk
    lopped the claws lopped the hand a second time
    cut off Unse-Sek's hand a second time
    freed Immakuk
    sliced Unse-Sek's bat wings
    so he could fly no more
    lopped off his sword claws
Unse-Sek who could not fly could not crawl
    he cried out for his mother
    the Queen of the Night
    cried out
    died

Brave Immakuk and Noble Ennikar took his head
    brought it to Hylas
    hung it there above the gate
    eyes still gleaming

When I was done, the Attolian thanked me.
"Very impressive, that Ennikar," he said.

"So, so, so," I said, and he smiled at the Attolian slang.

"Is he always rescuing Immakuk?" he asked.

He was probably remembering Ennikar pulling Immakuk into Anet's Chariot at the end of the play in Ianna-Ir.

"Not at all," I said. "They save each other. And when the Queen of the Night sends Death to take Ennikar to the underworld, it's Immakuk who rescues him."

"I'd like to hear that one next time," he said. Then he yawned, stretched himself out on the hard ground, and slept. I watched him for a while, and he never moved. His breathing never changed—deep and even and completely relaxed. I looked out at the wide world around us and thought about the Namreen on our trail, and the ordinary robbers who might be at hand, about lions and starvation and death from thirst if we didn't find water away from the trade routes—which, after all, are trade routes for a good reason. Then I lay down and tried to sleep like the Attolian.

The rainy season was well behind us, but there was still water cached in rocky depressions to supplement what we carried, and the sun was not too hot. As we moved away from the hills, I saw that there were indeed signs of life on the rolling terrain—thin grass and the occasional scraggly plant that fed the caggi. Without a trail to follow, we moved slowly. If the Attolian was impatient, it still didn't show.

I hated caggi. I hadn't really liked it the first time the Attolian had offered me a bite on the end of his knife. Within a few days I was so sick of it I would have almost preferred to starve. I didn't like the taste, but what I hated more was the sad look of their small bodies when the Attolian carried them back to camp and skinned them. He often killed three or four of the creatures at a time. Stripped of their skin, they looked distressingly like little men lying in a row waiting to be cooked.

"You are Unse-Sek to the rodents," I said, watching him work.

He bared his teeth and raised his hands like claws. "Nonsense," he said. "I am a much tidier eater." It was true. We picked those bones clean and buried them when we were through. Then the Attolian carefully scattered the ashes of the fire.

"We'll have to turn west and try now for a more traveled route," he said. We hadn't seen any water for two days and the Namreen's waterskins were almost dry. A little later the Attolian left me in the shade of a gully while he climbed up a nearby hill looking for a sign of a road or any man-made thing.

"Nothing," he said when he came back. "We'll rest here, and when it's cooler, we'll start west. Eventually we must hit the route between Perf and Traba and there will be water somewhere along there. If I give you the last of the water, will you tell me about Immakuk and Ennikar and the Queen of the Night?"

It was an obvious ruse to give me the last of the water, and I gratefully accepted it.

"So, the Queen of the Night, angry that her son had been killed, sent Death, her brother, after Ennikar. Death wrapped Ennikar in his wings and carried him away to the underworld."

Brave Ennikar Strong Ennikar
    taken like any man by Death
    to the gray lands
    through the gates of Kununigadak which none may pass
    twice
    none leave who have entered by way of them
    on the road from which there is no way back
    to the land wherein the dwellers are bereft of light
    where dust is their fare dust and clay is their food and
    their drink
    the gray lands
Grieving Immakuk lost his friend
    a loss more powerful than a great river
    bowled him over
    sharper than a sword
    cut him through
Loss led Immakuk from his journey home

THICK AS THIEVES

Death stalked the land as Unse-Sek had stalked
    had carried away his friend Ennikar
    left Immakuk nothing

Why do men die why does death take them
    Immakuk asked
    asked Nuri who had no answer
    asked Shesmegah goddess of mercy
    asked Anet to bring his friend back

The goddess of the moon heard his cries
    took pity on Immakuk
    took pity on him and
    sent him to the stepwell of Ne Malia
    lit his path there
    to the underworld
Step by step Immakuk descended
    to the water of Ne Malia followed the moonlight
    below the water
    into dark lit by moonlight descended
    to the gray lands and the empty banks
    before the eternal river
    that has no beginning and no end
He walked the banks of that river
    who knows how long
    who can know how long

until he met a ferryman
Immakuk asked and the ferryman answered
    two coins to cross the eternal river
Immakuk asked and the ferryman answered
    all may enter none may leave but those unseen
    by Kununigadak the Devourer
Only the anointed return from the gray lands
    anointed with the oil from the land of the gods
    only the anointed are unseen by Kununigadak
    as they pass through the gates
    to return to the bright lands all others remain forever
    within the gates in the gray lands
    bereft of light where clay is the food and
    dust their drink

Two coins to cross the eternal river and Immakuk had none
    tricked the ferryman
    promised to pay and cheated him
    rode across the wide river jumped to the shore
The ferryman said Immakuk two coins you owe me
No said Immakuk two coins I promised for a trip
    across the river
But here I jumped You did not bring me across
Immakuk turned his back on the ferryman
    walked who knows how long
    who can know how long

to the gates of Death's kingdom

gates guarded by Kununigadak

who allows any who choose to enter

none to leave

Immakuk passed through the gates

sought Ennikar

sought his friend

asked the gray people of the gray lands

for Ennikar

for the ointment of the gods

Found the palace of Death

brother to the Queen of the Night

Found the bottle that held the oil

that makes man immortal

that makes him invisible to Kununigadak

oil from the land of the gods

Death would not give up the bottle

would not let Immakuk

find its secret and steal it away

wanted all to come to the gated lands

All come None leave

wanted to rule over all

Immakuk was canny

coaxed Death to cajole his sister

inveigle induce convince persuade his sister
    to give up Ennikar
The Queen of the Night said
    where is my son where is the scion to my kindred
    where is Unse-Sek
    he is destroyed his head a decoration
She said she would not give up Ennikar
    until she had a son to beautify her house
    set up stelae to her spirits kindred to her kindred
    a scion to free her spirit
    to guard her footsteps
    to carry her when she had drunk
    to smother the life of her detractors
Ennikar gave her a son
    and she gave up Ennikar

Immakuk and Ennikar
    they anointed each another
    with the oil of the gods
    made only for the gods

"Wait," the Attolian interrupted. "How did they get the oil?"

"No one knows," I said. I explained that the tablet in the temple of Anet was broken and there were no copies of it. No one was sure how Immakuk got the bottle of oil from

Death, what bargain he made. "When people tell the story or they put on the play of Immakuk and the gray lands, they make up different ways Immakuk might have tricked Death or different promises he might have made. Or they skip that part."

I started again.

They anointed each other
    knew the ferryman would not take them across the river
    knew they would swim
    knew the waters of the eternal river would wash the oil
    away
Brought the bottle to anoint themselves
    and to anoint themselves again
    anoint themselves and others in the world
    make all invisible to the Devourer
So that none must go to the gated lands without leaving
    all shall come and go as they choose
    said Immakuk

Before they could pass the gates
    the ferryman spoke to the gray people
    told them Immakuk had that bottle
    that contained the oil of immortality
Kununigadak was blind could not see them
    only Kununigadak could not see
    the gray people not so blind

They pursued the heroes
 faster went Immakuk
 the gray people followed
 grappled trapped seized
 Ennikar Strong Ennikar
Trapped him the gray people
 as the great are brought down by the weak
 when they are many
As the hawk is mobbed by the roller birds
 as the great sea eagle is brought down by gulls
Immakuk saw Strong Ennikar held
 slowed his steps
 noble Immakuk turned back
Give us the bottle of oil said the gray people in the
 wind-filled whispers
 the bottle give it give it to us and we will let you leave
 the gated lands
 all will leave the gated lands
 never to return
Immakuk remembered his promise to Death
 threw the bottle far away
 deep into the gated lands
As the gray people weakened their hold
 seized Ennikar and drew him through the gates
 as they receded wailing
 seeking the bottle lost that made a

man invisible to the Devourer
Wailed as the Queen of the Night
    affrighted the gray people
    seized with her claws
    lifted the bottle
    flew back to the palace
    of Death her brother

Together Immakuk and Ennikar passed through the
    gates
    as no man has before or since
Immakuk and Ennikar
    swam the eternal river
    came into our world together
    climbed the stepwell of Ne Malia
Because Immakuk had saved his friend but lost the
    bottle of oil
    no man has escaped Death since

"That Ennikar," said the Attolian. "Always with a maid."

"Sometimes it's Immakuk who gives the Queen of the Night a child. It depends on the tablet and who is translating it."

"Translating it from the old language?"

"Yes, from old Ensur, from before the Mede, then into Attolian."

"Who translated what you have told me, then?"

I rocked a little, embarrassed and proud at the same time. "It's my translation."

His eyebrows went up. "All the translations—yours?"

I nodded again. I tried on a few feelings of superiority, telling myself that the Attolian was an uneducated audience who couldn't really appreciate the work involved, but I couldn't push that to a sticking point. I fell back on the embarrassment and pride. "I'm glad you like it," I said.

"Are you translating it just now, as you tell it?"

"No, I translated it from the Ensur into the Mede a long time ago. I was in Attolia when I translated it into your language. I used to sit sometimes in the kitchens, and the workers there liked to ask me about where I came from. Once when they were telling stories of the Attolian afterlife, they asked me if there were stories of the Mede afterlife. One of them kept asking until I translated Ennikar and Immakuk and the Queen of the Night for him. I liked doing it, so I kept at it."

The Attolian poked at the remains of the caggi in front of him. "In our stories of the underworld, it's important not to eat anything, or you will be trapped there forever."

"You'd be doomed," I said.

"I would. I think I'd trade immortality right now for a jug of wine and a plate full of nutcakes."

I remembered those cakes. I had been wrong to say that

the only beautiful thing in Attolia was the queen. She was as beautiful as the Queen of the Night, but the Attolian nutcakes, with their tops decorated in loops and swirls of sticky honey, were even more beautiful—and they wouldn't kill you.

I sighed. "I'd trade the plate of nutcakes for a bath," I said. He nodded. We'd washed as well as we could in the springwater we'd found, but I think our pursuers, if they were out there in the wasteland, could have found us by smell and without needing a dog.

"When we get to Traba, if we transform that chain into coin, the first thing we will do is have a wash and a shave," the Attolian promised. "May you dream of it tonight," he said, and I lay down hoping for just that but instead was haunted through the night by visions of the Namreen.

I was still asleep in the morning when the Attolian sat up suddenly, waking me. Before I could speak, he held up a hand. There was a sound. Very faint. A clinking noise, a sort of tapping, not the jingle of a harness, but almost musical in the same way. I couldn't identify it, but it was tantalizingly familiar.

The Attolian scrambled to his feet, pulling the strap of a waterskin over his shoulder. He leaned down briefly to ask, "Can you whistle?"

I said yes, not sure why he wanted to know.

"If I cannot find you again, I will whistle. You should whistle back. Two notes, one higher, then one lower. I will find you more easily than if you shout, and we won't announce ourselves quite so obviously to anybody else nearby." Then he scrambled out of the gully and was gone.

It was several hours before he came back. As time passed, I listened more and more intently for a whistle, wondering if I'd missed one while dozing or distracted by my thoughts. I considered how easy it would be for the Attolian to just go home to his king, leaving me—slow, annoying, and insufficiently appreciative of his caggi dinners—behind in the wilderness. I concentrated on his earlier refusal to leave my dead body by the side of the road to Perf and strained my ears for a sound floating through the air.

Finally, not far away, I heard a whistle and answered with one of my own. The Attolian appeared at the lip above me with one of the waterskins full again.

"I found a water seller," he said.

The road was north of us, and we could have walked parallel to it for some time before it curved south to cross our path. As it was, the Attolian led me to it fairly quickly, and we followed it all day. There were a number of towns between Perf and Traba, and the road had more travelers and conversely fewer caravans than the one between Sherguz and Perf. The need to travel in groups for safety was less pressing.

In the evening we reached a small community with campsites all around it. Quietly we joined other travelers at the shared fire and listened for gossip. There was no talk of the Namreen hunting an Attolian and a runaway slave—or of a murderous slave escaped from the capital either. I had a story prepared, ready to dismiss the second version as the inevitable exaggeration of rumormongering, but I didn't need it.

The Attolian thought it safe enough to stay at the campsite and continue on the road the next day. Mixed with the other traffic on the road, our presence would be unremarkable.

In the morning I watched as a medicine seller, his wares tied to a wooden yoke, lifted it to his shoulders. All the bottles—different sizes, shapes, and colors to indicate their contents—swung on individual strings, lightly hitting one another with a delicate musical sound, the noise I'd heard the day before, carrying through the open air.

The Attolian looked into his wallet and after a moment of indecision pulled out a coin to pay for two bowls of food from a man wheeling a giant pot through the camp. It was a soupy mix of grain and vegetables. The merchant apologized for the lack of meat, but I didn't mind. I thought it was delicious and ran my finger around the inside of the bowl before I gave it back to him.

"It's only three days to Traba on the road," the Attolian said. "Four, maybe." He meant at the rate I traveled. "I think we can stay on the road without being too noticeable, especially if we keep our ear to the ground for word of the Namreen." He was taking stock of our provisions and our resources. "We can fill our waterskins at the wells for free." He looked at me apologetically. "And then to eat there's—"

"Caggi," I said wearily.

CHAPTER FIVE

We looked up at the walls of Traba. I had reluctantly agreed that we would need to part with the slave chain.

"We'll need to find a money changer with a questionable reputation," said the Attolian. He approached a group of city guards where they were passing the time dicing against a wall in a game of Pits and Monsters. Not hiding his Attolian accent, but flaunting it, he joined the game, chatting comfortably about the dreariness of guard duty and the universal stupidity of superior officers. He'd staked our last bit of money and won at first, but the longer he played, the more he began to lose. At one point a loan from another player was all that kept him going. By then the other guards knew he was a soldier doing a favor for his father, traveling out to check on business matters with one of the family slaves.

I waited nearby like an obedient dog, with my eyes on

the ground, keeping my surprise to myself: I hadn't heard the Attolian say so many words in all the days we had been together. He'd not been this voluble even with Roamanj's caravan guards. By afternoon the Attolian had any number of new friends and was substantially in debt. When one of his new friends, a man with a scar across the bridge of his nose and several of his teeth missing, put a friendly arm around him, he dwarfed even the Attolian. The giant smiled as he said with unsettling intensity, "It would disappoint me to win that much money in a lucky game and not be paid what I am owed."

As the Attolian explained his very regrettable lack of coin, he hooked a finger through the chain on my neck. He and the Traban exchanged a speaking glance while I stood there with a watery smile. The giant suggested a money changer who might address the problem.

"Master," said I, bobbing along beside the Attolian as he strode into the market, "I strongly suggest you reconsider."

"Shut up," said the Attolian. They were the first rude words he had spoken to me, and they cut, though I knew they weren't meant to.

Like a dutiful and long-term house slave, I hung on the Attolian's shoulder all the way across the market to the small stall with a striped awning over it and a sign with the traditional scales that indicated a money changer, urging him to reconsider his plans. I stood wringing my hands while the

Attolian explained his errand in a penetrating whisper.

"Master," I positively whined.

"Shut up," said the Attolian again, and turned back to the money changer. "And I'll need another slave chain, somewhat cheaper, to fix the ownership seal to."

"Your honored father—" I said.

"Is a thousand miles away," said the Attolian.

"But when we return—"

"I'll get another made before then. I always win my money back."

My face eloquent with discontent, I fell silent and obediently leaned forward so that the money changer could grasp the chain and with a sharp jerk pull it from my throat. I had never noticed its weight until I felt it slide from my neck. Next, the money changer threw a cheap imitation gold chain around my neck to replace the one that was gone. In a moment he'd run Nahuseresh's plaque onto the chain and used a crimp to seal the links together.

In less time than it takes a cup of coffee to cool, we were on our way. The Traban guard waiting for his money just outside was quickly paid off. He offered another game, but the Attolian asked instead where we could find a place to have a bath and spend the night, promising to return for a game in the morning.

Once outside the market, the Attolian led the way into one alley after another until we were alone.

"You are sure you don't want another game with your

nice new friends?" I asked him.

He shook his head. "No, thanks, I'm all for the quiet life."

Grasping the chain around my neck with one hand, he yanked it hard, but the chain didn't break; he just pulled me off-balance, and I had to steady myself on his arm or fall over in the street.

"The cheaper the chain, the harder to break," I said, rubbing my neck. The gold in the chain of a high-status slave marks not only his value, but also his master's trust in him.

Using both hands, the Attolian gathered the links of the chain, and with muscles bunching under his skin, he wrenched it apart. He walked along the narrow alley until he came to an opening for the city sewer and dropped the chain to rattle through the grating. It was almost gone when I pinned it in place with my foot. Kneeling, I caught the little gold plaque with my master's seal on it. Pure gold, it was easy to twist free.

"It's small enough to keep hidden," I said.

Looking down at me, the Attolian shrugged. "Keep it if you want," he said.

We walked through Traba and picked out a bathhouse for ourselves. The Attolian chose a prosperous-looking place, more expensive than a common guard was likely to afford. With my chain gone, we didn't want to run into any of the men he had been dicing with earlier. Even after giving away almost a third of the money to pay our debts, we were suddenly very well off. When we were clean and shaved, we asked at the bathhouse for a good inn. We ate a prodigious amount and then staggered to our beds. In the morning, after the Attolian had checked them over carefully, we purchased two mules and some provisions. There'd been no sign that anyone from Perf had caught up to us, and we knew we would make good time riding instead of walking. We threw the Namreen's saddlebags across the mules' backs and left Traba feeling we were well ahead of any pursuit.

"Have you been a slave all your life, Kamet?"

We were alone on the road and could speak freely. It wasn't a polite question, and the Attolian knew that, but we had been together long enough that he must have thought we had reached a point where we could ask uncomfortable questions—that *he* could ask uncomfortable questions, rather. I considered what I should answer—yes, I had been beneath contempt since birth? Or, on the contrary, that I had once been a man as worthy as himself and had become less of one at some time in my life?

I waited a moment to see if he would retract the question, but he didn't.

"I was taken from my home as a child by raiders and then sold to the Mede."

"So you are not a Mede."

He seemed surprised. I wanted to ask him if I looked like a Mede.

"I am Setran by birth."

The Attolian shook his head. "I don't know anything of Setra."

"When you sailed from the Three Cities on the Isthmus to Iannis, if you had continued east you would have reached the city of Ghoda. Setra is in the highlands northeast of there."

"How old were you when you were captured?"

It wasn't as if I knew. I shrugged. "Old enough to have begun training as a scribe—I was on my way to lessons the morning the raiders came. Young enough that I ran back to my mother instead of on to the temple." I remembered her shouting at me that I shouldn't have come home to our fragile little house made of dried mud and reeds.

"I see." Then he considered, the way he often did, thinking things through before he spoke again.

"The temple was fortified, then?"

My memories were a confused jumble of what had been seen but not fully understood by a child. I hadn't picked my way through them in years—I'd just taken my mother's words for truth. I would have been safe with the priests, she had wailed, as the raiders literally tore our home apart. I had blamed myself for my fate—if only I had run toward the temple instead of away—but when I looked back as a grown man, it was obvious that the temple had been no more secure. Perhaps its walls had stood, but that was all. At the end of the day, there had been too many other acolytes in captivity for the priests to have repelled the raiders. The temple had been overrun, the priests were dead and dust— not carefully transcribing their records and setting them out to dry on the temple's porches, as I had been imagining them for years.

"I suppose not," I said.

The last time I had seen my mother, she had clutched at my head as if she could hold the memory of me in her hands if she only squeezed me tight enough before she let go. She was taken with my smaller brothers and sister by one man, but I had been selected by another. She had told me over and over again as they led her away, carrying my youngest brother in her arms, shouting it over her shoulder, "Tell them you are a scribe. Tell them you can write."

So, after we had been led away from the wreckage that was my village to a central camp that was a city of tents, I had dared to look my new master in the face and then carefully write my name with my finger in the dirt. Seeing it, the man had immediately squatted down beside me. Frightened, I had tried to scuttle away. He had grabbed me with bruising fingers and pulled me back. Wiping away my name until the dirt was smooth again, he had said in heavy accents, "Draw me a *hu*." He said, "Now *shee*, now *ur*." They were probably the only three letters the man knew, but I put them in the dust, and he smiled, showing all his yellow teeth. He nodded at me and stood up. That was all. But I rode one of the mules the next day when the camp city was packed up. I got no more food than my master's three other slaves, but I did get an extra cup of water. None of his other slaves were from my village, and they looked at me with sullen resentment every time I drank. At night I slept as far from them as my tether would allow. I would never be one among them again. I was something different.

"And how did you come to Nahuseresh?"

Why could a rock not fall out of the sky on the Attolian's head? "I was sold to the emperor's agent in Ghoda and brought to Ianna-Ir with other slaves. Nahuseresh purchased me in the market there."

I had been purchased as an apprentice and eventual replacement for my master's secretary, who had grown old and nearly blind. Jeffa taught me how to keep records and how to calculate, not just with the triangular marks of the reed, but with the more elegant strokes of ink and pen. Jeffa was gray and bent and remote, as if his life had already drained away and only a husk was left to instruct me, but he knew everything, and he passed it on to me, not only numbers and figures, but our master's habits and hints of his dangerous moods. All the wisdom a slave needs to survive in a palace, he gave me, asking nothing in return.

"You will go further than I did," he told me, patting my head. "Our master's father trained me to keep his records and little more, but he was an ambitious man, ambitious for his sons. They will be great men, and the slaves of great men wield great power as well. See how our master takes care that you learn other tongues? And takes you with him wherever he goes? He will make much of you."

I knew that Jeffa hoped to be retired as some faithful slaves are, sent off to our master's country estate to be cared for as he aged, but he died instead of a putrid throat. The morning after his death, I moved my belongings into his office alcove, ran my hand over his desk, and called it mine—though of course, both the desk and I belonged to my master.

Jeffa was the one who had warned me that I must be out in the sun every day if I didn't want to grow blind as he had, that the dark room where we kept our accounts, the smoke of the lamp, would damage my eyes over time. In the years after his death, I tried to follow his advice, but my eyes had weakened anyway. I was by no means blind, but it was difficult to make out expressions on people's faces from across a room. In the imperial palace, I hadn't realized the Attolian was lying in wait for me. The other guards in the caravan had recognized the Namreen long before I did.

The Attolian was watching me. "You know, back home I have a reputation for being closemouthed," he said. He wasn't the chatty Attolian I had first taken him for, it was true, so I nodded politely and then sank back into my thoughts as the mules carried us along.

Koadester sits at the intersection of two of the empire's great roads. The one we'd been on, going east to west, ran through Traba to Koadester on its way to Zabrisa on the coast. The other came down from the north, from Zaboar to Koadester, continuing south to Menle. The Ianna River is navigable only as far as Menle, but its source sits nearer Koadester where the meltwaters from the Taymets begin to come together. Those meltwaters bring the floods every year to the dry south, and the fertile ground around Koadester supplies much of the food consumed in the capital and by the emperor's armies.

First off, we had no need to go into the city. We only needed to buy food and move on, but the Attolian had developed a tourist's desire to see the Stepwell of Ne Malia lying within its walls. Our road had risen steadily after we left Traba and once we reached the broad open plain on which Koadester sits, there were more and more people traveling with us. We had ridden for some time next to a farmer with a large cataract that had turned his eye as white as the onions filling his cart. He smelled as strongly as his produce, and I'd been secretly relieved when he struck up a conversation with the Attolian, not me. Bragging about his city, he'd told the Attolian about the stepwell, the very one in which Immakuk had descended to the gray lands—as wide at the top as the forecourt of Anet's Great Temple and seven stories deep, with stairs going down on all five sides. In all of history, it had never been dry. Royalty came to sit in a pavilion near the water on hot summer days, and Ne Malia, goddess of the moon, would tell a man's fortune in exchange for an offering at her altar.

He was a most eloquent onion farmer.

I did point out that we were not on an educational tour visiting monuments of the empire like wealthy adolescents, but the truth was, we both felt safe. The Namreen were far behind, and we thought ourselves well hidden, indistinguishable from other travelers on the road. The Attolian gave me the same stubborn look he'd given Roamanj, and into the city we went. We stabled our mules at a livery outside Koadester's walls and walked through the open gates in the dry, hot afternoon. The city stank, but there were cool spaces in the shade cast by the buildings. We had no trouble finding the well, as there was a crowd of pilgrims come to ask the goddess for her help, and it was easy to follow them. We each purchased a token for the altar from an acolyte in the plaza, a flat ceramic plaque with eyes scribed across the top and a circle inside a pentagram set in the middle.

"That's you," I said, pointing to the Attolian's token. "And that's Ne Malia's symbol, the moon reflected in the water." I traced the pentagram and the circle. "When you offer it to the well, the Goddess's favor is on you." Together we walked to where a raised course of stones prevented the rainwater from washing across the filthy plaza and falling directly into the purer waters of the spring below. The dirty water was diverted into pits under the paving stones of the plaza. The pits, filled with sand, filtered the runoff before it seeped into Ne Malia's waters farther down.

The well was just as impressive as the onion farmer had suggested. Each of its five sides was made up of interconnecting staircases descending to the water and then disappearing into it. Some staircases had risers only a giant, or a god, could comfortably use, while others were more suitable for mortal traffic. One could pick any staircase to start, but as some disappeared at each level, many routes at the top led into fewer and fewer options as the well narrowed toward the bottom. The miscellaneous crowd of pilgrims descending from all directions was funneled into just one line that snaked around four sides of the well, turning back on itself when it neared the fifth wall—reserved for the royal pavilion—and arriving finally at the altar just above the water. The altar was stone, but pieced together, so that as the water level dropped, it could be disassembled and rebuilt farther down. The line of pilgrims approached it from the side and made their offering to a priest, who carried each token out over the opaque green water and dropped it in. He waited for a message from the goddess and then returned to whisper it into a pilgrim's ear before moving on to the next offering.

I thought it quite likely the priest spent his day saying the same things over and over, but the Attolian, standing on the lip of the well, was suitably awed. We spent an hour or two standing in line. It was magically cool, even in the hot sun. To me, the priest said, "Your journey will take you farther than you imagine"—a safe prophecy even if my journey had only been across the city. The Attolian looked a little mystified, and I asked what he'd heard. He repeated the words as he'd understood them: "Remember Immakuk. Pay the fastener." I tried to figure out what the priest had really said and the Attolian had misheard, but I couldn't puzzle it out.

Then, as we were climbing out of the well, the Attolian's sandal strap broke, and he wanted to look for a leatherworker to repair it. We walked through the markets nearby and found a craftsman with a booth and a collection of slaves at work on benches under an awning. The Attolian handed over his shoe, then walked on one bare foot to a wineshop just down the street to wait in the shade while it was fixed. The wineshop was on the opposite side of the street from the leatherworker's shop, and I could watch the slaves at their labor, my eye on the one who had the Attolian's sandal.

He sat at a slightly finer bench, with a cushion underneath him. Usually a head slave like this one has authority over the others, but I wondered if it was a recent promotion that had made the other slaves jealous. They treated him so abominably that I could see it from across the open ground between us. As I watched, they jostled his elbow, pulled his work askew, and, while he was distracted, substituted a broken tool for his awl.

When he ruefully offered his broken awl up to his master, the man smacked him on the head and regretted aloud the money he had wasted on a trained slave when he could have had an untrained one doing better work by a month's end. That ended the mystery and should have ended my interest; the slave was new and resented by the others. Still, I liked the look of the new slave and didn't particularly like the snake-eyed amusement of the most pernicious of his tormentors. When the Attolian went to retrieve his repaired sandal, I exercised my new authority as a free man and pointed out to the leatherworker the drama his slaves were acting out in front of him.

The leatherworker turned to look ominously over his slaves. The new one threw me a grateful glance before he hunched back down at his bench. The leader of the tormenters was more bold, and he stared at me with a look that would have boiled lead, but when I stared back, he had to drop his eyes.

It was a trivial thing, and I was used to wielding far more power than this. I had bought and sold slaves for my master and sent miscreants to be punished and had occasionally rewarded those who served my master well. But then, I had been wielding my master's power for him. This was my first exercise of my own authority as a free man, and I would be lying if I said I didn't enjoy the feeling.

By this time it was too late to be leaving the city. We agreed that we would buy our provisions and find an inn to rent us a room for the night. Thinking no more of the leatherworker, we walked the market stalls, buying up dried meat and fruit and grain that could be stewed quickly in a pot, which we also purchased. The Attolian carried all this, having declined my offer to take the parcels as we made our way down the streets, looking for a likely place to spend the night.

As we walked through the twilight, we saw stepping out of an inn doorway just ahead of us the slave from the leatherworker's stall. The Attolian recognized him before I did and stopped in the street. I saw him shift his packages to leave his right hand free, and my heart pounded in my chest. Only then did the leatherworker's slave come close enough for me to make out his face and then close enough to speak without being overheard. He addressed the Attolian, quickly and quietly. "The Namreen are in the city looking for an escaped slave, a Setran—with a foreigner—they have posted a bill in the judicial square." He looked at me. "Few would have noticed Bahlum's tricks, and only another slave or a freedman would have mentioned them to my master." He ducked his head politely, as if he'd done no more than offer us a greeting in passing. Then he was gone.

Both the Attolian and I continued walking as if the message were of no particular importance. In unspoken agreement, we passed by the inn where the slave had probably just made inquiries that would draw the landlord's attention to us if we were to stop in so soon after he left.

"There are other foreigners in the city," said the Attolian. That was true. They were quite common. But an Attolian and a Setran were a less common mix. And just because the slave had said "foreigner" didn't mean the Namreen hadn't more specifically said "Attolian."

"We may still make it through the city gates, and better to try now with the twilight to disguise us," said the Attolian. "We should try the main gate, though. It will be more crowded."

I followed, thinking of the bill the slave had said was posted in the judicial square, where the punishments authorized by the empire's courts were carried out. We would cross through the square on the shortest route back to the main gate. If the Attolian passed the bill, he would see the printing that declared me a murderer, and then the fat would be in the fire. I would not be able to pass off the official description of my crime as an exaggeration born of rumormongering.

Though he showed no sign of haste, the Attolian had picked up speed, and I hurried to catch up.

"We'll need water," I said, which was true. We'd left our

waterskins with the mules after agreeing that we needn't buy the higher-priced water inside the city—supposedly blessed by Ne Malia. We'd intended to buy cheaper water out on the road or wait until we reached a public well.

"We can still get our skins filled at the stable," said the Attolian.

"It will be faster to pay for new skins with Ne Malia's water than refill ours." If the Namreen were nearby, we wanted to leave as quickly as possible, and crossing the city by way of the water sellers would keep us well away from the judicial square.

The Attolian didn't agree, and I had to persist even though I knew I might be arousing his suspicions. We had reached the edge of the square before I convinced him to turn aside toward the street that led to the water sellers, and then, fool that I am, I let my eyes be drawn to the bills pasted on the side of the steps leading down from the governor's justice building to the plaza. To me, they were incomprehensible blurs, and I immediately pulled my gaze away, but it was too late. The Attolian noticed and turned to look as well.

"Never mind, Kamet," he said. "No one but that slave would connect you and me with the notice, and we'll be outside the gates in no time at all."

I nodded my head sharply a few times, thanking the gods he wasn't calling me a murderer and a liar. "Yes," I said, "everything will be fine."

"I'm sorry we came into the city," he said, blaming himself for bringing us to see the stepwell instead of blaming me for giving us away. "I thought we were well ahead of any pursuers from Perf. I did not think we would leave a trail in a city this size. I took a stupid risk."

I should have apologized—it was my fault as much as his—but I didn't. I was too busy thinking of the bill, wondering if he could have seen it and not understood its implications. Maybe my bill had been posted on the other side of the stairs and he hadn't seen it. Maybe he had seen it but couldn't read it from that distance. Maybe he couldn't read at all—the bills were read aloud every week because many people couldn't. Very likely he was as illiterate as most Attolians. I breathed again. He hadn't yet learned how I had deceived him.

At the main gate we separated, each of us tagging along in a different crowd. Once we were through, I turned to walk along the city wall, and the Attolian followed. When we reached the stables, I felt him take my elbow and kept walking. I could see the Namreen in their distinctive vests and didn't need him to explain—the mules and our saddlebags were lost to us. It was a good thing, after all, that we'd bought Ne Malia's water in fresh skins. We walked on in the growing darkness away from the city on the road leading west, among the farmers and merchants who had come to the city markets for the day and were on their way home.

"I can be silent if you can get a place for us," the Attolian whispered in my ear.

I started onward, looking for a likely group to approach, but his hand on my arm slowed me. "You must not give us away," he added. It was said without censure, but his meaning was clear. I had revealed too much in Koadester. My pride wanted to remind him we shouldn't have gone into the city to begin with, but I swallowed it and instead led the way through the discrete groups of people around us, looking for an opening to join one.

My problem was a lack of familiarity with ordinary free people. I knew how to be a humble slave around my master and how to be an arrogant slave as I did my master's work. None of that would help me now to pass as a free man. I thought about how the Attolian treated people, but I didn't have the bulk to move with his confidence. I thought of the leatherworker dealing affably with the Attolian, but his demeanor came with age. I considered the tailor Gessiret, back in the city, and his long-suffering response when I had retrieved the money I had given him the day Nahuseresh died. The tailor hadn't complained to me, but I didn't doubt he had complained to someone that day—his wife or his mistress, or a friend in a wineshop—just as slaves complained to each other. Everyone complained. Complaint was universal.

I picked a farmer walking beside the horse that was pulling his two-wheeled cart. I assumed it was his wife and daughter traveling with him. Slowing my pace just a little, I fell in next to him and nodded when he briefly looked up. "A good day?" I asked. "Or more money going out in taxes than comes in for profits?"

As I'd hoped, the prompt was all that was required. We walked together—the silent Attolian, the farmer, trailed by his wife and daughter, and me—while the farmer cataloged his woes and railed against the officials who ran the markets in the city and took away his money as fast as he made it. I only needed to nod my head and say something agreeable as it grew darker and darker around us. Nothing could have been more companionable than all of us traveling down the road until at last the farmer came to a turnoff and we bid him good-night. No one would have guessed that we didn't share the farmer's interest in city management. That we had taken every opportunity to glance behind us, checking for the light of torches issuing from the city gates. That our ears perked up at the sound of hoofbeats, no matter how slow moving.

Once the farmer had left us, we continued only a little farther and then, under the cover of the ever-blacker night, picked our way over the road's drainage ditch and a low stone wall onto a freshly plowed field. The land around Koadester was green and profitable, not dry like the plateaus farther south or on the road to Perf. Afraid of leaving footprints in the tilled dirt, we walked along the harder ground near the stone walls, moving away from the road until we found a cluster of pomegranate bushes the Attolian thought it was safe to sleep underneath. We crept in, the branches scratching at our exposed skin, until we were confident we wouldn't be seen as soon as the sun came up. Then we settled down for the night.

I lay looking up through the branches at the starry sky striped with filmy white clouds like bed-curtains and a few denser clouds like pillows, thinking of the comfortable beds in the inns back at Koadester. I'd been dreaming of them on the road from Traba. I admitted, if just to myself, that the hard ground I slept on was not the Attolian's fault. I had wanted to go into the city, too.

We'd seen no sign of the Namreen on the road. Heard no rumors about them from other travelers. They hadn't set out after us from Perf and must have come up directly from Menle. I should have considered that possibility, but I'd been imagining them following in our tracks, as if I were leaving a line across the landscape behind me like a crack in a china cup. I'd only been looking over my shoulder, not thinking of the emperor's command as a stone thrown in a puddle, scattering drops in all directions, sending the Namreen east to Perf, north to Koadester. Were they in Zabrisa looking for me now? Were they at Iannis on the Southern Ocean? We were lucky. We could have met them on the road with no warning at all, and if we hadn't gone into the city, we might have. Better sleeping in a field on the hard ground than in the Namreen's tender care.

"They are very determined," the Attolian said beside me. I knew he was mulling over the same thoughts.

In the early-morning light we crossed more fields until we came to a narrow footpath that paralleled the road we had left the night before. We hiked all day at our best pace, continuing into mostly uncultivated land. The ground was flat and open all around us, and I felt very exposed. There were no other travelers to hide among. The only comfort was that people on horseback were easy to see from a long distance, and all of them were far away on the main road. Eventually our narrow route curved toward the north, where the land rose as the scrub grew thicker and higher. Ahead were the first of the hills that lay between us and Zaboar, and our path soon joined a wagon track that skirted their southern flank. We stopped there for a rest and to eat.

"The trade route to the north is behind us now," said the Attolian, thinking aloud. "And it will be crowded with Namreen. If we continue to go west on this track, there may be some smaller passages over the hills that we can find. It's a risk, as we might be seen, but we will move faster through the hills if we find a beaten path going north. I don't think we should go overland unless we have to. What do you think,

Kamet?" Flattered that he thought my opinion worthwhile, I agreed. The hills ahead of us looked to be rocky and filled with canyons and chasms, just the sort of place to get lost in. I hoped we would find an easier route, and I still had no idea how we were going to get over the Taymets, which would make these hills look like ripples in a blanket by comparison.

We hurried, the Attolian keeping an eye out and sending us to cover any time he saw or heard other travelers. The wagon track was for local traffic, and there was very little of that. In the evening he found a hollow and said we could have a small fire, but it must be out before full dark. I asked if we'd continue after we ate, but he said there was no point—we'd likely pass any trail over the hills without seeing it.

As the grain and dried vegetables were bubbling in our cookpot, the Attolian said, as if it were no more than an idle observation, "My king thinks that the emperor must attack the Little Peninsula or die."

"He is dying either way." That was an open secret. The emperor had hidden the signs of his disease, but the Tethys lesions only worsen over time.

"His heir, I meant," said the Attolian. "Once he becomes emperor, my king says he will not live out the year if he cannot conquer the Little Peninsula."

I eyed him in some consternation while I considered his words.

"My king says the empire has absorbed all the little countries like your Setra to the east and is at a standstill in the Unshak Mountains. It cannot expand south beyond the Isthmus—not across the desert—and my king says that if the emperor fails to enlarge his borders, there will be an internal war to replace him. If the expansion can be stopped, even for a very short time, the empire will break apart under its own weight."

My king says . . . What a parrot, I thought, feeling worldly-wise. I knew better than the Attolian the reach of the empire.

"My king," said the Attolian again—and then he stopped, waiting for me to realize that he knew just what I was thinking. He was amused, not offended, and I wasn't afraid, but I was a little embarrassed that he read my mind so easily.

"I am sure your king is a wise man," I said apologetically, willing to consider that my prejudices had blinded me to his finer points.

"My king," said the Attolian, with a very serious expression, "likes to pretend that he doesn't recognize the Mede ambassador. Whenever they meet, the ambassador has to introduce himself—with all of his diplomatic titles and his qualifications."

"No."

"Yes." And when I stared, aghast at this juvenile and frankly rude behavior in a head of state, he added, "Sometimes twice a day."

"*You lie*," I said, certain he was mocking me.

He held up a hand. "My sacred oath." He didn't seem the least bit mortified.

I had been giving the Attolian king's idea serious attention, but now rejected it. There was always unrest, of course. Fear of the poor and of slave revolts, the occasional corn riot. Demagogues rose and fell, and the empire was always cutting down one or another. It would be possible, I supposed, for an outsider to see disruption and think the empire might collapse, but it was too all encompassing, too well sewn together to come apart. As each smaller nation was absorbed, it was integrated into the whole, enjoying all the benefits of being in the empire. It would be the same with Attolia, I was sure.

"The Little Peninsula cannot hold off the empire even for a short time," I said.

"We have the Greater Powers on our side."

He was naive.

"That only means that one of the Greater Powers of the Continent will control the Peninsula instead." I shrugged to indicate the unstoppable nature of this process. After time spent with the caravan guards and with the Attolian, I was more aware of the work and of the cost, but I still did not doubt the superiority of the Medes and the inevitability of their success.

"There are advantages to the empire," I reassured him.

"Stability and peace, an increase in trade, the exchange of art, advances in medicine." A decent sewer system, I almost added, but bit my tongue in time.

"Is that how you felt when the king of Setra gave over his country to the empire?" asked the Attolian.

I had been many years a slave by then. When the empire had put down the raiders who had taken me from my home, I had been happy to hear it. "Look at the Little Peninsula with its constant wars," I said. "It obstructs the land route between the Continent and the empire. Every time a squabble erupts, it disrupts the trade. Every time a land war flares up, the piracy on sea routes doubles. All the civilized nations want is a reliable trade route. They want something safer in the windy season than sailing. It's not about conquering, it's about business and prosperity. Prosperity for everybody."

With a sharp sweep of his hand, the Attolian dismissed prosperity and civilization and the Medes entirely. He said, "Nothing is certain in this world."

"True," I agreed, myself an example of the maxim, "but the emperor breeds that uncertainty and uses it to his advantage." I thought of the times he had elevated a member of the court only to turn around and humiliate him a short time later. I thought of the death of my master. Oh, what consternation that was going to cause! The emperor was probably chortling himself into phlegmy coughing fits. I said, "The longer it is unclear if he means to invade, the longer he can prepare his armies without drawing the Greater Powers in."

The Attolian took a swallow from the waterskin. "My king believes that your own master is a threat to his brother."

"I don't think so," I said. Although maybe that was why he'd been poisoned, for all I knew.

"Perhaps he will lead a rebellion."

Well, that wasn't going to happen, because he was dead. I thought the rest of what the Attolian had said was equally unlikely. If there were threats to the empire, then the emperor eliminated them. The Attolian king was a fool and, as a fool, hoped his enemy might magically disappear overnight. I wasn't that silly.

In the morning, we found a path that turned off our road and headed north into the hills. The Attolian asked me what I thought of it. "Shall we press on and see if we can find something more traveled?"

The hills were steep and rocky. Eroded by the winter rains, they were ridged with ravines and punctuated by cliff faces. I would have preferred to stay on the more easily navigable wagon track, but the Namreen might ride along at any moment—and moreover, the track wasn't going to carry us in the direction we wanted to go. It would eventually merge with the road from Koadester to the western coast, and that road would certainly be traveled by Namreen.

We took the path and struggled upward. I imagined the Taymets as I climbed, worrying about what their slopes might be like. The trade road we had been making for, the one we had been diverted from at Koadester, was known as a hard and narrow way over the mountains. It had to be hard or there wouldn't an independent Zaboar on the other side. If the trade road was narrow and hard, I hated to think what any other route was going to offer us.

Our path wasn't wide enough for a wagon, but it seemed quite reliable at first. It rose quickly, and became rockier, until it was no more than a broken ribbon twisting into the hills. We lost the track for a while and veered off course. We ended up retracing our steps, and that's when we first saw our pursuers—or at least, the Attolian did.

"There's a party out on the road large enough to throw up a dust cloud," he said. "And a smaller group coming up behind us."

"Namreen?"

"I can't tell," said the Attolian. "Try not to silhouette yourself against the sky. We'll wait here until they have gone past." He led the way to a spot where we could be unseen and still overlook a bit of the trail below.

When he next saw them, they had made up almost half the distance between us. "Probably coincidence," the Attolian said, trying to sound optimistic as we waited for them to go by.

It was a tense wait. I wasted it being anxious instead of enjoying the rare opportunity to sit down. Eventually we saw them again as they crossed below us. I relaxed, but the Attolian didn't, insisting we wait where we were. We were sitting there, sweating gently in the sun, when the party of men came back down the trail, watching the ground carefully as they came.

Hissing, the Attolian pulled me from where I was sitting and hustled me higher up the hillside.

"Not a coincidence," I whispered.

"So," the Attolian agreed, and proceeded to haul me bodily uphill.

As we climbed, we came to an open expanse of solid rock where we could move quickly. I thought this was lucky. The Attolian, still with his hand under my armpit, pulling me faster than I could safely go, didn't seem to feel the same way. He risked many anxious glances over his shoulder as we went at a breakneck pace. Only when we reached cover did he slow and begin to pick his way more carefully.

They couldn't possibly follow us, I told myself. We'd left no footprints behind on the rocky ground. Hadn't the guards on the caravan been extremely watchful in similar hills—because bandits could disappear so quickly into the hills? Surely we could do the same.

When he thought we were well ahead of our pursuers, the

Attolian tucked me into a rocky crevice and told me to wait while he climbed up to get another look at those hunting us.

"They aren't Namreen," he said as he dropped back down beside me.

"How can you tell?" I asked.

"If those ratty pieces of trash are Namreen, I'm emperor of the Medes. They are slavers and bounty hunters." He appeared to be considering a fight.

"There are still—what, seven, eight of them?" I said, thinking that the Attolian had killed two Namreen, but that did not make him invincible.

The Attolian reluctantly took his hand off his sword.

"Have they found our trail?" I asked.

"Not so far," he answered.

"Then we should keep going," I said. I started up the steep-sided valley that would carry us farther into the hills, and the Attolian followed.

CHAPTER SIX

It was clear by sundown that we were in desperate trouble. I could no longer pretend to myself that we could escape. We'd run up against a cliff and moved as quickly as we could along the face of it, weaving in and out of rockslides that had come down. We'd found an opening that we'd thought might lead us upward, but the ravine had narrowed as we climbed, and we'd reached a point where the ground rose too steeply for us to continue without using our hands as well as our feet. Even the Attolian would find it a challenge, and I was almost out of strength, hunched over and gasping, when he looked up in alarm and dragged me backward under an overhang.

"What is it?" I asked. "What did you see?"

"They've skylighted themselves, probably on purpose. I'm sorry, Kamet, at least three of them are at the top of the slope above us."

"Can we go back?"

"No. They revealed themselves because they know we are trapped." He dropped the bag he'd been carrying, with the remains of our purchases from Koadester, and the waterskins as well.

"What now then?" I suppose I thought he'd produce another lion's den for us to shelter in.

He didn't. He loosened his sword and began to draw it out.

"No," I said, pulling his hand away. He looked at me, startled, while I racked my brains.

"We've hardly seen them, and they haven't had a good look at us. Take off the sword belt and your breastplate. They aren't the Namreen—they don't know for certain who we are. If we are *two* escaped slaves instead of one, then maybe we are not the prize they are hoping for." Stripping the Attolian as I talked, I took his belt and the sword and the plate and hurried to push them deeper under the overhang where they would be out of sight, then directed the Attolian to empty his purse. Making a face, he tipped almost all of our coins out into the grass and replaced the purse in his belt. Then he helped me pile what loose rocks there were until our cookpot—I was really going to miss that pot—and his armor were well hidden.

When we were done, the Attolian stood staring at the rocks, like a man bewildered. I had to take him by the shoulders and turn him away.

"Don't look anyone in the face," I warned him. "Don't say anything if you don't have to. Let me talk. Don't disagree with anything, don't even think to yourself that you know what they do not because it will show on your face. *Everything* shows on your face, so just try to think of nothing at all. Look at the ground, do you understand?"

He nodded. I helped him to reshoulder the bag that had held our provisions, hoping that the men who pursued us would not notice any decrease in his bulk now that his armor had gone. Then I had to think how I could pass off someone with muscles like his as a slave. That he was a foreigner was not a problem—many slaves were. He was a field hand, perhaps, but that only raised the question of how he and I might be escaping together. Field hands would have little contact with the house slaves. If I'd ever planned an escape from my master, it would not have been with one of his ditchdiggers. The Attolian was very good-looking, though, and I chose that fact to guide my story. He might be a field hand brought into the house as a pet for the mistress. That was not uncommon, and it would only be helped if he played stupid and kept his mouth shut. I could only hope he would do so. He was far from arrogant, but his stubbornness might do us in.

Confident that they had us pinned, the slavers made no attempt to hide their approach. When I heard their voices, I began to berate the Attolian, blaming him for everything under the sun. He was slow, he was stupid, if he'd done as I'd told him, we would have been safe and—in ridiculous counterpoint—that we never should have tried to escape and it was his stupid idea and I shouldn't have listened when he suggested it. The Attolian went along with me, punctuating my rant with bumbling attempts to interrupt me or accept the blame.

"Morik," he said, giving me a common name, "Morik, I didn't know. I'm sorry," he said humbly.

Trying to conceal his Attolian accent, he spoke each word with deliberation that made him sound appropriately thickheaded. His accent really had improved, I noticed, but gods save us, he still had his earring in his ear. I fell silent, staring, and the Attolian hastily pulled it out of his ear and popped it into his mouth. Better to have thrown it away with the coins, but there was no time to argue with him.

"Ho," said the leader of the men hunting us. "What have we here, a slave and his friend thinking they could run off?"

Only then did it occur to me that he could very well mention the death of my master. I was completely unprepared to have that revealed. Panicked, I began to babble. I blurted out an invented name for our mistress and the farm outside of Koadester where we had come from, explaining that our disastrous mistake was entirely the stupid field hand's fault. He'd been brought into the house as the mistress's pet and it had led him to ideas about his own importance and I was terribly, terribly sorry to have been misled by him and was prepared to be taken home and would be a very good slave in the future.

I was so frantic and so stupid that I think this alone convinced them I could not be the murderous, conniving slave described on the bills posted in Koadester. The slavers looked shocked as I rattled on, at first merely skeptical that the hulking Attolian could be the mastermind of our escape and then disappointed.

The leader of them, to my surprise, swore in Setran, and I wondered if all of the men were Setran. Their features were indistinct, but they may have been from the Goli tribes, who'd scattered after being put down by the empire. The Attolian looked at me, but I ignored him, praying that if the Setrans talked of my master and his death, they might do it in a language the Attolian couldn't understand.

Behind us, we heard clattering rocks as the slavers who'd been on the heights above us finished making their way down.

"This isn't them," said the disgusted leader in Setran.

The men cursed, casting their hate at us, their disappointment dangerous.

"Two of us could have collected these," said one burly slaver. "We've left the rest with Kepet, and he's probably asleep again." He reached for his sword, and the Attolian tensed. He didn't need to understand the language to know that the slaver meant to kill us outright. I turned a little to lay a warning hand on his arm and leaned against him, retreating from the slaver and discreetly nudging the Attolian back as well.

I licked my lips and said, "I am my mistress's majordomo and amanuensis. Q-quite valuable."

"Put up, Shef," another of the slavers said.

"They're still worth more than the others put together," added another.

Shef lowered his sword back into its sheath, but then he punched me so hard that I fell straight to the ground, leaving the Attolian without any guide. I could only cover my head and pray that he would follow my example and take the blows he had coming to him.

Evidently he did. I heard him grunt as he hit the ground. We might have suffered longer from Shef's disappointment, but someone above spoke after only a few more blows. "Let's go. We still have to catch up to Kepet, and you're right that he is probably asleep by now."

The slavers pulled us to our feet and efficiently tied our hands, looping a rope around our necks to make a leash to lead us back down the ravine and from there back to the trail we had been following. Even in the dark, they seemed familiar with the terrain. I fell several times and heard the Attolian go down as well. I winced as one of the slavers said, "Oh, you don't like that, do you?"

We followed our previous trail only a little while and then left it to travel overland. The slavers led the way to a much wider path, a clearly well-used cart track we would have come to if we had continued along the road skirting the hills just a little farther. We walked uphill until we reached their camp on a patch of flat ground just off the road with a curving rock face behind it, like an outdoor room, made by chance. It was obviously a regular stopping place, with iron staples sunk into the rock at head height to tether the mules. There was a mortared fire ring in the center and a stack of firewood next to it. A lively fire was burning, and as predicted, a man was asleep beside it.

The slaves they were transporting were chained together, as close to the fire as they dared get, close enough to attack the man in his sleep, but he was hardly in any danger. When I saw the slaves, my heart constricted, and I squeezed my eyes momentarily closed.

There were perhaps twelve or fifteen of them. They were skeleton thin and covered in filth and sores, their clothes only rags. These were not the slaves of the imperial city or even of the outlying farms. They were the cheapest of slaves, the most miserable souls of the human race, bound for hard labor in the mines. They could have been anchored to the staples in the rocks, but weren't. Even with surprise on their side, all of them together would not have been a match for the healthy and well-fed Kepet. They sat or lay, indifferent, as the Attolian and I were brought into the circle of the firelight and chained at the end of their row.

One of the slavers cursed and lifted an empty ankle cuff. A slave had slipped away, and not for the first time evidently. The slavers kicked Kepet awake and swore he would pay for the missing slave from his share. Kepet argued that the man wasn't worth any money anyway, but the other slavers drove him off into the dark to fetch the missing slave back. Then they argued about who would make food.

One man was finally bullied into the task. He put a pot onto the fire, pouring in water and dried meat and a few vegetables to make a thin soup and then adding a scoop of grain. When it was obvious that nothing was coming to either of us from that pot, I told myself that the meat in it was probably caggi.

I heard the Attolian whisper under his breath, "Not nearly as tasty as grilled rodent," and essayed a weak smile.

The other slavers' dinner had been cooked and eaten before Kepet came back. He was alone, but carried something in his hand. He walked along the group of slaves, kicking each awake and showing it to him, and then moving on to the next. When he reached me, I saw that what he held was a severed hand. He walked to the fire and threw it in.

"Gods all damn you," the other slavers shouted. "Why did you do that?"

"You said you'd keep his price from my share, so keep it. I told you he wasn't worth the trouble he makes."

"You didn't need to throw it in the fire," snarled the man who'd been doing the cooking. He fished the hand out and threw it onto the road.

Then Kepet sat and ate what was in the pot, complaining that the other slavers hadn't left much. Only when he was finished did they feed the slaves. I saw there was another pot, not in the fire, where they had put grain to soak. Shef carried it along the row of chained men, scooping out a handful of grain, then squishing it into a cake and dropping it into the outstretched hands of the slaves. Each time he held it in the air first as the slave begged for it. He was followed by a man with a water sack and a cup who did the same.

"Please, please, master, please"—the whispered supplications like the voices of those already in the gray lands.

The Attolian wouldn't beg and got neither the grain nor the water. I took the wet lump the slaver had given me and divided it, handing one half to the Attolian. Then I picked out the grains from the cake and ate them one at a time to make them last. The slavers meanwhile passed a wineskin among themselves. As the drink loosened their tongues, they talked about their new slaves and where the best place to sell us would be. Dishonest to the core, they would make no attempt to return us to our supposed owner. They were on their way into the hills to take the slaves to a tin mine, but that wasn't the place to sell a trained slave and a healthy field hand. They would take us with them to the plains below. One suggested that our invented owner might have posted a reward, but none of his colleagues thought it worth the time to go back to Koadester to see. Better, they thought, to see us as a windfall, take us west to the first market, and sell us there. As we had no slave chains, they could plead ignorance of our owner's identity if they had to. Unethical but predictable. After a while the talk turned to the Attolian's good looks, and I grew more concerned. I had been too successful perhaps in casting him as the pampered lover of our imaginary owner. Swigging from a flask of wine, one of the slavers stood up and strolled over. He passed me and squatted next to the Attolian.

Oh, I thought hopelessly, this isn't going to end well.

I swung around toward the Attolian and without warning shouted in his face. "This is all your fault, isn't it?" I shouted. "I would be safe at home if I hadn't listened to you." The Attolian looked at me, as bewildered as I had expected. He hadn't understood the Setrans. "I am sorry," he said, as if an apology in this predicament was helpful. He didn't call me Morik, and this wasn't an act. "You would be better off if you had stayed with N—"

Not even these stupid slavers would believe our story if he mentioned my master by name. I shifted my weight, and using both feet, I kicked him as hard as I could between the legs.

The Attolian screamed. For an eternal moment his face was frozen, wide eyed, in shock and pain. Then he clutched himself and rolled to his side, curling up like a newborn over his injured manhood. Meanwhile, I continued shouting, calling him vile names and cursing him for his imaginary faults. The slavers laughed. The man with the flask swung it at my head, but by then I was already retreating as far as the chain would let me, even as I kept up my name-calling. The Attolian lay on his side gasping. When he could talk, he spoke in Attolian, so hoarse and so shrill that the men nearby were more likely to think they'd misheard than that the words had been unfamiliar. "—kill you," were the only ones clear to me.

Laughing with the other slavers, the man with the flask stepped back to watch what would happen.

I could only pray that the Attolian would realize the reason for my actions. Or that if he didn't, the slavers wouldn't really let him murder me. I couldn't be sure what to expect from men who would kill a slave rather than take the trouble of chaining him properly.

Very frightened, I tried to retreat further as the Attolian got himself up on his knees and crawled toward me. It did little good. He lifted the chain attached to my ankle and pulled. He was still too hunched to sit up straight, but the muscles in his arms tightened and I slid helplessly toward him.

I curled into a ball, the only defensive measure I could take. Rather than smashing my head with his fist, the Attolian seemed more intent on getting his hands around my neck. Like a plated lizard, I curled even tighter. The Attolian grunted as he pulled my arms away from my face. I took a chance and flipped myself over and scrambled away, but he pulled me back. We repeated this maneuver several times, to the hysterical amusement of our captors, until suddenly it was over. The Attolian had gotten a hand around my neck, and I couldn't move. He pressed me against the ground as I tried to pry his iron fingers away.

I would have tried to explain myself at that point, I would have said anything to persuade him to let go, but my breath was no more than a whistle, and then even the whistling stopped. All I could hear was the blood pounding in my ears. It grew louder, and the Attolian's face grew darker and seemed to be receding.

Then the darkness began to clear. The slavers had pulled the Attolian off, and I could breathe again. Sobbing for air, weeping with relief, I looked around to see if they had had enough entertainment or if they meant to release him for another round. It seemed they had had amusement enough, because they dragged the Attolian as far as the chain permitted and hammered a spike through one of the links into the ground, pinning him in place. They should have secured him to one of the iron staples in the rock wall, but it would have been more work, and they were too lazy. Instead, they added another spike to the chain just out of his reach, fixing that link to the ground so that he couldn't pull me toward him. Then they went away to sleep, leaving the grumbling Kepet on guard, warning him to do a better job or the Attolian might work his way free in the night and kill his little friend.

I sat rocking, holding my throat, not once looking toward the Attolian. The slaves around me curled up on their sides, shifted briefly on the hard ground before they fell into exhausted sleep. Through all the noise and the fighting, they had paid us little attention. They were too far gone to care much. I watched Kepet as he, too, fell asleep.

In the silence I heard the dry scratching as the Attolian worked at the spike that pinned him in place. I didn't look. Nor did I look at the soft slithering click of the metal links in the chain as he moved across the ground to the second peg. The chain pulled at my ankle, and I lifted it so that it would make no noise as he approached, but instead of growing slack, it stayed taut. I turned to see him moving catlike in the arc described by the length of his tether, heading for Kepet. He reached for him, and there was a popping sound, so small even the noise of a cricket would have obscured it. Then the Attolian carefully lowered the body to the ground.

The rest of the slavers were farther away, beyond the

Attolian's reach. Holding my breath, I turned to the slave sleeping beside me. Gently I shook him awake. He looked up at me, confused and exhausted. I put my finger to my lips and then pointed. The slave sat up, saw Kepet's body and the Attolian standing over him. He could have warned the slavers in hopes that they would reward him, but he did not. Silently he woke the man next to him. Any one of them could have given us away, in hope of a reward, perhaps his freedom, but the slavers had sealed their fate. Not one slave made a sound. Lifting the chains and holding them, they gave me room to move closer to the Attolian so that he in turn could move closer to the other slavers.

One after another, he broke two necks. Each time there was a frenzied but nearly soundless kicking and a quiet crunching sound as the bones gave way.

Sickened, I pulled on the chain, like a panicked man trying to rein in a runaway horse. The Attolian, feeling the tug at his ankle, turned to me, murder in the set of his shoulders. Spineless, I let him have the slack he needed. He faced me a moment longer, then took up a log from beside the fire and, swinging it hard, clubbed the next man and the next. The slavers were finally aware of their danger, but it was too late. As those remaining leapt up, the Attolian swung his club and laid each one out in turn.

"Tell them to sit on these men," he said to me, and waved at the slaves. They didn't need a translation. With a rattling of chains, they jumped onto the slavers. If they'd had any strength at all, they might have torn them apart, but the most they could do was hold the men while the Attolian reached for the hammer and pry bar that had been left lying nearby. In a few strokes, he was free. He freed each of the slaves next, leaving me for last.

Once the restraint on my ankle was gone, I went to the packs dumped on the ground near the mules and began to go through them. There was no bread and there was no time to cook the grains, but there was dried meat and some dried fruit. There was a leather bag filled with tin coin, probably their payments for recent sales they had made at other mines. Behind me, the Attolian began hammering the cuffs around the ankles of the slavers he'd left alive. Cursing, they strained to get free of the slaves piled on top of them. One man did get loose, briefly. The Attolian downed his tools and seized him by the head, then hauled him struggling across the campsite to where Kepet lay with his neck broken. The Attolian never said a word, only held the slaver there, face to the body, before he dragged him back and threw him down beside his colleagues, where he lay without moving and without speaking.

Once the slavers were chained, the slaves came to me for the food I had found in the mule packs. There was little water left in the skins, but one of the slaves, speaking for the first time in a hoarse voice, said that the skins had been filled earlier that evening at a spring by the road, so more water was not far away.

I went through all the pockets and purses of the slavers and emptied out all their money. "Thieves," snarled one of the slavers. "You won't get away with this."

One of the slaves laughed harshly. "And if you catch us, what? We will be sent to the mines?"

The Attolian took up the hammer again and dragged the end of the chain to one of the rings set in the rock wall around the campsite. Once he'd secured it, using an ankle cuff to make a closed loop, he stood. Muscles straining in the red glow of the firelight, he pulled until he was certain it would take a hammer to get free. Then the Attolian threw the hammer as hard as he could into the dark.

"You cannot leave us here," protested one slaver.

I translated for the Attolian.

"Tell him he's next to the road," said the Attolian. "Someone will come by."

"And if no one does?" said the man, when I repeated the words in Setran.

The Attolian snorted, guessing what the slaver's words meant. "Then maybe Kepet will have got off easy," he said. I didn't bother to translate that.

We packed up the mules, and the Attolian herded all of us down the road. The slaves moved slowly, but the Attolian was patient. He and I could hardly move faster anyway in the pitch dark over the rough surface, and we would have missed the spring on our own. One of the slaves warned us when we were close, and we listened for the sound of water murmuring over rocks. We stopped there to fill waterskins— two of them our own, taken back from the slavers. The Attolian explained that he and I would take some of the provisions and head back up the road toward the mines. "We go north," he said. "We are hunted, and our hunters will come after each of you. You may want to try to hide in the hills or make your way down to the plain. I can't tell you which is best."

"And the mules?" The slaves were resting in the dark all around us and I didn't know who spoke.

"You can have the mules," said the Attolian, "but ride them hard, and abandon them in the first village you come to."

"Those slavers will be out for blood," said another voice.

"And our pursuers even more so," the Attolian warned.

Diffidently I said, "There is a temple of Amrash at Nerket. Go west on the wagon trail below here, and when it joins the emperor's road to Zabrisa, go back east. It's not far from where the roads meet." The temple at Nerket was a sanctuary for escaped slaves, which would have angered local slaveholders more were it not that the slaves, once received in the temple, were forbidden to leave. The priests of Amrash were very poor—it was a subsistence living a slave faced within the temple walls. Common decency should have allowed such a haven for those so abused by their masters that they would choose that life. Cynicism made me think the sanctuary was tolerated because the slaves there had so little value. For the men crouched in the darkness around us, a life of peaceful service to the god and a roof over their heads would be a haven indeed.

There was quiet while each considered the risk and weighed it against his good fortune in being free at all.

"I'll take a mule," said one of the men.

"I as well," said another, "but I have the strength yet in my legs to get along on my own. I won't take a mule if there is someone who needs it more."

No one else, weak though they were, was willing to risk being mistaken for us. We stripped the packs from the mules, passed out what was valuable in them, and then handed them over to their riders.

"When you reach the first town, ride through it, so you can be seen to be a gray-haired slave on his way to the sanctuary—not an Attolian, not a Setran house slave. Then abandon the mule and hide for a while, or go overland. Those hunting us should not follow you further."

Odd that he called me Setran. I had not felt myself a Setran in a long time. Nor Mede either, for that matter. Our earlier conversation seemed to belong to a different world now, when the Attolian and I were comrades by the nighttime fire. Setra was no homeland to me. I had no homeland, but perhaps the Attolian only wanted to think of me as something other than Mede because he hated the Medes, or because he hated and respected the Medes but merely hated me. I didn't know.

With two waterskins between us and much less than our share of the food and money, we started back up the road toward the mines. The Attolian had not dithered over the disposition of the food and money, and I think that he gave most of it away. We each had a blanket roll and a set of spare clothes, useful but smelly. The Attolian was armed again with one of the slavers' swords as well as a hunting knife and a small bow and its arrows. We were better equipped now than we had been on leaving Koadester, except for the Attolian's missing breastplate and our cookpot and all our money gone.

I would miss the cookpot. We should have taken the slavers' when we had the chance, but we'd left it in the ashes of the fire. I know the Attolian was thinking of his sword and his armor, buried somewhere under the rocks to the east of us, but there was no time to go hunting them and little chance we could find them anyway. He said nothing, but I could guess how much it pained him to abandon them.

I had a long knife and a very small one that I had taken because it was just like one I had used for years to shape my pens. I felt I was more likely to get something done with the smaller knife in the right place than with the larger one, which I was afraid even to draw from its sheath. I did not discount the possibility that I might be using the knife on the Attolian, who had not once looked at me, though he had addressed several remarks meant for me to the air above us as if I were floating somewhere overhead, and several to the ground as if I were reclining somewhere to his left. Even if it had saved us, I did not expect him to forgive me that kick to the groin. I would pay a price, I was sure.

Head down, I followed him back up the road. When we got close to the slavers, we could hear the sullen argument going on as they tried to twist the pin out of the cuff and work the iron staple out of the rock. It was easy, in the darkness, to pass by without being noticed. The ground was dry and hard, and I doubt we even left footprints.

We went on as quickly as we could without risking a fall. As the sky began to lighten, we came to the end of the road. It opened out, to our right, into many smaller tracks around the tips and tailings of several mines. Sheds scattered across the hillside were dark and silent and still in the predawn air. Ahead of us, only a thread of a hunting track continued up the rocky slope. Without speaking, the Attolian began to climb. With the growing light, it was not impossible to find the way, and by the time the sun cleared the horizon, the mine was some distance below us.

The hunting track began to cut farther and farther to the right, headed toward a stretch of scrubby bushes. It was probably a loop that would eventually return to the mine, whereas we needed to make our way uphill. The Attolian picked a likely saddle in the ridge above us and began moving toward it. The whole hillside was rocks. As we moved higher, there was no more soil, just an unending pile of stones, all of them rounded, even the ones as big as a bull, unstable and threatening to roll underfoot. Picking a way, step by awkward step, was exhausting. I fell farther and farther behind.

Finally, the Attolian passed out of sight behind a large boulder, and I stopped to catch my breath, seeking some hidden reserve of strength that I didn't find. While I was still looking for it, the Attolian moved back into view and waved at me to catch up. I put my head down and focused only on my next step and the one after that. When at last I reached the place where I had seen him, I found behind the large boulder a flat area the size of a large tabletop, mostly level. The Attolian was already lying down on it with his back to me. I dropped beside him.

CHAPTER SEVEN

I woke as the sunlight was dimming. A breeze made my skin rise in goose pimples, and I shivered. I opened my eyes to see the Attolian already sitting up, wrapped in a blanket. I began to unroll my own.

"Kamet," said the Attolian in a low voice, "I am sorry. I hope you will forgive me."

I looked up at him, speechless. How many times had he apologized to me already? "I'm sorry," he'd said on the riverside in Ianna-Ir at the very start of my deceit, when I let him believe he had misspoken "after noon" for "after dark." He'd apologized when it was the Namreen who had sliced open my head, apologized for having only caggi to offer me, apologized for leading us into Koadester. I'd paid little attention, assuming his apologies were the result of habit, not intent. How many times does a slave hear the word "sorry" made meaningless? "I'm sorry, Kamet, but you must fetch another scroll, bottle of wine, set of linen, robe from the tailor. Kamet, I am sorry, but the accounts must be completed by morning. I'm so sorry, but there's no bed for you. Sorry, Kamet, there's nothing left for your dinner." How many times had my master used that word? As many times as I had bowed my head and said, "Yes, master, of course, of course."

I opened my mouth, and no words came. I didn't know what to say when "sorry" meant something, what to say to an apology that was so obviously sincere.

I fell back on habit and apologized myself. "I'm sorry," I said. "I was afraid."

"I know," said the Attolian. "I understand. I made a poor slave." He smiled at the irony, both of us thinking of Koadester.

We sat quietly for a while after that. There was no wood for a fire, and we couldn't make one anyway as we couldn't risk being seen. We also couldn't move out from behind the rock that was hiding us from view. From where he was sitting, the Attolian could watch for new activity at the mine. He said there had been no sign so far that the slavers had been discovered, so we just sat, each picking at our meager handful of dried food, trying to make it last. I noticed the Attolian's earring was back in his ear. I'd feared that it had fallen from his mouth when I'd kicked him or that he'd swallowed it.

"Is it because they are your enemies that they are so easy to kill?" I asked hesitantly.

The Attolian looked up, and then down again at the sliver of dried meat in his hand as if it were going to crawl away if he didn't watch it carefully.

"You have seen men die," he said. "You were not so squeamish about the Namreen."

"I've seen many people die," I agreed. "I've never held a man's life in my hands." I looked down at those hands, scraped and very dirty now, but still free of calluses except the one that came from holding a stylus. "I was no threat to the Namreen, certainly, and I was too worried that I was dying, I suppose. But last night's work was . . . different."

"I wondered when I was training to be a soldier if killing a man would be hard, but I learned that it's usually very easy. It's like throwing up a hand when you are startled, or wrenching at something that is stuck. You do it in a moment and without a thought, really. Afterward it can be like an avalanche . . . sometimes. In the nights after a battle, we always drink. A condolence if we've lost and a celebration if we've won, but it's always a little of both. I think mostly we drink to drive the ghosts away. We all know it. When you think of all the deaths—our comrades, and the men who were someone else's comrades—you drink to get through the night, because you won't sleep otherwise. Some men haunt you longer than others. I haven't thought much of the Namreen, though I suppose I will tonight." He turned his head to look across the rocky hillside toward the open sky.

"Will these slavers stay with you?"

"I hope not. I have killed better men."

"Because they were Medes?"

The Attolian looked puzzled. "But they weren't Medes. I couldn't understand a word they said."

"They were Setrans."

"Your countrymen? Kamet, I am more than sorry. I didn't realize."

"I don't care," I said, and I didn't. I had no connection to those men just because we might have been born in the same place. "I meant, if they had been Attolians?"

He shrugged. "They could just as easily have been Attolians, buying and selling slaves here in the empire. I am sure there are any number of Attolians equally despicable. Were they enemies of my king, then I would kill them. I am a soldier, Kamet. I am sorry if that distresses you."

He was quiet for a time before he continued, as if he were sorting his thoughts.

"I might have been more reluctant to kill them if they hadn't been murderers, but I wouldn't have killed them just for that. That is not my right. I couldn't have fought all the men if they had awakened, but I couldn't honestly say when, in killing, I stopped doing the work of a soldier and began doing . . . some other thing." He looked away, uncomfortable. "Battles are more straightforward."

He was quiet again.

I thought of my master, Nahuseresh, in a rocky tomb by now at his family's estate. That was one death I didn't want the Attolian to know about. I wished more every day that I didn't have to lie to him, but I saw no other choice. I knew that I had to separate myself from him in Zaboar. To go all the way to Attolia would be to invite my own death at the hands of the king when he found that he'd been tricked. Or at the hands of the emperor when he learned where I was.

"Kamet, is there nothing that you liked about Attolia?"

Startled by the change in subject, I again had no words.

The Attolian laughed a little at me. "You won't hurt my feelings. Why do you hate it so?"

Gods help me, it was his home. "What makes you think I don't like Attolia?" I asked disingenuously.

"You said so. After the fight with the Namreen. You called it a backward, stinking cesspit."

"I did?"

"So."

"I was upset," I said. "I didn't mean it."

He looked me in the eye and called my bluff. "You did."

I searched for the least insulting thing I could say. "In Attolia," I explained, "slaves are used for physical labor. Even free men rarely read and write. I was . . . an anomaly." I wasn't sure he knew what the word meant. "I was the only slave in the upper palace," I said. "Free men in Attolia have nothing to do with slaves, so they had nothing to do with me. And the few slaves in the palace had just as little to do with a man who was educated and a secretary to his master. In the empire, the Medes respect their slaves."

He looked as if he disagreed. "And fear them," he observed.

That was certainly true. There was little that frightened the citizens of the empire like the possibility of a slave revolt.

"What of the queen's indentured?" the Attolian asked me.

"They especially wouldn't have anything to do with me." The queen's indentured, those who were paying off their families' seven years of freedom from taxation with the same number of years in service to the crown, were snobs of the highest order. Their families had indentured them to pay for their educations, to raise their status, not to hobnob with slaves. "They will be free men and quite powerful when they go back to their provinces."

"I see. You were lonely?"

"No, not lonely." He deserved what truth I could give him. "I was unappreciated."

He snorted and covered it with his hand. I ducked my head in embarrassment.

There had been friendly people in Attolia, but none who were impressed by any of the things I thought were important. I toed my shoe in the dust. "I am a little vain," I admitted.

"I had no idea," said the Attolian with an impressively straight face.

"I am used to being respected."

"And no one was awed that you speak four languages?"

"Five." I corrected him automatically, and he laughed outright.

I laughed myself. I said, "Remember that I told you I had translated the tablets of Immakuk and Ennikar?"

He nodded.

"There was an errand boy at the palace—he was supposed to fetch and polish boots and sandals, stir vats in the laundry, that sort of thing—but he was more often hanging about in the kitchens or somewhere else out of sight, avoiding work. He was the one who pestered me to tell them a Mede story in Attolian. Well, I knew the Ensur language because I'd studied the texts for years. I had the translations into the Mede because I'd made them myself. I could tell him that story in Attolian because I had trained my whole life for it. I expected him to be impressed."

"And?"

"He said he thought any idiot could do it."

It had all been very humbling, but I smiled now at the memory. "He was one of the queen's indentured," I said as that tidbit came to my mind. I shouldn't have forgotten it because it was a point of such pride for him.

"Not if he was a sandal polisher," said the Attolian. "He was lying to you, I'm afraid."

"Well, he was certainly a liar," I said, "but no one in

the kitchens contradicted him when he bragged about it. Evidently his family took the queen's tax forgiveness and used the money to educate his older brother. Then the brother was gravely injured in a wagon accident, both of his legs broken." If he had died, the family's debt would have been canceled. As he hadn't, the debt had come due. "They sent the younger brother in his place."

"He was educated as well?"

"No," I said dryly. "That's why he did the grunt work."

The Attolian guessed from my tone that the boy, raised as the free son of a landholding family, had made a poor servant, as indeed he had.

"To my certain knowledge, he bit the man in charge of Attolia's kitchens not once but twice," I said.

"Well, good for him," the Attolian responded promptly. "More people should bite Onarkus," and I realized that of course he knew that overly proud petty tyrant of Her Majesty's kitchens. I think everyone had admired the sandal polisher that day. He'd paid for the bite with a terrific beating and then promptly bitten the man again.

"You were often in the kitchens?" the Attolian asked, and I wondered if we had passed each other there without noticing.

"My master brought very few servants to Attolia. There was just me to see to his food and his clothes, as well as the usual work of a secretary." Another reason I hadn't liked Attolia. "I was in the gardens often as well—when I was allowed time to myself." Grudgingly I admit here that the gardens are also beautiful, that there are more beautiful things in Attolia than I was willing to recognize at the time. The gardens—their lush bounty of green and growing things all meticulously trimmed to perfect order—filled my heart with a kind of contentment I had never known. They were so different from the tiled courtyards of the emperor's palace—also beautiful but sterile in comparison.

"My king liked the gardens," the Attolian said. "He was almost assassinated in them, and I don't know if he walks there anymore. The queen didn't want him to."

I would have made a snide comment about a man ruled by his wife if I hadn't myself been terrified of the queen. Instead, I said, "That work-dodging kitchen boy, he liked the gardens—for hiding in. The first time we met, he was under a bush trying to avoid stirring vats of piss in the laundry. When I asked how he would explain his absence, he said he'd tell the people in the kennels he'd been in the laundry, and the people in the laundry that he'd been cleaning out the kennels."

The Attolian shook his head in amusement. "And did you tell him a story while he was hiding?"

"No, I only told him the one story of Immakuk and Ennikar before he went home."

"Home? How? I thought he was indentured?"

"He said he had run away before and meant to try again." I cast a significant look at the Attolian. "He said the palace guard had hunted him down the first time."

The Attolian looked surprised. "Not while I was at the palace."

"He told me quite the tale—chased into the hills, swords, guns. Are you sure?"

The Attolian laughed. "Surely his family would have sent him back," he said. He knew that you don't cheat the queen of Attolia of her due.

"He didn't return. I assume they found some other way to repay the crown. I even got a gift from him later."

The Attolian's look was speculative.

"I might have given him a coin to help him on his way."

"So?" he prompted.

"His family was in a fishing village some way down the coast, past Ifrenia. It was a long way to go with the bloodthirsty palace guard after him. When he made it home, he recopied one of his brother's scrolls and sent it to me." The handwriting had been atrocious—I could see why the scribes hadn't let him work with the rest of the queen's indentured—but the text had been by Enoclitus, and I'd never seen it before. "It's the one thing I took with me when my master and I fled the fortress at Ephrata." I'd rolled it tight and forced it into a bottle. The stopper had leaked but the scroll had still been mostly readable.

Intuiting much, the Attolian said, "You had to leave it behind in Ianna-Ir."

I dismissed his concern, guilt-bitten by my own lies.

"What else did you leave?" he asked.

My death, I thought. I left my death behind.

I shrugged and said, "Nothing of any importance."

The twilight had deepened, and the Attolian thought it safe to move on. We climbed on toward the saddle in the hills above us and descended across much the same kind of ground on the far side. It was more treacherous going down than up, and I fell when a stone that appeared perfectly safe rolled out from under me.

"I'm fine," I called to the Attolian, some distance ahead.

"Of course," he said back.

I rubbed my leg resentfully. It's funny how this works. We do better when we are praised and worse when we feel unappreciated for our work. I'd hated being in Attolia and hadn't at all enjoyed the months at my master's family estate, when I'd had little to do and too much time to do it. When we'd returned to the emperor's palace, I had reveled in my work and in the respect I received from those around me. Now I was nurturing a sense of pride in my growing strength, but I feared the Attolian would expect too much of me.

We hadn't gone far, but it was already pitch dark when we reached the bottom of the next narrow valley. We stood on a thin line of soil, a dry streambed that barely supported a few scraggling bushes and had failed to support a tree that stretched its dead branches into the air. In front of us was a rocky hillside just as high as the one we had just descended. There was no sense in moving farther unless the moon rose, and even then we would have to proceed with caution to avoid breaking a bone among the rocks.

We still couldn't risk a fire, but the Attolian collected what fuel he could find. He used his blanket and his belt to make a bundle of it that he could carry on his shoulder; then we ate the last bites of dried meat we had from the slavers and waited to see if the moon would give us enough light. When it rose, we began climbing again, moving even more slowly than before, the moon shadows more treacherous than their daytime cousins. I looked longingly down the valley, along the relatively flat streambed, but the Attolian shook his head.

"We've no idea where it will lead us. If we keep heading north, we will eventually leave the empire and cross over into Zaboar."

"Assuming the way north is passable."

"Assuming that, yes."

We climbed the next hill, and from its crest the Attolian could see signs of a road below. I had to take his word for it.

"Probably leads to another mine," he said. We started carefully down. This hillside was as treacherous as the one before, and as we got closer to the bottom, I could see that the roadway was partially blocked by a slide. In spite of our care, we both lost our balance and rolled down in a shower of rocks. Sitting up at the bottom, the Attolian asked if I was all right and, when I didn't answer, hurried to my side. I was staring at the rocks and what they had partly covered over.

"A slave escaped from the mines," said the Attolian.

"He didn't get far," I said. Like us, he'd fallen on the hillside, but unlike us, he'd died of it. He must have hit his head as he fell, or the rocks came down on top of him once he'd hit bottom. The side of his head was crushed and black with blood.

"No, not far," said the Attolian. He reached to lift one hand of the corpse. "Just recently dead," he said.

"Could it be one of—"

"The men we freed? I don't see how. I can't believe any of them could be moving faster than we are, not in the state they were in."

Reluctantly I stood, wishing I could do something for this corpse, but there was nothing to do that would make any difference to him now. So we walked away, again choosing the rocky climb up the next hillside instead of the deceptively inviting road. The road would lead us nowhere we wanted to go.

When I woke the next morning, the sky over me was gray. Thinking it was just dawn, I fell back asleep and woke again to find it still gray. The Attolian was standing with his back to me, staring upward as if he could pierce the clouds like his god Miras with a magic arrow.

"This is unexpected," he said.

We waited for the skies to clear, but they did not. There were brighter spots, but it was impossible to tell if this was the sun itself shining through or only a thin place in the clouds. In these irregular hills we needed the sun to guide us.

"I'll climb to the top of this ridge," said the Attolian, "and see if there is a landmark we can navigate by. Watch for my signal."

He came back without having signaled, but I hadn't wasted the time he was away.

"Is that edible?" he asked when I held up the ring snake I'd caught.

"I think so," I said. I was certainly hungry enough to eat it.

"There's another valley just the same beyond this one. Why don't we go that far and, if it seems safe, cook the snake? I can make a fire without too much smoke. If the skies clear, we'll push on, and if not, we'll just have to wait out the clouds. We can't afford to lose our sense of direction."

I nodded. It seemed as good a plan as any. So I wore the snake draped over my shoulder as we climbed. The Attolian already had the wood for our fire balanced on his. Hunger lent skill to my feet, and I picked my way quickly up the hill. Whatever unpleasantness I might have encountered in my life, I'd never been this hungry for this long, and I deeply resented the clenched emptiness in my middle. I refused to think of the emaciated slaves we'd left behind.

I was concentrating so hard on not thinking of the poor men laboring in the mines around us that I nearly jumped out of my skin when the Attolian grabbed me by the arm. Heart in my mouth, I looked where he pointed, but it was no armed enemy watching us from the far side of the next narrow valley. It was a wild goat.

"Much better than snake," whispered the Attolian. Stripping the bundle off his back, he lowered it to the ground with only a slight sound of wood bumping against wood. Catlike and much faster than we'd been moving together, he made his way down to the flat ground at the center of the valley and then up the far slope. The goat didn't seem alarmed, but it didn't wait for him either. It moved off across the hillside, the Attolian following after. I descended more slowly to the bottom of the valley and arranged the wood for a fire and looked over the snake. I'd had ring snake before, but it had been cooked in a tureen. I wasn't sure what to do with it out in the wild. Instead of making a bad job of slicing it up, I went hunting down the valley for more firewood while I waited for the Attolian to return.

He was gone most of the afternoon, but when he came back, it was with the goat over his shoulder. I nearly cheered and pitched the now thoroughly unappetizing snake up the rocky hillside. The Attolian was less happy. When he reached the fireside, he threw the carcass down with a grunt.

"There are Namreen everywhere," he said abruptly. "I

think that road we saw must lead to some sort of passage into the Taymets, and they are watching it. We can't have a fire. We have got to get out of here in a hurry, and I can't carry the damn goat, but if we leave it here, they are sure to find it and guess we are nearby."

He rubbed his face. "I didn't see the Namreen until after I'd killed the goat. I haven't gutted it yet. Maybe we can eat the liver, but then we've got to be on our way. I'll hide the carcass and hope for the best."

I suggested we could go back to the rockslide we had caused earlier and hide the goat underneath a new one. So the Attolian cut out the liver with as little mess as possible, we split it between us, and then he carried the rest of the goat back over the hill and I carried the firewood. While we climbed, I had another idea, and when we reached the dead body of the slave, I told the Attolian to leave the goat next to it. He went up the hill to start another slide that covered the goat completely, and most of the body of the slave. I added a judicious few more rocks until only an outstretched hand remained visible. Beside it, I placed the gold plaque from my slave chain, set just deeply enough between the rocks that it would seem to have fallen from the body during the slide, but not so deeply set that it would be missed by an observer.

The Attolian crouched nearby, his hands on his knees. He looked between the rocks to the shining gold plaque and said, "Perfection." I ducked my head, more proud of myself than was probably warranted.

Then we hurried down the road, afraid of who might have heard the rocks coming down, hoping that we were moving away from any Namreen, not toward them, and that any footprints we left would be obscured by the other traffic. Fortunately the road did move more north and east for a while, so we were no farther south from our goal, at least, and after we'd traveled some distance, we again took to the rocky hills and hid for the night among them. We still had no fire. There was some dried grain in the slavers' bags, and we had water to soak it but no pot to pour it into, so we chewed it as it was. I thought longingly of the slavers' pot, stupidly left behind. Still, I had little to complain about, and any consideration of the poor slave we'd just buried under a rockfall would have silenced my complaints anyway. I think the Attolian sensed the bleakness of my mood. After he'd licked the last flecks of grain from his hand, he asked for another story of Immakuk and Ennikar.

It took a minute to gather my thoughts. "So, Ennikar and the witch of Urkull," I said. I thought he would like that one. "Ennikar in trouble with a maid again."

"What a surprise," said the Attolian.

Immakuk climbed the steps of the temple
    climbed to the altar of the people

climbed to the altar of kings
    climbed to the altar of priests and climbed onward.
Immakuk climbed to the heights of Shesmegah
    prostrated himself there
    begged the goddess her goodwill
    begged her aid
Wise Immakuk said she
Speak to the goddess tell her your need

Said Immakuk Brave Ennikar suffers
    suffers and is weak with suffering
Angry is the god Tenep
    Ennikar begat Tenep's anger
    He is the cause
Tenep who made the rain and the river
    Made the cow and the calf
    Made the grain and the nut
    The tree and leaf the house and the hearth
Tenep who is mild in her aspect
    Who is gentle before the other gods
    Who is good natured above all other gods
    And kind to us
    Has changed her face
    Has shown us the face of her anger
Tenep's anger falls on us all
    The river is stifled

The grain is stifled and the nut is stifled
The cow ignores her calf
The tree bears no leaves the hearth no fire
The witch of Urkull
Came to Brave Ennikar
Came to the city from the forests
Led him away from the city led him into the grain
Enticed him there and enchanted him
Persuaded him cajoled him inveigled him
Induced him to steal the sphere of light
Tenep's sphere and its power Ennikar took it
Gave it to the witch
Now Tenep's anger falls on us all.

Wise Immakuk you ask my aid
Who am I against the anger of great Tenep
I who was once mortal as you?

Goddess yours is the way of gentleness
Lead great Tenep away from her anger
Show us the road to mercy and forgiveness
Turn Tenep's face of kindness toward us again

Where is Ennikar who is the cause
Of Tenep's anger?
Where is he?

THICK AS THIEVES

He lies in fever stifled by great Tenep
The witch of Urkull where is she?
 The witch of Urkull cannot be found
 The sphere of Tenep cannot be found
 No mercy can be found no kindness no forgiveness

Shesmegah who knows the road to mercy
 Shesmegah goes to Cassa to ask her bees
 Cassa's bees hunters and seekers
 To seek everywhere find the witch
Shesmegah puts away her kindness puts away her forgiveness
 Sends the bees to sting the witch sting her
 Her feet and hands until she comes to Shesmegah
Why? asks Shesmegah
 Why cajole inveigle induce Brave Ennikar
 From the path of the good from the way of the right
 From the light of Tenep into the darkness of her anger?
Why does the cow ignore her calf why is the river stifled?
Why does the tree bear no leaf and the hearth have no fire?

Brave Ennikar the witch of Urkull did possess him
 Loved him in her forests until
 Shesmegah in her pity for Wise Immakuk turned his
 path to Ennikar
 Turned Ennikar's path from the witch
Grieved the witch

Longed she for Brave Ennikar

    Came to the city enticed him into the grain

    Led him from the light into the darkness of Tenep's anger

Foolish witch lost her love

Find your love witch said Shesmegah see it waits

    In Ennikar's heart the path is there follow it

    Your love is waiting for you

    Give Tenep her sphere and enter

    Ennikar's heart It will be your heart and his then

Shesmegah showed her the road to Ennikar's heart

    The path of forgiveness led her to it

The witch gave up the sphere and Tenep

    turned her face of kindness to the world

The cow took care of her calf the tree opened its leaves

The rain filled the river and love filled Ennikar's heart

The witch felt his love and carried it with her to the forests

    Ennikar followed

His path led him away from the city to the forest and he

    stayed there

Seven months until the moon called him back to the city.

"In trouble with a maid, indeed," said the Attolian.

"So, so, so," I said. "Who would be so foolish?" Together the Attolian and I raised our eyes to the heavens, both of us the picture of sweet propriety. Then we looked at each other and waited to see who was going to speak first.

"It so happens," said the Attolian, "that sometimes a young soldier comes to the city from deep in the country and he meets a man in a wineshop who offers to show him the town and introduces him to a 'lovely girl.' And after the lovely girl has soaked him for all the money in his pocket, the man will offer the soldier a loan. The really naive ones get into so much debt to their 'friends' that they have to ask for a touch from the guard's treasury, from funds set aside by everyone in the cohort for emergencies like this. Until the money gets paid back, they eat their meals standing up in the dining hall."

I wondered if the Attolian had ever been a backward boy from the country eating his meals standing up. When I saw the flush creeping up past his collar all the way to the roots of his hair, I knew he had.

I said, "I fell in love with my master's favorite dancing girl." If he was willing to admit to an embarrassing indiscretion, I could do the same.

"Eh?" said the Attolian, as if he thought he'd misheard. I repeated myself.

He said, "Surely that was—"

"—Spectacularly unwise," I agreed.

I expected a laugh, but the Attolian asked very seriously, "Did she love you?"

I nodded. Marin had, I was sure of it. "She loved my master as well, though." That was misleading. "She saw something to love in everyone. She was . . ." I really couldn't explain. "She was beautiful in spirit, like Shesmegah. I wanted her to be happy. I wanted to give her the happiness she deserved, and I asked her to run away with me."

"Is that when you were flogged?" He put up his hands. "I'm sorry. Never mind."

"No, no fear," I said. It was easier to talk about flogging than about Marin. I almost wished I hadn't spoken of her, but it was both bitter and sweet to say her name again. "I was flogged years ago for taking a piece of cake from my master's plate."

"He flogged you for *cake*?"

"Not really. He knew I wouldn't have touched his cake. He flogged me for being too full of myself."

"Marking an expensive slave seems—poor economy." His voice was low and edged as it hadn't been since Sherguz.

I shifted and looked away, uncomfortable with his anger even if it was not directed at me. "The emperor's personal slaves are more powerful than almost any free man in the empire. He relies on them and they must be . . . perfectly trained. It was a painful lesson, but necessary. It made me more valuable." In light of the remchik incident, it was a lesson I needed to relearn from time to time.

"The emperor's very powerful personal slaves are killed when he dies, aren't they? Replaced by the slaves of the new emperor?"

"The new emperor chooses a few to be freed and serve in his household. Not all die."

"Most do?"

I shrugged. "We all die someday."

After a long uncomfortable silence I abruptly said, "My master could be very kind." I had no idea why I needed to defend him, but it was true. Part of being capricious was that quite often he had been capriciously kind. "Once I dropped a figure of Tenep made by Sudesh. It was a gift for the emperor's birthday, very rare, and I had no business touching it, but I'd wanted to hold her just once." I cupped my hands, remembering, how strong and how beautiful Tenep had seemed, flawless, because my master and I had conspired to have the figurine stolen from the workshop before any part of it could be broken by Sudesh. Then she had slipped through my fingers and smashed into three pieces on the floor.

Still ashamed of myself, I admitted to the Attolian, "I thought of blaming someone else, but my master came into the room just then."

"And?" said the Attolian.

"He laughed. He said I may as well have the pieces glued together and keep it. It was of no use to him anymore." I wondered what had become of the little figure of Tenep. I had packed her very carefully every time we traveled to be sure she was not damaged further. "He almost killed me when he overhead Marin and me talk about running away, but he wouldn't have hurt me so much if he hadn't loved her, too."

The next morning, when the houseboy had come in, he'd seen me lying on the floor and said, "Is Kamet dead?" I still remember how my master had leapt from his bed and sent for his own doctor to care for me. How upset he had been and how carefully he had watched over me until I was better. "He felt very bad," I said.

"Of course he felt bad," said the Attolian. "He nearly did himself out of a well-trained secretary."

I wanted to believe it was more than that. "He sold Marin." When I had recovered and rose from my bed, she was gone.

"I'm sorry," said the Attolian.

His sympathy made me as uncomfortable as his anger, and I shrugged. "He could have kept her. I was more important to him than a dancing girl."

"More valuable," corrected the Attolian.

I conceded. I was much more valuable than a dancing girl, but I knew what it had cost him to let her go.

A year later he had made up a silly excuse to visit a vineyard in the country, and I'd seen Marin there. He'd sold her to a man he knew would be kind to her, one who would free her and make her his wife. We didn't have a chance to speak, we only exchanged a glance as she carried in a tray of coffee, but

I could see that she was happy. I told the Attolian this, but he just shook his head. Maybe he was right. Maybe I gave my master too much credit for his kindness. Maybe he had gotten rid of Marin to keep me focused on my work.

There was another uncomfortable silence. The Attolian broke it, with characteristic consideration. "I think the Mede ambassador in Attolia has a piece by Sudesh. He's the artist who always breaks some part of his figurines after they are made?"

"Yes, that's him. He breaks them to appease the gods who might be angry at him for striving to match their perfection."

"The ambassador's statue is missing its right hand. The king often remarks on it, hinting that the ambassador should offer it to him as a gift. The ambassador watches it like a hawk, afraid the king will steal it." He admired his fool king, and yet he generously held him up for my ridicule.

I obliged. "At least my master had a sense of decorum," I said. And the awkward moment passed.

CHAPTER EIGHT

"Well," the Attolian observed, "they are green hills at least."

We had made our way through the valleys and ridges of loose rock, climbing higher after each descent until we'd reached a ridge where we could see across a patchy plain to the mountains on the far side. The Taymets. It was true, their lower slopes were misted with green, unlike the ground behind us, so they had at least some soil covering them, but their summits weren't green—they were shining cloudlike white. Their winter snows never melted.

It was impossible. I looked at the Attolian. He had to know it.

"There will be water on the far side of the plain," said the Attolian. "I think I see a lake."

The idea of washing was a pleasant distraction, but an

improbable one. The plain below was barren, only the lightest stretches of scrubby plants, and the ground was a mottled gray and white.

"It's a salt pan," I explained. "If there is a lake out there, it will be filled with salt. We'll have to find a stream of snowmelt if we want fresh water."

The Attolian hefted his waterskin. It was half empty. We'd filled them earlier that day at a small spring he'd found by following animal tracks to it. My skin had a little less water, though I'd been trying to drink no more often than he did.

"It's flat ground," he said, "so we can make good time across, but we'll need the skins full." He told me to wait and rest while he checked for another spring nearby—or, if that failed, went all the way back to the spring we'd found earlier. "I'll set a snare before I go. We haven't seen any Namreen since we buried the goat. I think we can cook this time." He was trying to reassure me.

The raw goat liver we'd eaten hadn't been that bad. On the other hand, the raw caggi we'd had that morning had been so disgusting that once I'd choked it down, I almost brought it right back up again. I agreed that cooked caggi would be highly tolerable by comparison.

We waited until night was falling and then headed out onto the plain. We made good time and stopped when we found a group of rocks that would shelter us from the sun and from the eyes of any watching Namreen during the day. The sky was just lightening when I fell asleep. I woke in broad daylight and found the Attolian staring out over the salt pan.

"There are buildings," he said. "We'll make for them when the sun sets."

We dozed the rest of the day, and then headed toward what turned out to be an abandoned farm. There was a ring of flat stones set in the ground that might have been the top of a well. It needed no cover to keep people from falling into it, though, as it was filled to the brim with sand. The night was not yet over, but we decided to save what water we had and to rest inside the stone walls of the empty farmhouse until the next evening. We started walking again as the sun was sinking toward the west, and our shadows seemed to stretch as far as the horizon on the other side of the world. By dawn the Attolian could see what he thought might be inhabited farms ahead, supported by the seasonal runoff from the hills. We kept moving as the sun grew brighter and brighter on the salt and around us darkness seemed to rise in shimmering waves from the ground. I stumbled over a clump of dry weeds. The Attolian took my arm to steady me.

With the sun high overhead, we cautiously approached a shepherd out with his goats. Our water was gone, and we hadn't eaten in two days. The goats were nibbling a bare sustenance from the scrubby grass we had seen more and more of as we left the salt behind. The shepherd was standing in the sparse shade cast by a few dry willows. We moved closer, stopping a stone's throw away to call our greetings.

I explained that we were heading north and hoped to buy food and water. I gestured at the Attolian, and he pulled a coin from his purse and gave it to me to hold up as a sign of our commercial intentions. After wary consideration, the shepherd pointed us toward the farm and said that his brother, Hemke, might let us use the well.

Reaching the farm buildings, we stood in the yard, formed by the main house and its various dilapidated outbuildings. We held our hands away from our bodies, the Attolian's far from his sword, and waited until a man stepped from a slanting ramshackle goat shed and roughly asked what we wanted. We waved back toward the shepherd and said he'd told us to seek out Hemke if we wanted to use the well.

"I am Hemke," said the farmer, "but the well's not deep. It only provides for us."

"We can pay," I said, holding out the coin the Attolian had given me.

Grudgingly Hemke, still not coming any closer, agreed we could take a single skin full of water. "There's little to spare," he said, "and we can't drink a coin. You can go east and find water at the emperor's road."

We couldn't do that, and with so little water we'd be in trouble even if we made it to the hills. We had no way to know how long it might take to find a stream carrying fresh water.

The Attolian meanwhile had turned to look at an unused hearth at one corner of the yard. "Ask if we can offer him something more useful than a coin."

"You think he maybe needs a letter written?" I asked, skeptical.

"Maybe he has pots that need tinning."

"Do you know how to do that?" The Attolian had given the slaves most of the money when he'd divided up the slavers' possessions, but he'd kept the bag of tin coins from the mines. I certainly didn't know what to do with them.

The Attolian nodded. "My friend was the son of the village tinsmith. My father wouldn't let me apprentice there, he wouldn't hear of it, but I learned a fair bit in spite of that."

That was an interesting tidbit about my Attolian. I'd thought soldiers were born to be soldiers.

"Tell him I can re-tin his pots so they can be cooked in, but no guarantees on how pretty they will be."

I explained to the farmer what the Attolian was offering and asked if he had any pots in need of new tin. The farmer was just saying no when a woman's muffled shout came from inside the farmhouse.

There was a heated exchange between indoors and outdoors that ended with Hemke throwing up his hands and agreeing that we could have a meal and as much water as we could carry if we could re-tin their largest baking pan. "You'll have to make her happy," warned Hemke. I could guess that wouldn't be easy.

"I'll need lye," said the Attolian to me, "and some tallow or beeswax. And fireplace tongs."

Hemke had already headed back into the goat shed, flapping a hand in introduction over his shoulder as he went. We hesitantly poked our heads around the corner of the low stone building to find the matriarch of the family in the doorway there. Some years older than Hemke, his mother or perhaps an aunt, she was gray haired and whip thin, with the wrinkles brought both by age and by hard work in the sun. She gave us the once-over.

"You can do this, tin a baking pan?" I asked the Attolian under my breath.

"So, so, so," said the Attolian. He sounded entirely confident, but I noticed his hands anxiously rubbing together as he spoke. The old woman noticed, too, and rolled her eyes before she invited us into the kitchen to gather up the pan and the material the Attolian would need.

"Vedra will bring the lye and the tallow. How much lye?"

"We'll need to soak the pan in it. Half as much lye in the water as if we were making soap," said the Attolian.

The woman nodded. "Eat first," she said, and we gratefully fell on some bread and cheese while she and the woman she called Vedra found a container large enough to hold the baking pan—a monster of a pan. As wide across as the length of my arm, it probably weighed more than my master's cashbox when it was brimming with coin.

The Attolian handled it easily. Carrying it and the ceramic bath the old woman found to soak it in, he went out to the hearth and set up his tin shop. Vedra followed with a jar of powdered lye and a lump of beeswax. She was a grown woman, but clearly under the thumb of the matriarch, who we later learned was mother to her and her brothers—one of whom was Hemke and the other of whom was out with the goats.

The Attolian filled the ceramic bath and measured the powdered lye into it, stirring with a wooden stick before he set the baking pan to soak. Then he started a fire in the brick hearth and put a long-handled pot of beeswax to heat on its flat stone top. The hearth bricks had once been covered in plaster, but most of that now lay in flakes in the dirt below, and the stone top was cracked right across. The disrepair didn't seem to interfere with its function, though. Where the heat leaked up through the crack, the Attolian set the wax to melt. Most of the heat still came up through the circular hole the size of a dinner plate in the middle of the stone.

The foot pedal for the hearth was broken, so first the Attolian repaired that with a new piece of wood and the spare sandal leather he still had from Koadester. Then he fed the fire and worked the pedal until he had something that was even hotter than the sun out on the salt pans. He was dripping with sweat, and the old woman unbent enough to send Vedra out with ceramic cups of cool water scented with lemon for both of us. I hadn't earned it and gave him mine.

The Attolian checked the pan occasionally, pulling it out of the lye bath and looking at the color, then letting it slide back into the acrid liquid. When it was bright pink, he decided it had set long enough and dried it above the hearth before he rubbed the beeswax all over the interior surface. While he worked, he sang in a surprisingly tuneful voice a song about a girl a soldier left behind.

He sent me to get a cloth from Vedra, whom I found leaning against the doorpost with the old woman, both of them listening to the song with expressions soft and distant. The old woman slapped Vedra on the arm and sent her to fetch a rag. Then the Attolian began to work in earnest, pumping the fire with the pedal and holding the pan over the heat with the fire tongs until it was heated through. He turned it up on edge, slightly tipped, and set it into the hole in the hearthstone so that he didn't need to bear its entire weight as he threw the flattened pellets of tin a couple at a time onto the side of the pan. He rotated the pan as the tin melted, and after dipping the folded rag into the liquid beeswax, he rubbed the melting tin smooth. Again and again he threw in the tin until the entire inside edge of the pan was coated.

It's all very straightforward to tell it, but there was a great deal of wobbling of the pot and swearing in Attolian. The beeswax and water mixture steamed like a miniature storm cloud, and the cloth caught fire several times for added excitement and more swearing. The Attolian had a wide-ranging vocabulary, really. Curses from at least four languages.

Out of the corner of my eye, I caught the old woman and Vedra still watching, very amused.

When the sides were finished, the Attolian tipped the pan onto its bottom and flung an entire handful of tin into it. Elbow grease and the beeswaxed cloth smoothed the tin down, and he added another layer and another. It was late in the day by this time, and Hemke's brother had come in from the fields, as well as several other men bringing in their goats. They'd probably been sleeping for most of the afternoon in the shade of a rocky outcrop. They looked curiously at the Attolian working in the heat and conferred with Vedra before disappearing into the farmhouse and the other outbuildings.

Finally, the Attolian let the pan cool, and when it was safe to touch with a bare hand, he held it out for the old woman's appraisal. The interior shone like the sun, but the tin had overreached the edge in places and run in untidy streaks down the outside of the pan. The old woman pointed these out. The Attolian shrugged.

Vedra looked both anxious and hopeful, but the Attolian seemed at his ease. At last the old woman nodded her conditional approval, and Hemke invited us in to dinner. He told us we could spend the night in the shed with the goats and even suggested we make ourselves at home in the washhouse, the concerns about water scarcity evidently having faded. I believe he had worried less about the water and more about appearing weak in front of strangers, especially one built like the Attolian.

After dinner there was singing. The Attolian sang another song, a slower mournful one, which I translated for the company. It was about a man who missed his home, and I didn't really need to say more than that. By the time we left the next day, we were all friends. The old woman told Vedra to give us a large package of food for our trip, and we left her the remaining bits of tin to mend her pots in the future. We filled our skins again at the well, then turned toward the Taymets. We'd reached the first slopes by noon and rested in the shade before we began to climb again. I was sure we were doomed, but I was determined to go on until I dropped.

To my surprise, the going was easier, at least at first, than in those hellish rocky gullies around the mines. There were trails to follow that climbed with some consideration for the people who might be using them, not just for goats. Hemke, without commenting on the Attolian's heavy accent or our somewhat unorthodox arrival at his farm, had casually suggested that there were ways to go north while avoiding farms on the route and without going by the emperor's roads. I had translated the directions quietly into Attolian, and the Attolian seemed confident he could follow them. He was picking his way along the hunting trails with little hesitation, whereas I could only guess how lost I would already be if I were on my own.

Eleven days later we climbed over a low stone wall and entered a grove of olives, the huge trees in orderly rows, their leaves casting deep twilight below them. I looked back through the twisting branches at the sun shining on the fearsome Taymets, now unequivocally behind us.

"I don't understand," I said. I'd been afraid to say it before, for fear of drawing down a curse on our heads.

It's true that some of the climbs had been terrifying, and we'd spent most of four miserable days with our feet in the snow, but there had almost always been a trail to follow, even if it was just the path of someone else's footsteps. We'd sheltered in caves where we'd found firewood stacked and waiting for us. Twice the Attolian had used his bow to bring down a wild goat. We'd eaten and slept well, and Hemke's detailed directions had delivered us safely to Zaboar. We might have seen no other human being for the entirety of our journey across the mountains, but we'd seen evidence of them everywhere.

Whatever lay ahead, I had climbed the Taymets. If I could do it, what stopped the Medes?

"There's a saying from Eddis," the Attolian told me. "Water finds a way. A few people at a time can trickle through, but you couldn't take an army on that trail. A man can't climb straight up with his face in someone else's feet and his feet in the face of the man below. It would take an army a month or more to cross the mountains. Not only would they starve, they'd be picked off by the locals. They'd never get enough men through to be of any use in a battle."

That made sense to me. "The Namreen can come through, right after us," I said. They were never not on my mind.

"They could. Or they could just use the trade road," said the Attolian laconically. "The oligarch might object—or he might not." He shrugged. "You won't be entirely safe, Kamet, until I get you to my king in Attolia, but we are out of the empire. That will make it harder for anyone, bounty hunter or Namreen, to take you back."

Side by side, we walked downhill between the trees to the lower side of the olive grove. The contrast between the salt pans behind us and the fertile country before us was diametric. The Taymets captured all the rain that blew south, and the water ran back down into Zaboar, making it a small but healthy city-state, with farms to feed its populations and the mountains to protect it. It was almost, but not quite, worth the effort to conquer, and it paid a tribute to the Medes to ensure they looked elsewhere to expand their empire. The oligarch might see the Namreen as a threat to his sovereignty—or he might see handing me over as a goodwill gesture to a dangerous neighbor.

Looking out across the green land, all the way to the coast, I could see the blue of the Shallow Sea. The Attolian said he could not only see the city on its shore, he could trace the man-made lines of the aqueducts converging on it.

"There is an Attolian trade house in the city," he said. "They will know me and will help find a ship that will take us at least to the Middle Sea and perhaps all the way home."

We walked along the wall to a broken gate and a beaten path outside it. The path led us onto another path, wide enough for a wagon to bring down the olives, and from there every step brought us closer to civilization. The air was cool and the sky clear. It was an easy trip down the farm tracks, and we eventually caught sight of a town below us. The Attolian insisted he could see a sign for a tavern in the open market square, but I suspected it was wishful thinking.

The town was unwalled. Wandering between the houses, we found ourselves at the open village square, not large, with a tree-lined edge and a central cobblestoned area around a spring-fed fountain. There was indeed a tavern with tables under a shaded porch, and the Attolian was smug. He led the way toward it without hesitation. He wasn't worrying about the Namreen. Inside, he chatted up the tavern wife— the people in Zaboar mostly speak the same language as the Medes—and if she had trouble with some of his heavily accented words, she understood he wanted to buy food. He understood in turn when she held her nose. Blushing, he admitted that we didn't have coin for a meal and a bath, but she kindly produced a ball of soap and a cloth and waved toward the cobblestoned area and the fountain. There were several buckets chained by the fountain and racks nearby where clothes were draped to dry.

"Give me your shirt," I told the Attolian, and filled the bucket in the reservoir below the bubbling fountain. I pushed his shirt and mine into water so cold it made the bones in my wrists ache. Scooping a bucket for himself, the Attolian dumped it over his head and then gasped.

"Snowmelt," I pointed out, too late.

"Gods all around us, I am not sure I want to be clean this badly." But he rubbed himself with the soap and then handed it to me to use on the shirts while he rinsed himself off, shuddering and swearing under his breath. Then he took over the scrubbing of the shirts while I did the same. Freezing cold and soaking wet, we both wrung out the shirts. As we spread them out on the racks to dry, we saw the tavern wife approaching with toweling for each of us. Shivering, we thanked her again and again and she laughed at our gratitude. She sent us to sit at the tables in front of the tavern and brought us each a bowl of stew from the hearth. We sat there in our toweling and ate, and I think it was the most restorative bath I have ever had in my life. I felt as if I could lift up and fly to the capital, like Immakuk and Ennikar in Anet's Chariot, but the Attolian was more down to earth, and he was worried about money. He asked the tavern wife if there was anyone taking a wagon down to the coast in the next few days, someone who might let us ride along. She called a boy out of the tavern, obviously her son, and spoke a few quick words to him.

The Attolian looked at me. "She sent him to the potter," I said. "To see if he could use a young man with a strong back."

While we waited, we took stock. We had a blanket roll apiece, and the slavers' spare clothes, odds and ends we had taken for camping, and their weapons. "We can sell my knife," I pointed out. The longer knife was of no use to me. The Attolian had done all the cutting with his own knife, while mine had hung at my waist since I had taken it from the slavers. I pulled it out so that the Attolian could look it over.

"It's nothing fancy. I doubt anyone here would buy it," he said. "We can probably sell it in the city, though, along with the bow and the arrows."

It turned out that the potter wasn't going to the city, but he was delivering his pots to an estate partway there. He not only agreed to take us along, he promised us two hennat to load and then unload his wagon. From the estate, we could walk to the city in a day or two. The tavern wife gave us a generous measure of bread and cheese for one of the hennat. There would be no more hunting with the bow and no more caggi either. Any goats we saw would have owners who would strongly object to our shooting their farm animals, while smaller prey would have plenty of cover. We wanted to waste no time on snares. If we took a day or two to reach the city, we had enough money to feed us on the way. Once we got to the city, the Attolians would provide.

We spent the night in the potter's shed and loaded his wagon in the morning. I'd been thinking of wine jars for serving in a tavern, but these pots were huge, almost as high as I am tall, made to hold grain, not wine. The potter was an old man bent by the years at his wheel. He couldn't have lifted a single pot, but he had an ingenious block and tackle to get them into the back of his cart. The Attolian's strength just made everything easier. Once the pots were loaded, we climbed up ourselves and sat on top of them. We chatted with the potter while his mules carried us at a brisk pace, and we were unloading the pots that evening, halfway to the coast. We spent the night in a stable at the estate and started again in the morning.

It was an easy walk. There was farmland on either side of the road and, in the distance, aqueducts bringing fresh water to the city. There were smaller ducts as well, carrying water to irrigate the fields and, in some places, to drive mills. All the people of Zaboar seemed to be engineers putting the runoff from the Taymets to good use.

Our waterskins were empty when we saw the mill, and it seemed reasonable to cross the drainage ditch by the road and approach the large stone building to ask for a drink and a chance to fill our skins. As we got closer to the mill and its sagging outbuildings, though, our steps slowed. The mill was in poor repair. The wheel wasn't moving. The elevated wooden race leading to it was bone dry. There was a garden laid out inside a low stone wall, but its plants were dried and withered, and the mill yard was empty. There was a well, though, in the center of the yard. Or at least there was a worm-eaten wooden well cover lying on the ground with a square hole in the center.

We caught a glimpse of children between the buildings, but a larger figure shooed them inside, and we heard a door close. Somewhere in a shed a dog, a large dog by the sound of it, began barking ferociously. I was ready to head back to the road, but the Attolian walked on toward the doorless entryway to the mill.

Tiptoeing hesitantly up beside him, I heard voices inside. The Attolian looked pointedly at me, and I cleared my throat and called a greeting. The voices fell silent. The Attolian stepped into the darkness.

Politely he called out, asking aid for travelers.

Someone laughed harshly.

My eyes had finally adjusted, and I made out five or six men leaning against the motionless mechanisms of the mill or sitting on the bags of grain. The mill smelled of mold and decay.

"Gentlemen," I said politely before my voice trailed off. These weren't gentlemen.

"The miller?" the Attolian asked. He bobbled the emphasis on the second syllable, but one of the burly men stood up.

"This is my mill," he said.

"We hoped to fill our waterskins."

The men laughed again, looking at one another.

The Attolian took a half step back and balanced his weight. He didn't put his hand on his sword, though.

"There is no water here," said the miller. "The carrion picker uphill stole it."

"Then we will go," said the Attolian. But before he could take another step back, all the men stood at once. The Attolian drew his sword. No sooner was it free of its scabbard than a man, unseen on the machinery above, dropped onto the Attolian's shoulders.

I had looked around already for a weapon. There was nothing that would serve as a club, but there was a half-filled sack nearby. As the men in the mill closed in on the

Attolian, I lifted the sack by its upper edge and swung it, first back behind me and then in a long, sweeping arc toward the head of the approaching miller. The first blow was the most satisfying. The bag was heavy enough and its momentum great enough that it knocked the miller clean over. The bag kept going, nearly pulling me over, too, while the Attolian was handling his attacker with ease, first backing hard against a post, pinning the man, and then stepping forward before slamming him again. His attacker was knocked back and front. He dropped to the ground, clutching his nose with one hand and the back of his head with the other.

My second attempt with the bag was weaker. I didn't have time to swing it back as far and instead danced a step or two forward to add some momentum. The sack was rotten and split just as it hit the man I was aiming for. It wasn't half filled with grain, as I had assumed, but flour. As the split widened, the flour erupted in a stinking cloud. To my great distress, the Attolian caught the worst of it—he retreated, struck blind. Our attackers retreated as well, but we couldn't afford to dawdle. I backed into the Attolian and was pushing him toward the door as the miller was climbing to his feet, wiping the flour from his eyes. There was still some left in the sack, so I swung again and again at him until all the flour had escaped. Finally, I was swinging an empty sack, and we were out of the mill.

I would have run for the road, but the Attolian planted

himself at the doorway, assuming the men would have to come at him one at a time. There was no time to point out that the mill would almost certainly have more than one entrance. I was pulling hard on the Attolian's shoulder, and thinking I would explain to him his stupidity at a later date, when the barking that came from some outbuilding suddenly grew much louder. The dog was already rounding a corner and loping toward us. It was a huge beast, black and as big as a donkey, I swear, with a ruff like a lion. I shouted a warning, the Attolian turned to fend it off, and the miller lunged from the doorway.

Parrying the miller's knife, the Attolian had no chance to use his sword against the dog as it went for his throat. Overwhelmed, he went down. He rolled onto his back and briefly made it to his feet, but the miller pushed him hard as the dog jumped again. The Attolian stumbled, then staggered under its weight. Struggling for his balance, he went backward, stepping onto the rotten well cover. There was a soft rending sound. He and the dog disappeared. We heard a heavy fall and a single sharp yelp, then a long silence.

The burly miller looked at me with hate-filled eyes. "No water," he spat. It was a dry well.

I turned and ran.

I leapt across the empty ditch and onto the road as if I had wings on my feet. I heard no one following me but still ran on until I was spent, finally stumbling to a halt. I tried to wipe away the stinking flour from my clothes. I tried to shake it out of my hair, but it mixed with my sweat and stuck to me. I could feel it on my face however hard I scrubbed with my hands, and my mouth was thick with the taste of it. I spit and spit again. Then I turned and looked at the empty road behind me. The Attolian was dead.

I'd meant to leave him in Zaboar. I'd liked him—more than I'd ever expected to, but I'd still meant to leave him. I would have slipped away—he would have boarded a ship back to Attolia. There was no other choice. There was nothing for me in Attolia. I'd never meant to go to Attolia.

Nothing about my plans had changed, but I stood for a long time staring down the empty road, my arms hanging useless at my sides, waiting, as if he would appear, as if the world would settle back into its proper course, like the wine in a tilting wine cup saved just before it tipped too far. But the cup was overturned, the wine spilled. My master was dead. Now the Attolian was dead as well. I was free to go wherever I chose, and at last I started toward the city.

The day grew hotter. I refused to think of water. When I came to the next town, I marched straight through without turning my head to stare back at anyone who might be staring at me. Eventually, though, I came to a spot where a wooden bridge crossed over a narrow irrigation ditch, and I slipped down beside it, ducking my head into the brackish water to wash away the last of the flour. I rinsed out my shirt and twisted it dry, trying not to think of the ice-cold water in the fountain just a few days earlier. I didn't notice the piece of waterweed that clung to the shirt until I unwound the fabric and saw the green stains. I sat staring at it, despairing, but in the end, instead of trying to rinse out the mess, I just put the wet shirt on and kept going.

The road was eventually hemmed in by the walls of gardens and stables and then by inns and shops and ever-larger buildings. There were blocks of apartments, three and four stories tall, and I still hadn't reached the city walls. Dusty ruts were replaced with paving stones, and intersections grew more frequent. When it wasn't clear anymore which was the main road into the city, I turned at random and walked blindly through the streets. I stopped for a drink at a public fountain and washed my face again.

I saw a weapons shop and went in to sell my knife. The man behind the counter offered me a pittance, far less than the knife was worth. Then he looked me in the face. Whatever he saw prompted him to quadruple the price and cautiously slide the money across the counter to me. My hands shaking, I swept it up and left without a word.

Later in the day I arrived on the waterfront. I still hadn't seen the walls of the city, having somehow circled around them. My rage at the hapless man in the weapons shop had drained away, leaving me embarrassed for myself and exhausted. All I wanted to do was rest. I found a spot of wall not blocked by a vendor's stall and leaned against it, closing my eyes. I would have sat there in the shade of the neighboring stall, but too many people had used the space to piss.

I had no money. I had lost the bundle with my blanket and supplies—it had fallen in the mill yard when I was running away—so I had the clothes I stood up in and nothing else. I could scribe, could offer my services for a fee, but I had no means to buy pens and inks, vellum or paper to demonstrate my skills. I had my life, I reminded myself. I had my freedom. I had followed others' directions long enough. But my thoughts were like birds that wouldn't settle, flying around in my head. I heard again and again the single yelp and the silence from the well, saw the miller's smug animosity, smelled the stink of the flour, and felt again the pounding of my footsteps as I ran away.

CHAPTER NINE

"You're certain he's dead?" someone asked.

My eyes flew open, and I straightened up. A stranger stood before me, taller than the Attolian and slim, very elegant. He had a long, narrow face darker than my own and a heavier beard than I will ever grow. The patterns at the edges of his soft skullcap, and the ones around the collar and hem of his belted shift, marked him as a traveler from beyond the Isthmus.

"Your pardon, sir?"

The man repeated himself, and this time I heard him say, "Is there a pain in your head? You look unwell."

"No," I stammered. "Thank you, I am quite well."

"Ah, I see it is grief, not illness, that strikes, but there are rumors of plague in the city. It is perhaps unwise to lean so sorrowfully against a wall, you see?"

I did see.

He said, "You have lost a friend?"

"He was not my friend," I said automatically, then wondered why I'd said anything at all.

"Hmm," said the man, thoughtfully tensing his lower lip. "You know, I think you are mistaken about that," and he smiled, very kindly.

I thought back to the many dead in my life. I had told the Attolian as we sat among the stones above the tin mines that I had seen many deaths, and I had. Young and old, the houseboys of a fever, Jeffa of the same—other slaves and free men, associates of Nahuseresh, by age or disease or violence. All were alive one day and dead the next, as instantly as the Attolian, and yet this feeling was new, this particular loss, as if some part of me had been hollowed out, leaving me at a standstill and directionless.

The man said gently, careful to avoid offense, "You will forgive a man who has given you one bit of good advice if he gives more, won't you? If you are wrong about whether he is a friend, perhaps you are wrong as well about whether he is gone, hmm? Sometimes we mistake these things." He laid a hand on my shoulder. "Be certain before you let go of him. I once was lost, and my friend came for me." He patted my arm and waved a good-bye before heading away into the crowded market.

I didn't dare lean back against the wall. He was right that rumors of plague could be dangerous for the sick and the well. They didn't always check for plague signs before they tossed anyone who appeared to be ill into plague houses. Better to be on the safe side, they would say, never mind the poor soul going to certain death.

The stranger had had an immense dignity about him. It had been inconceivable to be rude to him, in spite of his intrusion into my private affairs, but the Attolian had not been my friend. The Attolian had been no more to me than a convenience.

"Sometimes we mistake these things."

The Attolian was *dead*. There had been no sound from the well. Only the yelp of the dog and then silence, echoing up from the depths. I looked back over the crowd in the market for a glimpse of the man in the patterned cap, as if I could go to him and insist that he was the one who was mistaken, but by then he was out of sight. I closed my eyes briefly and saw an image of the Attolian lying at the bottom of the well, not dead but dying. His legs or his back broken, calling for help. For a drink of water in the dark. Begging the miller to save him. I shook the image away.

What could I hope to accomplish by returning except to waste a chance to put myself further from the reach of bounty hunters or the Namreen? He was dead. There was nothing I could have done but run away. I would have ended up in the well myself if I had stayed. How long might it take the Attolian to die, if he was alive in that well, if he was alone there? Someone bumped against me in the crowd. Startled, I lifted my eyes from the ground, looking around to see who had bumped me, but I couldn't tell. I looked up at the impersonal blue sky over my head, thought of flying up and away in Anet's Chariot, and then I began to retrace my steps to the mill.

It was past midnight by the time I got back to the mill yard. The full moon overhead made the walls of the mill stark and beautiful, and all the spaces between the buildings impenetrably black. It was quiet. The miller, it seemed, had had only one dog.

I stood by the side of the well, dithering. Finally, I lay down on my stomach and lowered my head through the irregular hole in the rotten cover. There was no sound from below. I stretched my neck and turned my head, listening for any sign of life, and impaled myself on a splinter of broken wood.

"Monsters of hell," I whispered sharply, pulling away from the splinter that was sticking into my skin perilously close to my eye.

"Kamet?" said a quiet voice from below.

I nearly jumped out of my skin and then froze, not sure if it was the Attolian or the ghost of him that spoke.

"You're alive?" I whispered.

"Of course I'm alive," he said, sounding peeved.

"Well, why didn't you say something?"

"I just did."

"I meant before I stuck myself with a splinter like an awl."

"Maybe because I thought you were the miller, you idiot."

"Oh, you were expecting him to sneak into his own mill yard in the middle of the night?" I didn't know why I was so angry.

"Kamet," said the Attolian patiently, "stop arguing, please, and get me out of here."

"How?"

"I have no idea," he admitted. "I've tried climbing the walls, but they are smooth down here, and I can't get a grip."

"I saw rope in the mill earlier."

"That would help."

I pulled my head out of the well and turned toward the yawning darkness that was the entryway to the mill. I'd seen the rope running through a pulley system deep inside, but I wasn't sure I could find it in the dark. Fortunately, the moon was shining a bright beam of light through a window or a broken place in the dilapidated roof, and that beam picked out the block and tackle hanging from a rafter. I picked my way across the mill and tried to free the rope as quietly as possible, but the pulleys, like everything else, were in disrepair. The wooden wheels stuck, and as they turned, they squeaked. I cursed the miller and his stinking mill under my breath.

In the end I couldn't free the rope entirely—the knot that held it to the final pulley was too old and too tight to be undone. I tried to cut the rope with my penknife, but the sun would have risen before I got the small blade through it. Cursing myself for having sold the longer knife, I scooped up the coil of rope I'd pulled free and carried it back toward the well, unwinding it as I went. At the well I dropped the remaining coil through the hole in the cover, hoping it wasn't too rotten to hold the Attolian's weight.

A whispered curse indicated that I should have given him some warning first.

Down on my knees, I stuck my face back into the well to apologize. There was a whisper of sound beside me, a footfall in the dusty soil, and I pushed myself backward onto my heels just as the miller's club swung down. It hit the well cover, very near where my head had been, and caught in the rotten wood. I still had my penknife in my hand, and before the miller could wrench his club free, I plunged the little blade into his thigh. It made only a small wound, but I stabbed him again and again. He shouted and struck at me, but his blows landed with little force. He retreated, and I got to my feet.

Limping heavily, the miller came at me again. I circled away, staying outside the swing of the club, while the miller hurled abuse. "Thief," he called me. "Stinking thief in my mill. Come to rob me, come to steal, nothing here for you but my club."

I held my hands away from my body and said as calmly as I could, "I mean you no harm. I just came back for my friend. I've only come back for my friend."

"He's dead!" the miller snarled. "You can't have him!"

Intent on hitting me with his club, he had turned his back on the well. He didn't see the Attolian rising out of it like a mechanical god in a stage play, shining white in the moonlight.

Oh, dear gods, I thought, he really was dead.

My stark terror must have been obvious because the miller whirled to face the apparition. Just for a moment we stood frozen: the ghostly Attolian, the miller, and me. Then the club dropped from the miller's nerveless fingers, and he produced a thin, whistling sound like a wounded toddler without the breath to scream. He tried again. Every breath brought a louder sound as he ran away, wobbling on his wounded leg. Staring back at us over his shoulder, he crashed full on into the wall of a shed and then staggered out of sight, still shrieking.

The Attolian looked after him, then turned his puzzled expression on me.

Emotions welled up in me until I was near drowning in them. I reached to touch his warm, living hand and swallowed a laugh and a sob. The Attolian cocked his head as if I were as inexplicable as the miller, but there was no time for explanation. If he was hale enough to climb out of the well, then he was equally capable of running. I grabbed him by the arm and hauled him toward the road, away from the cursed mill and its miller before any others came out to see the apparition and realized that he was no ghost at all, but a man still liberally coated in flour.

We ran until darkness and the high brush growing beside the road hid the mill from sight. Slowing, I turned to check on the Attolian. He seemed little injured by his fall—he had kept pace with me and appeared in every way whole. He was breathing heavily, but he smiled, realizing what had so frightened the miller.

"Woo—oo—hooo-o," he said, floating his hands in the air.

Something in my chest split then like an overfull wineskin, and I laughed out loud. The two of us stood there clutching ourselves and heaving with laughter. Every time one of us tried to catch his breath, the other would raise up his arms with a "Woo—oo—hooo-o," and off we would go again like children.

Finally, afraid that the miller might come to his senses and hear us out on the road, I waved a hand toward the city and, arm in arm, we staggered off. "I've still got my sword," the Attolian said, "but I left the bow in the well."

"We aren't going back for it."

"I guess not," he said.

I led the way past now-familiar landmarks: the small town, the ditch where I had washed my shirt, the last rise above the city. As the moon dropped toward the horizon, the sun rose—it would be hot later, but the morning was cool and pleasant. I looked forward to the bustle of the city. Then I glanced at the Attolian, surprised to see how far he had fallen behind. My happy spirits settled with a thump.

"You're hurt," I said, walking back to him.

"I'm fine," said the Attolian.

"No, you aren't," I said. He'd told me he'd landed on the dog—killing it and breaking his fall. He'd been senseless for a bit afterward but otherwise unharmed. Only now, he walked with his shoulders bowed and a hesitation in his step.

"I'm fine," said the Attolian again, more curtly. Then he seemed to rethink. "Actually," he said, "I am inches from death from a putrid sore throat and you should leave me in the nearest ditch."

"What?" I was mystified. "If I wouldn't leave you in a well, why would I abandon you in a ditch?"

He looked momentarily as confused as I felt. "I don't know," he admitted. "I was just trying to stop you from worrying and I've seen someone else do it that way. Actually, I don't know why you didn't leave me in a hole in the ground." He smiled at me, as if he might have laughed again at the miller, but he was too tired to make the effort. There were marks like bruises under his eyes. I hadn't seen them before in the dim light. "I'm fine," he insisted. "Let's keep going."

He wasn't fine. He rubbed his head as if it ached, and mindful of the rumors of plague in the city, I watched the people passing near us on the road to see if they noticed. I reached hesitantly to touch him, and his forehead was hot and dry. He brushed my hand away and stood a little straighter for a few steps but soon sank back again into silent plodding.

"It's just a sore throat," he said, his voice hoarse. "I'll be better tomorrow."

Better that he's ill, said a small voice in the back of my head—it would make it easier to slip away after we reached the Attolian trade house.

The day before, I had wandered without direction. This time I was looking for the fastest way to the center of the city, and I was hopelessly lost. Once we were among the buildings, the streets grew so narrow it was impossible to get any reliable guidance from the sun. All I could do was pick the widest street at every intersection, hoping to reach someplace where I could get my bearings. At last we reached a broad avenue and I could follow the vendors clearly headed for the market in the old city.

Horses and mules pulled wagons, and the occasional camel

was given a wide berth. There were a few chairs occupied by people rich enough to be carried but not so influential as to have the road cleared for them. As their attendants had sharp elbows, they were given a wide berth, too. Nonetheless, the crowd tightened around us as we approached the gates, and we were eventually at a standstill. I cursed the delay even before I saw the cause of it.

Just ahead of where we waited, a group of armed men stood by the open gates to the old city, surrounding another man in an official-looking robe. My heart leapt to my mouth before I realized the man in the robe was a health official— they weren't hunting me. Then it leapt to my mouth again. They were checking for signs of the plague, the tiny red dots that would grow into pustules. It was probably meant to reassure the population and calm the city, but if someone was pulled from the crowd, it was going to start a stampede. I had the Attolian close at hand and was holding him by the arm as if we were close friends traveling together. Head down, he was unaware of anything beyond the paving stones under his feet. He'd complained of a sore throat, so it wasn't plague he suffered, I was sure, but that might mean nothing if he caught the inspector's eye. I looked over my shoulder. Trying to force our way against the crowd would draw exactly the attention we wanted to avoid.

I looked forward again and saw a camel not too far ahead of us. The vile nature of camels was such that even in the

tight crowd there was space around it. Nudging the Attolian
along, I pressed forward into that space, then maneuvered
to put the camel between us and the official at the gate.
We had just drawn even with the camel's back end, and I
was watching it closely because it was much too close for
comfort, when I heard the man leading the camel say over
his shoulder, "Lucky fellow!"

It was the stranger, the gentleman from south of the
Isthmus who had questioned me the day before. "You have
found what you thought was lost, then?" he asked.

"Yes," I said, pushing the Attolian forward as discreetly
as possible. The Attolian, who'd been hunched before, was
suddenly standing straight up. I prayed he wouldn't do
anything to draw attention.

"Ennikar!" he said, as if greeting an old friend.

The southerner looked startled. He did look like
Immakuk's companion. Tall and dark skinned, with his
carefully groomed beard trimmed straight across at the
bottom, he was very like the actor who had represented
Ennikar in the play back in Ianna-Ir. I was afraid the man
might be offended, but he laughed.

"You know those stories?" the southerner asked. He threw
an arm around the shoulder of the Attolian and didn't seem
to notice the way the Attolian staggered. Anyone watching
would have thought that we were together and that the
Attolian's stumble was no more than the result of a friendly

embrace. Arm in arm, we proceeded into the old city.

Once through the gate, we walked in a narrow midway between the stalls of the market. Only the central space was wide enough to allow the traffic to pass through to the rest of the city.

The Attolian continued to be positively delighted by the stranger. I decided it would be best to make an exit before the Attolian said something rude and before the southerner realized how ill he was. I gestured to a space between two market stalls—the booths were constructed of interlocking panels with ceilings of striped fabric, a temporary city within the city, with even narrower roads.

"Our way is through here," I said. "Many felicities to you."

"And many to you, Kamet."

I turned away, only for a moment. No sooner had I stepped between the stalls than I looked back, but he was gone. Puzzled, I stepped out into the open again. The camel at least should have been easy to spot. How could he have known my name?

"You saw him, too?" asked the Attolian.

"What? Yes, of course."

"He's gone now."

"I see that." I was still looking, though.

"We should go, too," said the Attolian.

Fevered and weak, he had more sense than I did. "Yes,

yes," I agreed, and pushed him along between the stalls, among the merchants selling scarves and robes and bolts of cloth, but still looking over my shoulder every few steps until the open part of the market was entirely out of sight.

At a stall selling leather bags, I asked a woman for directions to the Attolian trade house. The answer came in a heavy accent, and I wasn't sure I understood completely, but I nodded and thanked her and moved on. She'd pointed in the direction we were already going, so I thought I could follow my best guess at what she'd said, then ask someone else. We left the market and made our way along a fairly open street. The whole city sloped downhill to the waterfront. The higher part of it, where we'd entered the gates, was where the wealthier people lived and shopped. The stores along the street were for ink and paper and fine tailoring. The trade house would be down near the waterfront.

I'd known that it would be difficult to get the Attolian to the harbor. When we passed a fountain with three stone dolphins, I was relieved that I'd followed the leather seller's directions that far. She'd said there was a road marked with a crowned lion, and there was. We came to a flight of steps, but I wasn't sure if she'd said to turn at the top or at the bottom. I'd hoped it would be obvious when we got to them, but it wasn't.

All I really needed to do was continue downhill—one way or another I would get to the waterfront—but I wanted, for the Attolian's sake, to get there as soon as possible. I parked him against a wall and went quickly down the steps to investigate the street below.

"Excuse me, kind sir," I asked a passerby. "Can you tell me how best to get to the Attolian trade house?"

The man pointed back to the top of the stairs. "Take Zam Street to the next set of stairs on the right, and go down from there to Sun Street, follow it to the first fountain and look for a cookshop called the Lady's Grace, go to the right of the cookshop for a bit, and turn toward the water at the cobbler's. There's another court there, with a"—something I didn't understand—"fountain, and the largest building is the trade house."

"Thank you, k—"

"They're closed, though."

Plague. They had heard rumors of the plague and cleared out, boarding up the doors and leaving the city for the time being. I thanked the man again, wishing he'd told me that first, and went back up the stairs to the Attolian. It was still morning and he could have been a drunk resting on his way home after a long night, but not for much longer. As the sun got higher, he was going to look more and more like a plague victim. I needed to get him out of sight.

I looked around, assessing our options. I couldn't take him to an inn. No innkeeper would give him a room. In the city of Ianna-Ir, I could have found a storage site, a warehouse, a stable, or some kind of shed, but Zaboar was a smaller city and inside its walls it was wealthiest. It would be hard to find a place where the Attolian could be tucked away. Even if he had the strength to make it to the shabbier parts of town outside the walls of the old city, I didn't dare take him past the health inspectors at the gates again.

CHAPTER TEN

"Need help?"

I turned, almost expecting my southern gentleman, but this was an unfamiliar voice. The man before me was out of place in this fancy part of town—even more than the Attolian and I. He was extremely dirty and short to the point of being stunted, with the shoulders and beefy arms of a laborer. He wore a freedman's cap and, judging by his leathery skin, had probably been a field slave for most of his life. He might have been well into middle age, but field workers have hard lives, and he could have been much younger.

"Excuse me?" I said in tones both polite and a little haughty. I thought he might be a beggar and meant to drive him away if he was.

"You need help," he said again, and it wasn't a question. He cut his eyes at the Attolian. "Best he go sleep it off," he said. Thank the gods, he thought the Attolian drunk and not worse.

"I've got no coin," I said sharply, and before I could wave him away, he held up a hand to stop me.

"Not a hennat? For a hennat I can give you a space for him to sleep it off. Quiet place. Out of sight. Celebrated a bit last night, didn't you, thought you were free and clear?"

I didn't understand. I was tired and worried, and obviously already past my wit's end. When the freedman said, "They'll be along soon enough—saw them up in the market," I still didn't understand. I thought he meant health inspectors and then read his direct stare more carefully. Leaning closer, he said in a greasy undertone, "They'll turn you over to slave catchers from the empire for a tidy reward."

Oh, gods, bounty hunters. Or worse, the Namreen, with the permission of the oligarch. I decided quickly. I had the money from selling my knife and whatever the Attolian had left in his purse. "A hennat?" I asked.

"Hennat apiece," he said, now that he had me on the line.

"I've only got five," I said, letting a little of my panic into my voice. I had more than that but wasn't going to let him know.

"Then you've got three," he said. "The other two are mine."

I lifted the Attolian off the wall and propped him on my shoulder—his weight made me stagger—trying to guess if the man only meant to lead us into the nearest alley to knock me on the head. The Attolian blinked his eyes to focus on something that wasn't there and said, "Immakuk?" Perhaps he was even sicker than I realized and this was delirium setting in.

The freedman looked him over. "Not Immakuk," he said. "Godekker."

Godekker—it's a decorative cord that fastens a scroll closed. No one, no matter how lowborn, would name a child after something so trivial. His master must have given him the name using the first word that popped into his head. I wondered that Godekker didn't change it now that he was a grown man and free.

With a sharp jerk of his head, Godekker led us across the square. He went quickly, without looking to see if we were with him. After a moment's hesitation, I followed. At every intersection I considered turning away but never did. The Attolian didn't protest, maybe because he agreed with my decision, or maybe because he was beyond disagreeing. His lips were dry and cracking, and his breaths were short. With most of his weight against my side, I could feel the fever burning in him.

So we went on, moving downhill through the streets until we were almost at the waterfront in a narrow space between two buildings. It was empty—and probably with good reason. The height of the building on one side was too great for its foundations. The stone walls had begun to buckle under the weight and belled out in swales that almost closed off the passage entirely. I had to turn sideways and pull the Attolian through behind me. When the passage widened again, a high barred gate, a remnant from a more prosperous time, blocked the way to a tiny courtyard. Our guide fumbled with a rusting chain and then shoved hard to force the gate open across the uneven paving stones.

"You're lucky I found you," he said, making us welcome with a wave of his hand. "I don't usually go up the hill. Got paid to deliver a barrel to the market." As we passed through the gate, I saw that its lock was no more than a rusted lump connecting two ends of the chain together. A broken link farther along the chain allowed it to be unwrapped. Godekker wrapped it back again, carefully tucking the ends of the chain in so that it looked solid.

Godekker caught me eyeing his work and shrugged. "The walls shifted in the last quake, so no one comes down here anymore. No one but me." Indeed, I thought. Anyone here when the walls gave way wouldn't be trapped in this tiny space, he'd be buried. "The chain just keeps out the stupid children," he explained.

For the first time, he caught sight of the sword the Attolian wore down his back and looked alarmed. "Can he use that?"

"Of course," I said, just in case he was planning to rob us and take all five of the hennat I had mentioned. It wasn't the

Attolian's original sword and was hardly as valuable, but it wasn't what an escaping slave would usually carry. "He stole it in a tavern," I added hastily.

Godekker approved. "Good for him," he said.

So I had fallen in with a criminal—I'd trafficked with them before, on my master's behalf in Ianna-Ir. I looked around at our hiding place. The yard was smaller than my master's rooms in the emperor's palace, and filled with heaps of junk and garbage, broken pots and bowls. There was a shed made of scrap wood with a doorway partially covered by a blanket.

"Few enough saw you come in," Godekker said, "and none of them are friends of the guard. You will be safe here until he sobers up."

He pointed to the doorway, and I maneuvered the Attolian through the mess. Inside was a lightless tomb in which even I couldn't stand up straight as the ceiling sloped down on one side. There was a bed—a mattress bag laid on ropes stretched across the low frame. As I lowered the Attolian onto it, he thrashed, struggling to get back up. "Ennikar?" he said clearly. I patted his arm, hoping he wasn't going to start raving and spoil his disguise of drunkenness. "Yes," I said. "Immakuk and Ennikar. I'll tell you more of the stories later." Thank the gods, he lay back down then and closed his eyes.

Godekker was waiting. Once the Attolian was down and

I left the shed, he put his hand out.

"Four hennat," he said.

"You said two before."

"I'm a fool to risk this," he said. "Damned stupid to risk my neck for runaways and you as obvious as a wart on a lady's nose."

That was heartening—did I have a brand I didn't know about, glowing on my forehead?

"Four hennat," said Godekker.

I had little choice. I opened the Attolian's wallet, keeping Godekker from seeing the contents, and pulled out two coins. "Two hennat now. Two more when we leave," I said.

He wanted four up front. I said no.

"Then three more tomorrow," he said, crossing his arms.

"That's all I have!" But I was already giving in. There was more in my purse, and I could see the indecision in Godekker's eyes. I didn't want him turning us in for a reward.

"You can get more," he said, his voice brimming with resentment. "*You'll* be able to go anywhere in the city—and so will *he*." He indicated the Attolian lying in the shed with a jut of his chin.

Why couldn't Godekker? That was when my sluggish mind finally put two and two together. He didn't usually go uphill, where his shabbiness might lead to unwanted attention. He'd noticed the talk of bounty hunters in the market, and when he saw me, at my wit's end, he'd known me for what I was. Not because I was so obviously an escaped slave, but because like knows like.

"You aren't a freedman," I said.

I frightened him. In an instant he had snatched up a club from a pile of junk, and all I could do was leap backward, my hands in the air. "Five hennat," I said. "You can have all five hennat."

He still looked as if he might swing at me.

"I'll give you all five of the hennat now. Right now. Can you—can you just give us something to eat?" I pleaded, and he calmed down. "I'm sorry," I said. "I'm sorry and I am very grateful to you for letting us stay here."

"Could have turned you over myself," he reminded me.

"Yes, you could have. Thank you for helping us," I said.

"Could still do it," he said.

That was what I feared most. I took a breath and let it out slowly. There was a fine line between frightening him and letting him think he had us entirely at his mercy. "No," I said.

I had directed my master's household for most of my life. I had managed his free employees and his slaves, and each person and each situation required a particular approach. Sometimes I could swing my master's authority like a club, but often I needed to persuade people to respect my position. I gave Godekker the look I used on slaves who resented me because I, too, was a slave and they didn't think I had any business ordering them around. Gentle with them, I explained my authority, always making them see that we were on the same side, both slaves, both capable of treating the other with the respect we were denied by free men.

"No," I said again, quietly but quite firmly. "Godekker, you cannot. I will tell them you are also an escaped slave, and we will all three be doomed."

He shuffled his feet and made to lift the club.

"We can work together, Godekker. My friend and I can pass more easily for free men. We can help you."

I lowered my hands and held them out to him, palms up. "Be my friend, Godekker," I said. "Be my friend in need, and as Shesmegah is my witness, I will repay you someday."

I waited while he wavered between fear and greed and a naked longing that made me pity him. At last he tipped the wooden handle back into the trash heap beside him and laid his hands on mine.

"Friend, Godekker," I said.

"Friend . . . ," and he paused and looked up at me expectantly.

In for a goat, in for a sheep, I thought. "Kamet," I told him.

"Friend, Kamet," he said. "But I still want the five hennat."

✦ ✦ ✦

I slept until Godekker came back with food. I think he meant to catch me unawares, but he should have known better. We slaves are light sleepers. He looked at me strangely where I lay on the floor, while the Attolian had the bed and both of our thin blankets, but he didn't say anything, just held up the bunches of carrots and greens he'd brought. I didn't completely trust Godekker, so I didn't dare sleep more. Eating a little of the food helped keep me awake.

There was a stack of stones to make a fireplace and a clay pipe to make a chimney in one corner. It was more functional than it looked. I used the single clay pot to cook up some of the vegetables in water so the Attolian might drink the broth when he woke. When I was done with that, I went out to pace the tiny yard. The walls above were windowless, which made the yard private but bleak. Two of the walls reached high above my head, while the remaining side of the triangular yard was lower, a single story with a sloping roof above it. Judging by a boarded-up door and dessicated piles of straw and manure, it was a stable and its stable boys had once wheeled barrows of used bedding out of the passageway before the quake had made the walls unsafe.

I paused in my pacing and poked through the piles of junk with my toe. There were some nice pots and a few very pretty floor tiles.

"Found those at a burned-out villa," said Godekker,

sitting on a broken piece of a stone pillar with his knees up around his ears and his arms hanging down in front of him. He looked like a buzzard. "I scavenge and then sell what I find." It was a living, but not a profitable one, clearly.

"How long?" I asked.

"Seven years," said Godekker.

"Field-worker?" I asked.

He nodded.

"From near here?"

"No, of course not," he said. "And I won't say where, so don't ask."

I shook my head. I wouldn't have asked.

Godekker rocked himself back and forth while I stood there thinking of the Namreen hunting me and the rewards they would post. Or maybe they'd found my master's plaque next to the slave dead under the rockslide and no one was looking for me at all. Maybe the bounty hunters in the market were after a different slave. I didn't know. I would never know. I looked at Godekker and wondered if he still worried about pursuit. He stood and stalked past me.

"You worry forever," he said over his shoulder. "You'll never feel safe."

That's what I'd thought.

Godekker ducked in through the low doorway but was only inside for a minute before he charged out again. "That's not a drunk," he said, outraged.

"It's not the plague, though. It's been all day, and there's no sign of it," I assured him as I jumped to my feet.

"How would you know? You've probably killed us both!"

I frankly stared. "What fool doesn't know what the plague looks like?" I asked, and then realized the obvious answer—an uneducated escaped slave living alone hand to mouth in the dead end of a disused alley. So I wiped the insulting expression off my face and carefully described the plague signs, trying to sound as reasonable as possible, and Godekker settled down a bit. I think the what-kind-of-an-idiot-look probably convinced him more than the rational explanation, though.

Godekker wouldn't come near the Attolian. He said he'd sleep outside, so the Attolian and I had the place to ourselves. As the sky darkened, I ate the cooked vegetables, leaving their broth in the pot. The Attolian hadn't opened his eyes all day. I lay down to sleep, reassuring myself that I'd wake if Godekker tried to drag the gate open to leave the yard.

In the morning I drank the broth and made more. The Attolian had tossed and groaned in the night. When I spoke to him, his eyes opened and he seemed to hear me. When he tried to talk, he made no sense. I spooned a little broth into him, but the liquid just dribbled out of his mouth again, and I was beginning to be afraid he was dying.

I was just wiping up the mess I'd made when the light in the shed dimmed. Godekker was in the doorway. He leaned over the Attolian, his eyes narrowing—he'd seen the ring in the Attolian's ear, and I couldn't pass it off as something we'd stolen in a tavern.

"He's not a slave," Godekker said. "You're a slave. He is not."

"He is helping me escape."

Godekker's face suffused with rage. "Patsy," he snarled. "Dog. Whimpering, bootlicking dog. Why do you need Godekker for a friend? Why be here in Godekker's shed? Go find an inn for your master."

"I told you."

"He isn't helping you escape. He's *stealing* you. When he gets you far enough away from your old master, you'll find out what that means. You're nothing, you're a horse ridden by whoever holds the reins."

"No." I denied it with a weak shake of my head.

Godekker pointed to a pile of debris near the doorway. "Take a rock from the pile and beat his head in. Then you'll be free."

He stormed off. Holding the pot in one hand, the spoon in the other, I listened for the sound of the gate, and relaxed when his anger didn't seem to have carried him farther than the yard. I couldn't help but wonder if Godekker was right. I was glad I'd gone back to the mill, but why stay with the

Attolian when he was ill—when it might be my best chance to leave? I could go down to the docks, find any Attolian ship, and tell his countrymen where the Attolian lay. They'd come for him. Godekker wouldn't slit the Attolian's throat if he knew there would be a reward—and there surely would be a reward from the Attolians. Meanwhile, I would be well aboard any ship that could carry me across the Shallow Sea to the north, farther from any retribution from the empire. I could go all the way to Oncevar, which I'd heard was civilizing itself. My skill as a scribe would keep me fed, and no one would pursue me there.

On the other hand, I would never know if the Attolian lived or died, and after all that worry getting him out of the well, I would spend the rest of my life asking myself a question I couldn't answer. I decided to wait just long enough to see if he lived. If he did, I would get him to an Attolian ship and then slip away. If he died, I would leave immediately for the north. It was a reasonable decision—I wasn't just rationalizing—unless I was. Maybe I was a patsy, as Godekker claimed. I had been a slave for most of my life. Was I incapable of acting as a free man?

I put the spoon and pot down and reluctantly went to talk to Godekker.

"Does he only have eyes for you?" Godekker called to me when I came out through the doorway of the shed. He sneered. "Does he tell you how much he loves you? Does he tell you how pretty you are? Just wait. His father will send a tidy sum to your master as compensation, and when he tires of you, they will sell you on to some new master. If you are that lucky."

I had misjudged Godekker. I'd thought money was all he cared for, but I could see that he had taken pride in the idea of helping fellow slaves. Now he felt betrayed, and for good reason.

"I'm sorry, Godekker," I said. "We have been bad guests."

"I should have passed you by, should have left you for the enforcers to pick up, but I thought I could help. I could hide you, and why not? Why not do a good turn? Because we don't, that's why. We don't do favors, do we?"

It was true. We don't do favors. I have in my time—for Laela and a very few others, but only because I was, or had been, powerful enough not to need those favors back, and the obligation to repay me was tempered by that. Even so, when I arranged for my master to make Laela mistress over the other girls in his household instead of selling her, I had kept it a secret at first, concerned that she would be angry at me. When you have no freedom, the last thing you want is some other slave who holds a debt over you. We don't do favors. Now I was indebted to Godekker, and I knew that was part of the reason I didn't like him.

"You are right, he is stealing me, but not because he loves me." I thought I might as well be as honest as possible. "He is taking me to his employer, and he will free me."

He snorted in disbelief. "You are an idiot if you believe that."

I admitted that was probably true. "I am not a fool, and if my old master catches me, I am a dead man. If I end up a slave because of this, well, I was a slave before. We don't get to choose much, do we, Godekker?"

With obvious reluctance he nodded in agreement, but then he said, "A well-placed knife thrust would buy you your freedom faster." He stood up and looked me in the eye—as much as someone even shorter than I am could. "Kill him," he said, his chin jutting out. "Bash his head in with a rock and be free. I will be your friend then."

I shrugged weakly. "He's valuable if he lives," I said. "He'll reward you, Godekker, and he'll get me out of here."

Godekker turned his back, and I retreated to the shed.

The Attolian woke in the afternoon. I heard him say my name and rose to check his fever. It had broken, and he was covered in sweat—I was able to give him some water from a cup.

"Where?" he asked after a sip, his voice hoarse.

"In the city," I said. "Zaboar. In a safe place. How are you?"

"My throat hurts," said the Attolian. "Not as much now, though."

I asked if he could drink the broth, and when he said yes, I lifted him and held the pot to his lips.

The pot was too wide to easily drink from, and he ended up with a fair amount spilled on himself. As he drank I explained in a low voice about the rumors of plague and the closing of the trade house, about Godekker and our hideaway. "When you are up to it, we can go down to the docks. There may be a ship to carry us to another trade house."

The Attolian settled back into the mattress and lay looking at the ceiling not far over his head. I sat on the floor beside him with my arms around my knees.

"Kamet, what is troubling you?" he asked, though it was obviously painful for him to speak.

"Nothing. Nothing at all. We are safe here."

With effort he lifted his head to throw me a disbelieving look.

"Everything is fine," I said.

I hadn't realized Godekker was listening from just outside until he thrust his face into view. "I told him to hit you on the head and be free of you. And if he doesn't, I'll turn you both in to the guard." Then he was gone again.

Horrified, I tried to reassure the Attolian. "Don't worry," I said.

"I'm not."

"There's nothing to worry about."

"Kamet—"

"I swear."

"Kamet. I'm not worried." His eyes closed briefly, but he forced himself awake. "Did he tell you that you are too weak to be a free man?"

"He's a fool," I said.

"So are you, if you believe him." His certainty was almost enough to convince me. He said, "If it were Nahuseresh lying on this bed, would you still be here?"

Instinctively I looked to the rock pile. I could see it through the open doorway. If it were Nahuseresh who stood between me and my chance of escape, I might very well smash his head in, as Godekker demanded. If it were Nahuseresh, though, I'd be long gone and Godekker be damned.

I looked down at the Attolian, whose smile was fading as he drifted back to sleep.

Huh. I'd meant for him to eat some of the vegetables as well as drink the broth, but that would have to wait.

The Attolian slept more comfortably that night while I stayed awake to listen for any sounds of Godekker leaving the yard. I heard nothing to alarm me. In the morning, the Attolian was awake and I was dozing when we heard heavy footsteps in the passageway. It could have been anyone approaching until we heard the distinctive sound of a metal breastplate scraping against stone.

"Godekker," I said, and rushed out to the courtyard, where Godekker was nowhere in sight. A ladder propped against the low roof of the stable told me how he had gotten away without alerting me. I kicked myself for telling him that the Attolian was valuable. I'd hoped Godekker would think it worth his while to keep us safe, but instead, he'd thought it worth the risk to his own freedom to betray us.

As a squad of enforcers came into sight, I threw myself at the gate, shaking it as hard as I could without actually causing the rusted chain to loosen and drop off.

"It's not the plague!" I shouted. "I swear! I swear!"

The men in front stopped dead in their tracks. Others, stuck behind them, tried to push forward.

"Please," I begged, twisting my entire body as if with desperation. "Please, it's not the plague!"

There was some very directed swearing, and the men nearest me popped forward a few reluctant steps to allow their leader room to pass, and there beside him, oh, heavenly graces, was Godekker himself, looking as trustworthy as a rat out of a sewer.

"Godekker," I shouted, as if surprised to see him, "tell our master that Noli is getting better. It wasn't the plague! We can come home now!" I pushed my face against the gate. "Master only said to sell us if Noli got worse, and he isn't getting worse. He's better, Godekker, I swear."

Well, that put the cat among the pigeons.

The officer in charge of the enforcers stared down his nose at Godekker, who threw his hands up in protest, looking like nothing so much as an unscrupulous slave palming off his master's plague-infected property for reward money before the disease became obvious. While Godekker shouted that we were runaways and that they should drag out the "foreigner," and I sobbed dramatically, the officer was doing his own share of shouting, accusing Godekker of trying to get him and the entire squad infected with the plague and insisting there was no way he or any of his men was stepping into that courtyard.

Finally, Godekker, maddened with frustration, crossed a line.

"Coward!" he screamed. "There's no Noli, it's a foreigner! And he's Kamet! I tell you, Kamet!"

"Coward?" The guard leader stared at him, and Godekker fell silent.

"No offense, kind sir," he said quickly, "no offense." But it was too late. With a single blow across the face, the officer knocked him down and when he was down kicked him.

"You like the plague?" the guard leader said. "Why don't you go in then?"

I fell silent and backed away as they lifted the protesting Godekker and threw him bodily over the high gate to land at my feet with a dull crack of his head on the pavement.

He lay unmoving as the guard leader looked me over through the bars.

"We'll come back in a few days. If you're still here and still alive, we'll sort out who you are."

Then he ordered his men about, and they left, squeezing one by one down the passage.

When they were gone, I bent over Godekker. He was still breathing and his head didn't seem to be broken, so I pulled his shirt off and tore it into strips to tie his ankles and wrists. The Attolian leaned at the doorway to watch, but I waved him back inside. Then I slowly dragged Godekker across the courtyard and into the shed.

"Better give him the bed," said the Attolian.

"He can have the floor," I said.

I made the Attolian lie back down to rest and made more broth with the last of the water and some carrots while we waited to see if Godekker was going to wake up or die. He'd begun to groan and pull against his bonds, but it was still some time before he opened his eyes and knew where he was. What he said then was impolite. I could believe he'd been a field-worker.

"I have enough left of your shirt to put a gag in your mouth," I said, unsympathetic.

Now that Godekker was tied up, I could do what hadn't been safe before. I unwrapped the chain from the gate and went out to buy better food and bring back skins full of fresh water. I went down to the docks to see if there was an Attolian ship but couldn't pick one out in the inner harbor. There was a vendor selling skewers of grilled meat, though, so I bought three and went back to the courtyard.

Godekker watched with silent hate as I put the small sack of barley and the basket full of provisions down by the hearthstones. I could almost see his mouth watering as I handed the Attolian the skewer of meat, and I thought his eyes would jump out of his head when I handed him one of his own. He held it in his still-tied hands. He looked at it and then at me. His eyes dropped, and he began to cry.

I'd been angry enough to beat Godekker myself when I heard the enforcers of the peace coming, but my heart was swept again by pity. That didn't make me untie him. Eventually he stopped sniffling and wolfed the meat off the skewer. I made the Attolian a decent soup with barley and vegetables and shared that with Godekker as well. I didn't expect an apology, and he didn't offer one. When he was done eating, he turned his face to the wall and ignored us.

The next morning I asked the Attolian if he thought he was well enough to travel. With Godekker still tied up and glowering in the background, we couldn't discuss our plans. All I could say was that we had no idea when the enforcers might be back, so we should move on at the earliest opportunity, and the Attolian agreed.

We shared one last potful of soup, and then we left the shed. We'd been there so long I felt I should have something to pack, but there was nothing. The Attolian paused in the doorway to look back into the dark where Godekker sat. I had retied one hand to the bed frame with a multitude of knots. He would get himself free once we were gone, but not quickly—we would be well away by the time he did. The Attolian held out a hand, and I gave him our purse. He tipped it upside down and then leaned to pour a handful of coins into Godekker's lap.

Once we had emerged from the dead-end passageway, I asked, "How much did you give him?"

"All of it," said the Attolian.

I stopped in my tracks as he kept on walking.

"So?" I asked when I'd caught up with him. It hadn't been much, but to Godekker it was no doubt an eye-popping amount and all we'd had to feed ourselves with.

He nodded. "So, so, so."

"The trade house is closed because of the plague rumors," I reminded him.

"There will be an Attolian ship in the harbor," he said confidently.

"I didn't see one."

"You can't see your hand in front of your face."

My eyesight was not that bad. "If there are none?"

"I don't know," he said with a shrug, still smiling.

"So we will burn that bridge when we come to it?" I asked, and he laughed as he threw one arm over my shoulder. If Godekker had betrayed us, he'd undeniably saved us first. I said, "Maybe he'll help some other runaway."

CHAPTER ELEVEN

"Do you think Godekker will have us back?" the Attolian asked.

"Not if he thinks he already has all our money," I said. Godekker might turn over a compassionate new leaf, but I doubted he would ever be any friend of ours.

There had been no Attolian ships in the inner harbor, and we had moved out to the docks beyond the city walls. Zaboar wasn't the trading city that Sukir was, but its docks were usually busy. Larger vessels came in from the Middle Sea and smaller ones traded up and down the coast of the Shallow Sea—collecting goods to resell at Zaboar, or buying in Zaboar to resell to smaller ports where the ships with a deeper draft could not go. Rumors of plague had reduced traffic, though. We had worked our way about half the length of the waterfront without finding an Attolian ship and were pausing for a rest. Two bollards, cast iron mushrooms cemented to the stone quay, provided mooring for the nearest ship and seating for us. As we looked ahead, it was clear we were running out of options—the tail end of the waterfront was mostly smaller local boats.

The day was warm, the sun breaking on the top of every wave in the harbor. There were a few clouds that proceeded across the sky like errant parasols, giving us brief moments of much-appreciated shade before moving on. I thought how pleasant it would be to move to one of the wineshops on the waterfront and sit there, watching all the traffic go by, but we had no money, and I couldn't forget that the Attolian was still recovering. He might yet be picked up as a plague victim. That he was on the mend was obvious to me but might not be so to a health inspector. As well as Godekker, there were the enforcers of the peace to consider. Gods forbid we ran into any of them out in the open air.

The Attolian got back to his feet, saying, "Onward then." I tried again to convince him to stay while I went and found a ship.

"I'm fine," he insisted, and when I looked at him skeptically, offered a more honest assessment. "I'm not fine, but I'm good enough for another few ships."

So we walked on until we came to a shabby little caravel, with a dolphin in peeling paint on its stern. A sailor told us it had an Attolian captain. "Though the crew comes from here and there." It was not the most prepossessing vessel, but as I said, we were reaching the end of the docks and the end of our options.

The Attolian led the way up the plank to the deck and spoke to a sailor there. Much to my surprise, when the captain appeared the Attolian pulled the ring from his ear and held it out.

"This is the private seal of Attolis Eugenides," he said.

Well, thank the eternal gods he hadn't swallowed it.

The black cylinder of stone that had dangled from his ear since we had left Ianna-Ir was not flat on the bottom as I had assumed, but engraved—evidently with the king's seal. The carving was much too small for me to make out, and I had to resist the impulse to bend over it to get a better look. The captain reached for the seal, but the Attolian pulled it back.

"I die before it leaves my hand," he warned, and the captain slowly nodded his understanding.

"We need passage home," said the Attolian.

"We are headed east," said the captain. "I can take you on board, but we will not see Sukir again for three or four months. It will be half a year before we are back in Attolia."

"We need passage now," said the Attolian.

"Find another ship," said the captain. He looked out over the water, as if one might rise up out of the brightly twinkling waves.

"Our king will pay you well," offered the Attolian.

The captain rolled his eyes. "Well enough to compensate me for the loss of trade on a six-month trip?" he asked, not believing it.

The Attolian nodded. I was quite impressed with his air of command. Even more impressed because he was still pale from illness, with dark circles under his eyes and his clothes quite filthy after his stay in Godekker's garbage pen.

The captain hesitated. Locking eyes with the Attolian, he weighed the dangers of failing us if what the Attolian said was true, if we did indeed travel under the private seal of the king.

"Very well," said the captain at last, and I let go of my breath. "I will take you as far as Sukir."

The Attolian opened his mouth, but the captain raised a hand to forestall him. "We will take this seal of yours to the trade house in Sukir and see if they verify it. Maybe you can find a better ship there. I am captain, not captain-owner, and I won't go farther than Sukir without more proof than some carved seal I have never seen or heard of before. I warn you, those who own this ship are powerful enough to hunt you down if this is fraud."

"They won't need to," the Attolian assured him.

The captain shouted for his bosun then and ordered the crew recalled from the shore.

The Attolian was unhappy—he stood at the ship's rail and glowered at the passing waves as we sailed. He'd wanted to bypass Sukir, saying we'd spent too much effort getting out of the empire to step back into it so easily, but I was secretly relieved. In Sukir, it would be easy to disappear. Twice the size of the Zaboar's capital city, it has twice the chaos to get lost in, and because it was on the north side of the Black Straits, I could slip away overland. I wouldn't need to pay passage on a ship to get me away from the empire. I did not want to leave the Attolian, but once he knew of my master's death, our brief friendship would be over. He might hear the rumors in Sukir, and he would certainly know the truth when we reached Attolia. I could not accompany him there, no matter what. I'd made a fool of a ruler so petty he'd stolen another man's slave for spite, so profligate he'd waste the profits of a six-month trading trip to have what he wanted. He wasn't going to free me, and might well kill me for it. I had to pray that because the Attolian was a favorite, he would be safe.

Even if the Attolian king didn't kill me, I wouldn't live long in his city. The news of my presence there would travel back to the emperor like an arrow shot from a bow, and when the Little Peninsula fell to the Medes, they would be looking for me. Bounty hunters might well arrive before that. Attolia was no safe place for me. I needed to leave the Attolian and the empire far behind, and as the days passed, I planned. I needed no cap, as Godekker did, to pass as a free man—I just needed to show a little more confidence. After asking the captain's permission, I had helped myself to some of his paper and pens. With those, I would be able to prove my worth to any merchant in the city of Sukir. It would not take long to find an employer who needed a trustworthy scribe to travel to a distant city and work his ledgers there. I could go as far as Mûr on the Black River or farther north to Oncevar.

We came to Sukir late in the evening. The Attolian had asked me to stay in our cabin during the time we spent there, and I'd agreed. We didn't know if the empire believed me dead in a rockfall, and even if the empire was unaware that I still lived, we didn't want to arouse any suspicions. I sat in the cabin, the Attolian beside me, and listened to the clatter and bang of the sails and blocks as we glided over the lowered chain into the harbor. It has always amazed me that something made out of cloth can make so much noise when it flaps, like cannon-shot or a lightning strike from a clear sky. Through the small round porthole, I looked out at a hundred ships moored around us, silhouettes against the orange and pink and translucent blue sky. Sukir is the largest of the empire's ports, larger even than Iannis at the Ianna river delta.

Navigating into a crowded harbor is a ticklish business, but the evening breeze was gentle, and the captain skillfully eased his way to a mooring and ordered anchors dropped. We slowly swung into alignment with the other ships as the sails were gathered in. Then we waited for the harbormaster's boat to come alongside, as it eventually did—when there was almost no light left to see by—to ask the captain's business.

The captain's business had been a point of contention. The Attolian wanted to leave as quickly as possible—we would not change ships, and once the seal was verified, we would rely instead on the *Dolphin* to take us the rest of the way. The captain was not thrilled with this plan—at the very least, he wanted to dump his cargo on the market at Sukir, to offset the costs of his commandeering. The Attolian had refused to permit it, afraid that people would ask questions about the unusual activity. Again I was taken by surprise by his confidence and his air of command. That he was more sure of himself in his native tongue was one explanation, but I think it was also the effect of the king's seal. When he held it in his hand, he did not doubt that he spoke for the king and that the king's authority was incontestable. Anyone could see it in his face, and I think his respect for that trivially small carved stone, more than anything else, persuaded the captain. Or perhaps it was just the obverse side of being such a terrible liar—his honesty was easy to believe in.

The captain might have accepted the Attolian's authority, but he still fought his losses. He'd argued that docking in Sukir and *not* doing business would be more likely to attract unwanted attention. Ultimately, he and the Attolian had worked out a story that would explain the unexpected arrival of the *Dolphin* in the harbor at Sukir—a change in the ship's ownership that required an immediate return home—and would permit the captain to sell off a part of his cargo, even if it wasn't at the best possible price. This was the fiction that the captain related to the harbormaster.

In the morning the ship was moved to the dock to offload whatever cargo the captain would be able to sell and take on whatever he could for the trip to Attolia. I pretended to yawn when the sailor knocked at our cabin door to inform us that the captain was ready for the walk to the Attolian trade house to present the king's seal. When the king took the throne, the imprint of that seal had been sent out on documents everywhere the Attolians traded. Unlike the public seals, only a handful of people would have seen it at each house, but it would have been carefully stored for just such occasions as this one.

"Sleep in," said the Attolian, already up and meticulously tidy, as if he were going to see the king himself. It was unusual for me to still be lying down and he'd asked earlier if I was ill.

"Just tired," I told him and I did feel tired, as if I were being pressed into the bunk by a tremendous weight.

"We won't be long," he assured me.

I lay listening until I was certain the Attolian had left the ship, then forced myself up. I pulled on a clean tunic, borrowed from one of the sailors, and carefully folded the dirty one out of habit. I wouldn't be taking it, or any of my clothing, with me. I took only my penknife and the pens and paper from the captain, secured in a roll. I looked around, seeing that everything was tidy, and then I left.

I made my way up the narrow stairwell to the deck of the ship. The morning sun was still on the slant and the sailors busy with predictable tasks. Trundling about the cargo that the captain still hoped to sell, they had no attention to spare on me. I nodded hastily to a sailor by the gangplank as I trotted past, as if trying to catch up to the men who had left earlier, and he never gave me a second glance.

Leaving the waterfront, I didn't dare take the larger avenues. I dodged into the more inviting side streets, forgetting that they weren't as familiar to me as the narrow byways of Ianna-Ir. Sukir for all of its size and wealth was similar to many small coastal towns in that it was deliberately difficult to navigate. The rough stone streets turning in hairpins and intersecting at odd angles all looked alike. Pirates who attacked the vulnerable towns on the coast rarely made it very far into their mazes before being thoroughly turned around and dumped back out on the waterfronts. Sukir hadn't had a pirate attack in my lifetime, but it still had the streets to thwart one.

Soon enough, I was praying that I hadn't gotten myself hopelessly lost. Never would I have guessed I could have so much fellow feeling for pirates. Twice I found myself back at the docks where I had started, as if the gods had cursed my wandering feet. Frantic, I set out a third time, risking a wider road, hurrying along it until I saw a glimpse of the city wall and turned toward it. Following the street along its base, I thought I must eventually reach a gate.

I had my head down, berating myself for an idiot, and I looked up only moments before crashing straight into the Attolian standing amused in front of me.

He laughed at my surprise. "Were you worried we were taking too long?" he asked.

"Yes," I said breathlessly. "Yes, you've been gone awhile."

He shook his head, disgusted. "The traders took forever to find someone with the authority to verify the seal. He had to be called in from his home, but he checked the dispatches and gave the go-ahead at last. The captain is over the moon to know that the king is going to pay him. We were just on our way back."

"I see," I said. "That's good."

The Attolian put a hand on my shoulder and turned me around.

"You shouldn't have come out after us," he said. "It's still dangerous. We don't even know for certain that the Namreen found that body in the rockslide."

The captain, the Attolian, and I walked back to the docks. The curving streets led us right to our ship as though the gods themselves had paved our way.

The captain was indeed in fine spirits and eager to treat us in style. The second mate was turned out of his cabin so that the Attolian and I needn't continue to share. The captain apologized for the tiny size of the cabin, but it was a blessing just to be alone. I could pray without the Attolian's asking why I was wringing my hands and what I was muttering under my breath. I promised a lifetime of dedications to a terrifying number of gods if they would just turn the ship away from Attolia. I prayed for storm and shipwreck. I prayed for a water supply gone bad or tanks holed so that we could put into a port for resupply. I prayed for plague or pirates. The only thing I didn't pray for was a ship full of Namreen. Nonetheless, we sailed untroubled from Sukir down the Black Straits to the Sea in the Middle of the World and then across it.

I couldn't bear to look the Attolian in the face. I couldn't risk him reading my thoughts, so I told him the motion of the waves out on the Middle Sea made me sick, and I stayed in the cabin. He, of course, came to sit with me, and I had to lie still and pretend I was asleep.

"Kamet, wake up," said the Attolian one morning, and showed me the pennant he'd asked the ship's sailmaker to sew. A black line made an oval around four oddly formed letters. "It's supposed to be Hamiathes's Gift," he said. "When we reach the Thegmis Channel, we will fly it from the mast. No one but the king and I know what it means, but when they see it at the fort on the mainland, they've been told to send a man on a fast horse to the capital. The king will know we are coming."

I didn't know what Hamiathes's Gift was, and I didn't care, either. "How long until we see Thegmis?" I asked.

"Only a day or two now," he assured me. Then he asked if I wanted something to eat, and when I said no, he finally left.

I didn't want anything to eat. I wanted to die. I would have thrown myself overboard into the sea if I'd thought it would have kept the Attolian from ever knowing that I had betrayed him and I prayed to Prokip, god of justice, that punishment for my deceit would fall on my shoulders, not his. At night I lay awake thinking about what the Attolian king might do. Throw me in a prison cell or kill me or send me back to the empire. Maybe he would sell me off to one of his barons in need of a record keeper. I had once had ambitions to run the empire—and the best I could hope for was that I might end my life in the wilderness counting sheep.

When the island of Thegmis lay ahead of us, I climbed up on the deck to see the pennant raised.

"My god, Kamet, you look terrible," the Attolian said. "Go back and lie down."

So I looked out the porthole in my cabin, and I thought of our upcoming reception in Attolia as we passed under the cliffs of Thegmis, no more than a stone's throw from shore. I wished for the hundred thousandth time that I could swim.

I could read and write in five languages. I could multiply and divide in my head, track a hennat out of place through an entire year's expense records, and turn a feather into a perfect pen with two cuts of my knife, but I could not swim.

We neared the capital as the sun was setting, and I returned to the deck to face the future. Everything was shining in the sun's dying rays—the headlands, the temples, the ordinary buildings of what I knew for a fact was a rather dingy city. The marble palace of Attolia, as we rounded the headland, glowed like another sun itself, but as we drew nearer, the shadow of Thegmis, lurking offshore, crept up from the sea to swallow first the port, then the city, then the palace. By the time we passed the lighthouse at the end of the mole, only the temples on the heights were still in the sun, and heading toward us at top speed were two of Attolia's war galleys.

The Attolian was puzzled. "We were supposed to get into the city without anyone knowing we'd arrived. Why would they send out war galleys?"

Before my hands could cover my treacherous mouth, the words fell out. "Because my master is dead—there's no need for secrecy now."

CHAPTER TWELVE

The Attolian dismissed this with a shake of his head. Then he took his eyes off the approaching galleys and looked at me instead while the words sank in.

"He was poisoned the day you offered me my freedom," I said to the deck under my feet.

Where another man might have shouted, or cursed, or questioned, the Attolian just stood silent. In Ianna-Ir, I had picked him for an idiot, but by this time I knew better. He was thinking everything through before he responded—the persistence of the Namreen, my fear that he would see the wanted poster in Koadester, the empire's well-known policy on the treatment of slaves of a murdered master. Every single thing that he had noticed, he was reevaluating.

"I wondered why you said Nahuseresh 'had' a sense of decorum. Did you poison him?"

Well, that was a question I hadn't anticipated. "No, it was his brother, probably at the emperor's direction."

"You would have left the *Anet's Dream,* but you couldn't swim." He hadn't been asleep when I went exploring on the riverboat.

"Yes."

"And you still meant to disappear in Sukir."

"Yes."

He nodded slowly. "I thought we were Immakuk and Ennikar, but we were just Senabid and his master, weren't we?" His words were more full of contempt for himself than for me. "Is that why you didn't want to tell me those jokes? You were afraid I'd see myself in them?"

"No," I protested.

"No," he agreed. "I wouldn't have. I'm that stupid."

Just then a bump shook the ship, the war galley wasting no time on a gentle interception. The captain shouted in outrage. The sailors looked over at us, suddenly uncertain. The soldiers came up over the railings, so many to collect just the two of us, their numbers proportional to the rage of a confounded king.

As I looked away, the Attolian leaned over me, planting one large finger against my chest. "If you had told me," he said quietly, equal parts betrayal and rage in his voice, "if you had told me in Sukir, *I would have let you go.*"

Almost as if he'd heard this declaration of treason, a

soldier as big as the Attolian, but older, with gray in his hair and a fancy badge on his breast, stepped up to the Attolian. It was Teleus, captain of Attolia's palace guard, and he said very loudly, "I hereby arrest you both in the name of the king."

This time the Attolian did shout. "What?"

"Think, you idiot," said his captain.

Two men grabbed me then and dragged me away. I tried to insist that it was not the Attolian at fault, but no one listened. I doubt the Attolian even heard over his own shouting. In moments I was tossed over the side of the ship into the war galley and the galley was pulling away. Someone tugged me to a bench where I sat down so hard I nearly fell over backward. The galley's high sides hid everything from view but the temples on the hillside above Attolia's palace. I sat watching it grow closer, wavering, as I blinked again and again.

The galleys stroked to the shore, cutting through the waves like a stylus across wet clay. We arrived at the dock, and I wiped my cheeks with my sleeves. The guards were gentler getting me off the boat than they had been putting me on—there was one at either hand to swing me across the gap between the ship and the quay to where even more guards waited, dressed in their breastplates and greaves, their helmets with the rounded tabs in front to protect the nose. They were impersonal and anonymous and stood intimidatingly close. I looked for the Attolian—I was still thinking of him as the Attolian, even surrounded by other Attolians—and located him at last arguing with the captain of the palace guard, poking him in the chest as he'd poked me—which was out of character and seemed like an excessively bad idea. The captain's only response was a series of curt orders that set the guards around him in motion. They hastily formed into groups, and each set off from the waterfront in a different direction. The captain led one group away while the Attolian was escorted to my side. He'd been saying something as he came, but when he saw me, he fell silent and looked pointedly away. Then we marched, surrounded by guards, through an eerily quiet city.

I noticed it immediately—there was no one lingering in the street. My view was limited by the armsmen all around me, but the few people I could see moved quickly and kept their heads down. I looked more carefully. The palace guards were watchful, but not of me. Their eyes were on the streets, the people, the alleys we passed. Their hands were on their swords. The hairs on the back of my neck lifted.

The Attolian, blinded by his anger, was oblivious until we had passed through the open space of a market and were making our way up a street of wineshops, all of them shuttered. It was probably where he'd once upon a time been separated from his pay as a country bumpkin, and it should have been crowded at this time of day. It also wasn't on any direct path between the waterfront and the palace. We were taking an exceptionally circuitous route.

"Where is everyone?" the Attolian asked.

"Silence," said the leader of our cohort.

"The queen," someone said under his breath.

The queen had gone on a rampage against her citizens? The queen had poisoned her second husband the way she had poisoned the first? Only two words spoken, but those two words said it wasn't either of those things. The words conveyed a world of grief, and the Attolians loved their savage queen.

The Attolian looked stricken. "Dead?" he asked.

"Silence!" said the cohort leader again.

"Shut up, Haemus," snarled the Attolian back. "Is she dead?" he demanded of the men around him.

Several guards shook their heads, not outright disobeying their commander.

"Miscarried," the man beside me whispered.

"A son, I heard," said another.

So we learned of the heir just as he slipped away. His sex might have been only a rumor, a reflection of the longed-for security an heir would have brought to the country, but talk of it meant the pregnancy had been far along. The queen was old for a first child, and late miscarriages were often deadly. The Attolians might lose her yet. No wonder the city was as silent as a held breath. How long would the Eddisian king rule without his queen? Not long, I guessed. If I weren't already doomed, I would have been planning to leave the city by morning. Civil war was coming and on its heels, no doubt, the Medes.

We continued up the streets in the silence the squad leader had called for—I wondered if he had been a friend of the Attolian—and reached the walls around the palace without crossing through the open plaza at its front. We entered the grounds by way of a side gate to a small courtyard. A door led to stairs down to the bowels of the palace—and the prison cells underneath it. At the bottom of the stairs the Attolian was led away without a backward look, while I was taken through a room filled with all the horrors I had fled in Ianna-Ir and out the other side to a warren of stinking, dimly lit hallways and a lightless cell. There was no door to the cell, only a barred gate, and far away one sad lamp to cast the flickering shadows of the passing guards onto the wall near me. I could also hear the Attolian shouting somewhere. He sounded angry but unafraid. I was not surprised.

Unfortunately, he was also getting closer.

I sat against the front wall of the cell, away from the barred door, hoping to be out of sight. The Attolian had stopped shouting, but I was certain I heard his stamping feet among the others making their way toward me. I heard keys jingle as a nearby cell was unlocked and then locked again and the guards awkwardly shuffled away. I sat quietly, breathing through my open mouth.

"I know you are in there, Kamet."

I twisted to peer out at him. He was sitting across the passageway, leaning, as I was now, on the bars of his cell.

"Costis," I said, using his name for the first time since he had told it to me, on board the riverboat at the start of our journey. "Costis, I'm sorry."

He crossed his arms and continued to look furious. "No one has spoken of your master. The king will not leave the queen's side, and my captain says he must keep you safe until the king sends for you." He seemed as angry at the captain as he was at me.

"And you?" I asked.

"And me," he spat. I think the argument I had overheard had been over the role of the Attolian—whether he would guard me from outside a cell or be guarded himself.

"The other guards at the waterfront. They were decoys?"

"Yes. I should have realized, but I was too busy feeling like an idiot."

Which suddenly made me furious.

"Well," I said, realizing that the strange feeling rising in my chest was anger, "you *are* an idiot."

"What?"

I didn't back down. He was securely locked in the cell opposite, after all, and I'd already lost his goodwill. I had nothing left to lose. "You knew what I thought of Attolia.

You heard me after that Namreen tried to take my head off. Did you not wonder why I met you at the docks? Did you ever think? Did you never ask yourself *why* I would want to come to your stinking backward country and spend the rest of my life scrabbling for a living on a vomit-stained street corner writing love letters for drunks and bills for tailors?"

He recoiled as if bitten by a rabbit. Then he snarled back at me, "What makes you think my king would have turned you out on a street corner?"

"Costis"—I flung out a hand at the distance the two of us had come—"he sent you halfway across the world to steal me out of *spite*. He doesn't care what happens to me."

He refused to concede, but it would have been difficult, if not impossible, to refute the pettiness of Eugenides. Costis could only mutter into his chest, "That's not true." He had so much faith in his silly king.

"If you had let me disappear in Sukir, you would have been a traitor."

Costis had uncrossed his arms without thinking, and now he sullenly crossed them again. "If your master is dead, then it wouldn't matter to the king where you went. I keep telling you, you idiot, but you won't listen."

Oh, I listened. I knew all I needed of the king of the Attolians. He was so incompetent he couldn't stop his servants from dumping sand in his food. He was so careless of the lives of his servants that he exiled Costis when he couldn't protect him. So careless of my life that he thought I would come like a dog to his hand when he sent for me. Like Nahuseresh, he cared only about what *he* wanted, and to hell with anyone else. I knew what men with power were like, even if Costis didn't.

"One of us is an idiot," I said. "I don't think it's me." I'd had no choice but to stake everything on a chance to escape my fate, and I'd lost. Scribing on a street corner would be a paradise compared with what I saw in my future.

We waited for a very long time. It was hard to tell how long in the darkness and the unbroken silence. The prison's guards brought us food. I slept a little, with my knees up and my head on my arms. Finally, the palace guards came again and unlocked our doors. They tried a joke or two at our expense, but the black look Costis gave them restored the silence as we walked the dark passageways and up the narrow stairs to the palace. We passed open windows in the corridors, and the sky above was a deep blue, like lapis. It had felt like years in the palace's prison cells, but perhaps this was just the dawn of the day after we had been taken on the war galleys. I didn't know if I would see the sky again, and I tried to capture its color in my mind's eye. I did not believe that the news of Nahuseresh's death had not reached Attolia. His guards might not have heard, but the king surely knew.

We were taken to a small audience room, one near the

great throne room. There were no windows, only candles in the iron chandeliers overhead and in the sconces on the walls to give us light. The room was full. Men and women lined the walls, leaving open only a narrow aisle that led to a throne on a raised stage. Costis stood frowning beside me.

My thoughts wandered—to the blue of the sky I had glimpsed and memories of the blue of the sea we had sailed across. I thought of the sandal-making slave in the city who had warned us of the Namreen, and the kind people on the desolate farm beside the salt pans who'd given us more for a song than they had for a coin. I hoped the slaves from the tin mine were safely arrived at the sanctuary and prayed that the other slaves of my master had been spared torture once I had fled like a guilty party. I thought of Laela and hoped she hadn't suffered. I thought of Marin and hoped she was happy.

All around the courtiers chatted and whispered, having easy conversations about horse races and trade ships and quieter ones about the queen. They cast the occasional glance in my direction, but I knew they had not gathered there because of me. Whispers had traveled through the palace that the king would have an audience—and they had come to see him, hoping for news of their queen. How appalled they must be to think that their queen might die and they might be left with the Thief of Eddis as their sovereign.

Then the king entered the room.

I couldn't see him at first, but I knew someone had arrived because every head turned in his direction and words died on every lip. It might have been someone else, some baron who was a power behind the throne, but no, the man who stepped out from among the attendants dropped onto one of the gold-leafed chairs on the dais with a clear sense of ownership. He was too far away for me to see him very well, but the strength of his personality was apparent—reflected in the undivided attention of every single person in the room. Great Anet, I thought, I have been deceived, and I looked over at Costis in amazement because it was he who had deceived me. This was not the weak and silly man he had described. This was not the king of the Attolians they talked about in the empire. This was a man who held his court in thrall as if he were the emperor himself.

"The queen lives and will be well," said the king, and everyone breathed again. In unison, they dipped their heads and turned their palms up, grateful to receive the blessing of their gods, but not because they would have abandoned Eugenides if she had died. No. They feared the worst because they cared for her and perhaps, as I later learned, because the king's health was also poor. The Attolians knew their precarious position and feared to lose either head of state. He was their sovereign as much as she. I could not doubt it.

Oh, my Costis, I thought, oh, my friend. I turned to him, panic filling my heart because he was as solid and unflappable as ever, and he *was* an idiot. Never in all his stories of the king had he shown me this man sitting on the dais—this man, who had seized a throne and in so short a time made it indisputably his own. I'd counted on the fact that Costis was the favorite of a weak and petty man—that the king who had forgiven him once would forgive him again and that any consequences of the king's anger would fall on me alone. But powerful men like this had no patience for those who disappointed them. I looked at Costis and only in that moment recognized—to my horror—that the expression on his face was not anger but stubbornness. He meant to lie to his king. He would try to conceal my master's death, sure that the king would free me and I could flee before the king learned he had been deceived.

"Great king," I said, turning away from him, shouting toward the far end of the room, struggling to advance, but held by the arms of the guard.

All around me people inhaled sharply—it was as if the whole room had gasped. I'd merely used the archaic form of "great," hoping to flatter him. "Great king," I repeated even louder, "my master, Nahuseresh, is dead. I have—I have deceived your servant to secure my freedom."

I heard Costis shout from behind me that it was his fault, not mine, and I could hear him struggling to come forward. The king waved one hand, and Costis was silent. The king waved again, and the men holding me back eased their grip.

I stumbled as close as I dared and dropped to my knees, hastily assembling in my head a story to persuade the king of Attolians that I had left the empire for no other reason than a desire to serve him.

"Kamet." He spoke with such familiarity, as if we were friends meeting at a wineshop, that I paused in my generation of my narrative and raised my head. I must have looked like a caggi checking for a hawk.

"I am reluctant," said the king slowly, studying his boots as if they were a surprise there on the end of his legs, and wriggling one, as if checking its polish before starting again, "I am reluctant to incur the wrath of the gods by claiming that a man lives when they may take any of us at their pleasure, but I believe that Nahuseresh is in perfect health."

I couldn't imagine what he meant.

The king shifted on his throne. "It is my fault. Let neither of us blame Costis." How amusing that both of us were absolving Costis, but it was nonsense. The king was speaking nonsense.

"Nahuseresh was not poisoned."

Of course he was poisoned. Laela had told me so.

"My ambassador in the empire, Ornon, arranged for Laela to meet you in the passage and misdirect you. We didn't tell Costis."

Misdirect me? Lie. He meant "lie to me."

I thought back to when Laela had stopped me before

I reached my master's apartments—had saved me from the inquisition. Hadn't she? I shook my head in disbelief. There had been no one to support or contradict her story. We had been alone. But it was impossible. It was absolutely impossible. Why would Laela lie?

We don't trust one another. We don't do each other favors.

Everything she said had made sense to me—my master was desperate to recover his place at court, and he had been failing. The emperor was unhappy, Nahuseresh's friends had turned away from him, and he was an embarrassment to his brother—so the emperor had gotten rid of him. It seemed perfectly clear, but I had taken it for truth, had believed Laela without question because I had believed *in her*. I had trusted her. I'd left the palace in a panic on the basis of nothing but her word. Oh, Laela, I thought. Did you lie to me?

She had.

She had lied. I could feel my heart breaking. When only she could have betrayed me, she had. Laela. Laela, I thought. Why?

"You would not have left Nahuseresh otherwise," said the king.

I wouldn't have. I was going to be a great man; I was going to direct an empire. Instead, played for a fool, I had run away from all my dreams, from my future, to this dark room lit by flickering candles and smelling of too many people in an airless place. Speechless, I curled around the terrible hollow feeling in my middle until my head knocked the floor.

"Kamet, she did it so that you could be free."

I didn't look up.

"As I knew she would."

How could he have known such a thing? I knew Laela and could not fathom it.

"Because you told me so much about her."

Never. I finally looked up. I had never spoken to the king.

"I know you don't see well, but I thought you would remember my voice."

I shook my head, shook off his kindness, his concern, his familiarity. He waited.

His familiarity. I squinted at him—much like a blind caggi, I'm sure.

Then I leapt to my feet. Eyes wide open and staring, I surged toward the throne—the guards clutching at me just a moment too late, and the king waving them back. I kept going until I could see his face, see every detail—the quirk of his eyebrow, the twist at the corner of his mouth, the mark on his cheek, where he'd said the Attolian guards had once shot him when he was running away, leaving the scar I remembered so well. I was almost on top of him before I stopped, but he did not recoil, only sat leaning forward so that I could get a good look at the queen of Attolia's errand boy and sandal polisher.

CHAPTER THIRTEEN

"Do they know?" I asked, gesturing toward all the courtiers behind me.

"Some," he said seriously. He threw his eyes over the crowd and then looked back at me. "More will know now."

He smiled.

I remembered him as a boy, small for his age. I found him taller, broader in the shoulder, much older than the intervening years would explain, with a hook where his hand had been—wholly changed, in fact, but for the scar on his face and that smile. Or perhaps, I thought, he has not changed. Perhaps it is just the world that has changed. Perhaps he was only by accident at the edge of this court and had slowly and inevitably drawn all of it into orbit around him.

"Why?" I asked. "Why bring me here?"

"Spite," said Eugenides frankly. He leaned back and

crossed his arms. "I have a great deal of ill will for your former master. And because you are my friend," he added, glancing up from his boots. "That should have been the first reason, but I will be honest now—it was not."

Was it the act of a friend to steal my future? To engage Laela in my betrayal? "Kings don't move mountains as a favor to a friend," I said aloud.

The king equivocated. "While in my experience, they do, I grant you—it's not what successful kings are known for. Sometimes a little bit of spite motivates what more kindness cannot."

The disobedient servant I'd found endearing and the king who'd stolen my future—I struggled to put the two people together in my head. Costis's stories of a weak and silly king and the confident and cunning manipulator before me—like misaligned papers, I could not shape them into a tidy stack. Like a bad ledger, it wouldn't tally.

"I'm sorry," said the king. "I know you wanted your chance at the emperor's side, even if it meant your death would come with his."

"We all die," I snapped.

"We do." He was suddenly so grieved. I remembered his queen and his heir and wanted to bite my tongue. He said, "I've taken something from you that I had no right to take. As Laela did. I hope you will forgive us both."

He waited, but I was still busy tidying my mismatched

impressions, adding his grief to the layering of them in my head. I looked around the room, evaluating the likelihood that this was actually a dream—I was asleep still in the cells under Attolia's palace. It was a wonder the entire room wasn't laughing, as I was the butt of the joke now. I looked for Costis but couldn't pick him out at that distance.

The wine merchant—the memory came to me, now that I knew the truth. I turned back to the king. "You sent the wine merchant?"

He seemed confused. "I did not send a wine merchant," he said—for whatever that was worth.

"He led me to the docks. He was in Sherguz as well."

"You would not have gone to the docks on your own?" the king asked. I shook my head.

"A coincidence, then," said Eugenides.

I shook my head again. I'd been quite sure there was something odd about the merchant, and I'd begun to doubt coincidences.

"I've upended your life for spite, Kamet. Will you let me make it up to you?"

He was the king of the Attolians. What was there to say but yes?

"As a token of my good faith," he said, offering me a coin. I knew, before I took it from his hand, that it would be the very one I'd given him when I thought I was helping him make his way home to a fishing village on the coast.

No doubt the whole court would hear the story—and how it ended with this small coin returned to me. All the Attolians would think that he had repaid me for my kindness—because the Attolians were fools. I wondered if he had a brother, if his brother was a scholar, if anything he'd ever said had been true.

"I'll get you a new copy of Enoclitus's scroll," said the king. "Someone with better handwriting can copy it for you this time. We will rebuild your library here in Attolia."

Then he waved forward an attendant with instructions to take me to my rooms as an honored guest. I was not headed for that street corner yet. I suppose that made Costis right and me wrong, but there was no chance for me to tell him so. Poor Costis. Now that he'd found himself played by his king as well as by me, he probably wanted to see neither of us ever again. Still in a daze, I was led away, leaving the king to continue his audience with others who waited for his attention.

I was walking up one of the wide marble staircases, still in the ceremonial part of the palace, trying to adjust to the idea of being an honored guest with attendants—who were attending *me*—when I saw the Mede ambassador. Melheret arrived at the top of the stairs and began to descend while I paused, one foot up and one down, and when Melheret bowed, I bowed back, a lopsided, wobbling attempt at courtesy.

"Kamet, what a surprise," he said. He'd stopped on a higher stair and looked down at me benevolently. "We thought you dead in a rockslide."

"No, sir," I said. I knew Melheret. He had been my master's commanding officer once. He was a mid-level army man who'd grown too old for battle and had been given the position as ambassador to the Attolians because no one else wanted it. After his appointment, he'd come to Nahuseresh's country estate to ask for advice. For Melheret, it had been a heaven-sent opportunity to advance his career—he need only avoid complete catastrophe and he could return to a much better position at court than he had previously held. He'd had every reason to expect some guidance from Nahuseresh, but my master had looked down his nose at him and been snotty. I think I had probably been snotty as well.

"We almost had you at Sherguz," Melheret said, conversationally. "You must have been on one of the boats that burned before they could be searched. The Namreen checked the inns afterward, of course, but they were looking for a Setran traveling alone. We didn't know about the Attolian then."

I swallowed, remembering the inn. I'd only gotten the Attolian out of the courtyard because the wine merchant from the capital had come into it. We could have been sitting right there in plain sight when the Namreen had come hunting. I hoped the wine merchant, wherever he was, would be blessed by the gods with a booming business, with health and wealth and an old age surrounded by his grandchildren.

Melheret smiled. "You've come from an audience with the

king, but before that from the prisons. Not how an honored guest is usually received."

I waited.

"Perhaps because you are less an honored guest and more . . . stolen property. I can restore you safely to your place, Kamet. You have been lost and are now found." He indicated his burly servants, and he held out his hand to me, offering me back the very future I'd just been grieving over. All I had to do was take his hand and I would belong to the Medes again, protected by all the diplomatic agreements made with the ambassadors of foreign heads of state. Here was the control of my destiny that I had been denied.

The attendants beside me stiffened, and the two palace guards who had been following at a polite distance surged forward, but they were powerless to stop me. I'll never know if Eugenides would have honored the diplomatic agreements because I didn't take the ambassador's hand. I just stood there, still halfway between stairs.

"No?" the ambassador asked.

"No," I said, and he withdrew his hand.

"Freedom tastes sweeter than you thought."

I nodded.

"May it always taste so sweet." The ambassador bowed. "Nahuseresh will miss you, I am sure."

My heart skipped a beat. I'd been so stunned by the king's revelation, and by the ambassador's offer, that this most salient detail had been neglected. Nahuseresh was still alive. Laela was alive. As betrayed as I had felt only moments before, a rush of relief flooded my body—she and the houseboys, the cook and the valet, they were all alive—and almost immediately after the relief, familiar fear. Did my master know that Laela had betrayed him? How long until he learned I was in Attolia?

"His Majesty's interest is unaccountable," the ambassador was saying.

It was. A weaker, more foolish king might have stolen me away from my master for spite, but not the man I'd just seen on the throne. A less ruthless man might have done it out of kindness, but Eugenides had dismissed that justification.

"The king does enjoy his little jokes," I said. There was a subtext to this conversation that I was missing. Whatever it was, I felt very strongly that I didn't want to talk to the Mede ambassador anymore. I nodded and twitched another moment or so, trying to think of a good reason to excuse myself before I remembered that I didn't need one. I was a free man. So I bowed again, said, "Good day," and continued past him up the stairs.

I wondered what it was that Melheret knew, that the king knew, that perhaps all the attendants and guards around me knew, that I did not. I wondered if I would ever find out. I was nobody's secretary with my ear to the ground. I had no connection to these people. No expectation that they might pass along rumors or information. Melheret was correct about one thing. I certainly wasn't an honored guest. I didn't know what I was.

The king's attendants led me to a set of rooms I recognized immediately. I had lived in them with my master when he was ambassador in Attolia. Indeed, the king did like his little jokes. One of the attendants, Lamion, I think, explained that there would be guards at my door, but only to be sure I was undisturbed. I was free to come and go as I liked. He pointed out the amenities of the rooms, with which I was already familiar, and directed me to the guests' bathing room with heated water for the bath. I nodded. I knew where the bathroom was, though I'd never used it, just carried my master's cosmetics to and fro. The dreamlike feeling of the day was only growing more intense. I realized, with just enough time to politely send the attendants out the door, that I was going to burst into tears. As soon as I was alone, I did. I sat there on a velvet-cushioned stool and sobbed like a child. I was a free man—with the favor of the king of Attolia as well as the undying enmity of my former master, and I had lost my only friend.

When I was done, I wanted a bath but was too exhausted to manage it. I crawled onto my master's bed, wrapped myself in the linen, and fell asleep.

I woke groggy. Recognizing the bed I lay in, I panicked, wondering what could have possessed me to commit such a transgression, before I came fully awake and found the king of Attolia sitting on the footboard. Another figure nearby held a lamp. It was deep twilight, and I had slept through the day.

The man with the lamp used the taper on the nightstand to light the larger lamp on the desk and then went from sconce to sconce until the room was filled with light. He set his lamp down on a side table and came to stand near the bed. He wasn't an Attolian. He had the clothing as well as the fair hair and skin of men from the north.

"It wasn't spite *or* friendship," I said, glancing sideways at the king.

"It wasn't *just* spite or friendship," he said. "Though I hope you will believe that both played their part. This is Yorn Fordad, ambassador of the Braels, come to have a chat with the two of us." The Braeling bowed silently to me.

The king said, "The emperor is preparing an army to attack our Little Peninsula."

I nodded. Everyone knew that.

"Everyone knows that?" prompted the king, as if, like Costis, he could read my thoughts.

I nodded again. "Yes."

The king looked significantly at the ambassador and then back to me. "Everyone knows except the Braelings and the rest of the Greater Powers of the Continent. Their official position is that the emperor is only rattling his sword and when he's rattled himself to death, his heir will have so much to occupy him that he will have no interest at all in our three little states."

This sounded unlikely to me. It was possible that the emperor would squander his resources on an army he didn't mean to use, but he would have to have some exceptionally good reason to do so, and I couldn't imagine what it might be.

"Our allies fear to provoke the emperor by arming Attolia. They make excuses, hoping the threat will melt away. They are busy with their own problems and won't deal with ours until the Mede is on their doorstep. By then, it will be too late for little Attolia, little Eddis, and little Sounis." The king pinched his finger and thumb together, under no illusions as to their significance in the conflict between the Continent and the Medes. Little countries get eaten up by bigger countries. Or crushed between them.

"However"—the king went on, clapping his hand against his leg—"my queen believes the emperor cannot bring his army against us without ships—many ships. She thinks he preserves the illusion of sword-rattling while he masses his navy—moving in secret to avoid open confrontation and hoping to take the Continent by surprise. If the allied navy came face-to-face with those ships, no one could ignore the threat they represent. We need the allies to see that fleet, Kamet." The king leaned toward me, searching my face. He asked, "Where are the emperor's ships?"

This was why I had been brought from the empire, and this was why the Namreen had hunted us so relentlessly. Not because

Nahuseresh had been murdered, but because the emperor feared I could tell the king of Attolia where he was hiding his navy. Melheret had made one last effort to retrieve me, to ensure my silence, but he needn't have bothered. I didn't know.

The emperor's fleet was in no correspondence that Nahuseresh had dictated or received. He'd been in disgrace, I wanted to remind the king. We had spent months at his family estate with his razor-tongued wife before he had been allowed back to the capital, and then all of his efforts had been directed at living down his humiliation. That was why I had been taken in by Laela's story—because Nahuseresh was obsessed with the emperor's good opinion, and I assumed he had lost it permanently—fatally. If there was one thing I was certain of, it was that Nahuseresh had had no part in the emperor's plans.

Eugenides let out a long sigh. "Well enough, Kamet. It was worth a cast of the dice."

But my sleep-sodden brain was finally tallying its account. "Hemsha," I said aloud, and the king straightened up again.

Hemsha. It had been such a humble request for my proud master to make of the emperor, to be governor of an undeveloped coastal province. I remembered my relief that he hadn't been overreaching as he often did and my mistaken certainty that he would be successful—overconfidence that had certainly cost me dearly. If Nahuseresh was not dead, if he hadn't sunk so low in the emperor's graces as to be poisoned by his own brother, why then hadn't he been made governor of Hemsha?

More certain by the moment, I said to the king, "Hemsha has only a tiny port at Hemet, but there is a protected strait along the coast to the northeast where you could put a hundred ships, two hundred ships. There's no water there to make it a usable port, but there are good roads to bring supplies and soldiers to Hemet, and they could then be ferried from there to the fleet. Hemet is far south, but they could sail for Cymorene. The emperor has agents there ready to betray the fort."

"Really?" asked the king, surprised.

"I burned the correspondence from them before we left that fortress at Ephrata. I'm sure they are still there." After resupplying on Cymorene, the fleet could sail north to anywhere on the Little Peninsula.

The king nodded. "Province of Hemsha," he said gravely. "Thank you, Kamet."

He continued to sit cross-legged at the foot of the bed a little longer, assuring me that I would be safe in the palace, even from the Mede ambassador. I remember that he rubbed his ear as he spoke. As he had no right hand, he rubbed it with his left while his hook stayed in his lap. It made him look very young, like a boy imitating a monkey, absolutely unlike the man I had seen on the throne early that morning.

"Melheret is more bark than bite, but we will keep guards at your door just in case," the king said. "You can trust them.

It's gold that makes treason, and the emperor hasn't given Melheret any. He can't afford an assassin to knife you in your sleep, and you needn't worry about something being slipped into your dinner. I had a little talk with the kitchen staff last night, so happily, neither will I." He rubbed his ear again. "The ambassador will have to assume that you have brought me the information I needed, but any message he sends back to the emperor will be slowed by the labyrinth of imperial correspondence—it's very likely Melheret's warning will be dismissed even if it reaches the inner court. This morning a hundred people heard me say that I stole you away for spite, and the Mede will want to believe it. All that Melheret or I can do is wait to see how this plays out, while you, Kamet, can begin a new life. Contemplate a new name, if you like, to start with."

He gave me an encouraging nod as he rose and left with the ambassador of the Braels—the Braeling never saying a single word. I didn't hear the outer door close behind them, and I believe that the guards, if asked, would have insisted that no one had passed by.

I hadn't gotten to my feet in the entire time Eugenides had been in the room. I lay back down, thinking how I might describe the encounter to one of the other secretaries in the emperor's palace, and began to appreciate Costis's difficulty in accurately representing the king of the Attolians. I looked around—except for the lamps, lit by the Braeling, there was no evidence that the king had been there.

A month or so later, an allied fleet sailed into the narrow bay north of Hemsha, ostensibly looking for a stream to refill their water barrels, and found instead the ships of the Emperor's navy neatly lined up at their moorings. Alarmed at the approach of the foreign ships, an unknown gunner on board one of the emperor's brigs fired his cannon without instruction. The allied ship *Hammer of Yeltsever* responded. Once the firing began, there was no stopping it. The emperor's ships, unable to maneuver, were destroyed by a fleet one-third the size of their own. Eighty or more of the emperor's ships sunk. Thousands of men lost.

The admiral of the allied fleet wrote a very regretful report to his king, calling the loss of the Mede fleet a most untoward accident. Rumor had it that Eugenides stole the report from the diplomatic correspondence of the Pentish ambassador and read it out loud to his queen.

The Attolians liked to point out with a snicker that there was no sign anywhere of the king's hand at work.

I took the king seriously and spent much time that night considering my new life. I struggled to name myself. I could be Jeffa, or Nish. Or Ashnadnechnamharr, if I chose, though the ghost of King Ashnadnechnamharr might haunt me if I were so bold. I began to understand why Godekker might have continued as Godekker—it was difficult to imagine answering to a new name. Kamet was the name my mother had given me, or so I have always believed, and I decided to keep it. Kamet the Setran? Kamet the Scribe? Nothing seemed to fit. I would be stuck with Kamet Freedman if I waited too long, but I resolved to wait anyway, in hopes of finding a name that felt right.

In the morning a boy brought me my breakfast on a tray and was scandalized when I took it from his hands and sent him on his way—I couldn't be comfortable being served. There were guards outside my door as promised, and one warned that I should expect visitors after breakfast.

Indeed, my first visitor was Attolia's former secretary of the archives, Relius. The guard announced his arrival, and I bowed and stepped back to admit him. We'd met before. He'd been one of only a few people who had understood my value to my former master. I was surprised that he was no longer secretary of the archives, the official title of Attolia's master of spies, but of course, I couldn't ask about the change. I invited him to sit on the elegant cushioned furniture and perched a little gingerly on a chair opposite him. As he pulled his robe around him before sitting, I saw his hands were misshapen, badly broken and healed, with two of the fingers missing. I looked from them to his face and quickly away. They had been undamaged when I had seen him last.

"There are some questions you might answer for us, Kamet. I am here to ask if you would be willing to do so."

I'd expected this. I knew more about the empire than just the location of its ships, and I'd thought through the night about what things I might tell the Attolians that would profit them.

Relius said, "The king wants you to know that you are under no obligation. You are his guest, free to come and go as you please, and welcome to stay—in the palace, or anywhere in Attolia—for as long as you like."

Or until Attolia fell. I still believed the Mede would roll the Little Peninsula as a lion rolls a gazelle, and I intended to be long gone when they arrived.

"You are thinking of driving a stiff bargain," said Relius, and he was right. I'd thought long and hard about what my information might be worth. "Don't," he advised me. "You will do better to trust the king—he will see you amply rewarded." I remembered Eugenides the night before, sitting at the foot of my bed, and earlier, sitting on his throne. I remembered how much I had liked him when I'd thought he was an errand boy—when he had ruthlessly tricked me into believing that was all he was. The only thing I knew was that I didn't know anything, really, about the king of the Attolians, and I didn't trust him.

"He's very tenderhearted," said Relius. "He'll feel quite bad about it as he cuts you up into little pieces and feeds you to wolves."

I laughed. Then I remembered Relius's hands.

He nodded seriously. "I myself would walk across hot coals for him." The Relius I had known had been fanatically loyal to his queen. "For either of them," he added.

I didn't trust Eugenides—I trusted my judgment of Relius. "What is it that you would like to know?" I asked.

Many more meetings followed. Every morning a messenger arrived at my door with a list of appointments, and I was asked to offer all my understanding of the entire empire as if I were a combination of oracle and travelogue. I described every port I had been in, and I had been in many. I laid out the roads for them, as if it were they who were invading the Mede and not otherwise. I told them about the hierarchy of the empire's armies and navies and described every member of the court in as much detail as I could—habits, commitments, and liaisons, both proper and improper. Significant details, trivial details, when the emperor rose in the morning, what the heir preferred for breakfast, the strength and disposition of armies, of their stockpiles, every rumor of unrest in the provinces. All the information I had gleaned from my master's correspondence. Everything I had learned as a slave—wholly attentive to any detail that might someday be used to my advantage. That information would be turned to the Attolians' benefit—and that was to mine. I had no loyalty to the empire that had enslaved me and none to the Attolians, either. This was a business arrangement.

Not content with a spoken version, Relius wanted a written record of my flight from the empire, so I began this narrative in the palace of Attolia but have only recently neared its completion. I will eventually send it to Relius, when I am sure it can be delivered without interception, and I hope he will be satisfied with my account, as I would be honored to have it added to his library. I think he is more truly the secretary of Attolia's archives now than he was when he carried the title. If events fall out badly, perhaps the scroll will go no farther than the library at the temple just up the hill from here.

While my day was filled with meetings, it was empty of other responsibilities—shockingly so, to me, who had never had time to call my own. I had hours to walk through the palace, revisiting the places I remembered, sometimes seeing them with new eyes. Mosaics, statuary, and the detailed carvings on railings and staircases that I had previously hurried past, unable to linger without appearing to be shirking my duties, I had time to fully appreciate. Day by day I found more beautiful things in Attolia.

If I had once been an anonymous secretary to a Mede master, I was no longer. People greeted me in the hallways wherever I went—the indentured were especially polite. The first time I heard my name, I was flummoxed and stood blinking as I translated its meaning in my head: Kamet Who Called Eugenides the Great King. It was even more of a mouthful than Ashnadnechnamharr and eventually shortened itself to just Kamet Kingnamer. I do not use it, as

I am living very quietly here in Roa, known only as Kay the Scribe, but that is the name they use for me in Attolia. I am delighted, and I don't care if Costis mocks me for it.

I spent much of my free time in the palace library, where several times I saw the youngest attendant of the king wrestling with his lessons. He had a pugnacious self-reliance that was unusual in such a body, and I suspected he was tying his tutor in knots on purpose. Curious to see if I was correct, I approached just after a lesson had ended and the tutor had decamped. I asked the young Erondites if I could use his slate, and he handed it over, amiable enough. I drew a bird and wrote three Attolian letters underneath it. "Which of these makes the first sound in the word?" I asked.

Very deliberately, he pointed to the one for *pa*, and not to the *ba* in bird. He knew it was wrong. I could see it in his face, and he, in turn, could see that in mine. After a moment, he shrugged with just the one shoulder and picked the chalk out of my fingers. Using great care, and his left hand, he added two more letters, one for *ja* and one for *ne*, next to the letter he'd chosen. Then he cast me a speculative glance from the corner of his eye and waited.

I conceded. "Indeed, it is a pigeon."

Rarely have I seen a smile so utterly transform a face.

When I was not exploring the library or wandering the interior of the palace, I wandered instead in its gardens—not the queen's garden, because that was private to the royal family, but the wide gardens that lay between the palace and the sacred grounds of the temples on the hillside above it. They were as orderly and as peaceful as I remembered, and I liked to visit one particular outdoor room where hedges enclosed a grove of mature trees and a deep pool was encircled by a ring of large stones. I enjoyed sitting there as the fish rose to the surface nearby, nibbling at the crumbs I dropped on the water.

One day I approached the grove so lost in my own thoughts that I didn't realize that others were there before me until I passed through the arched entryway in the hedge and two of the palace guards stepped in close beside me. They dropped the butts of their long guns into the gravel under our feet with an intimidating crunch, and I saw that the queen was resting in the garden, her attendants all around her. They turned to look at me, but I was already murmuring my apologies and backing away.

One of the attendants rose and followed me out. "Kamet," she called as I retreated, "the queen says you are welcome and asks you to join her." Attolia's request was my command, so I nervously trailed after the attendant as she returned to the group beside the rock-rimmed pool. Attolia lay on a couch that had been carried out from the palace—her beauty heightened by an unsettling frailty. She was surrounded by cushions of velvet and embroidered linen, and a boy sat nearby with a fan to cool her if she grew too warm, while one of her attendants had a woven cloth folded in her lap, ready to deploy if the queen became too cool. She was obviously ill, but her vulnerability only emphasized the nature of her power. It was neither her beauty nor her physical strength that made her queen.

I bowed low, and as I lifted my head, she indicated the ground by her side with a glance. I dropped to sit cross-legged on the grass next to her couch. She smiled at me, and her eyes seemed brighter for it. She asked, "Is it true, Kamet, that my king twice bit my head cook?"

I nodded and said gravely, "Indeed, Your Majesty. I witnessed it with my own eyes."

She murmured, "Anything worth doing is worth overdoing, it seems," and I ducked my head to hide my own smile. It was a most apt summation of the king's behavior. I knew by then that there was far more affection between the monarchs than I would have believed possible before my arrival in Attolia, and it was no surprise to me that she characterized him so well.

"Kamet," she said a little more seriously, "we have a saying in Attolian: the river knows its time. My king tells me that it came originally from the land of the Ianna and refers to that great river."

I nodded. "Indeed, I believe that is so, Your Majesty."

"My king says it is part of a longer piece of writing that he has read about, but has never seen. He told me that you might know it."

I nodded again. "It's from one of the tablets of instruction."
I knew what she was asking, and I recited the text quietly
for her.

Mother why does the River not rise
It is not the River's time
Why does the seed not sprout
It is not the seed's time
Why does the rain not fall
the leaf not unfurl itself
Where is the hind and why does she not graze the fields before us
It is not their time

The River knows its time
The seed knows its time
The rain the leaf and the hind
They know their time

The River will rise the seed will sprout
The rains come down and the leaves unfurl
The hind will bring her children to graze before us
All in their time

It was quiet then. The leaves of the trees overhead ticked
against each other in the light breeze. A fish flapped its tail in
the water as it dove deeper into the pool. The queen looked

down at her hands, stroking the soft velvet of a cushion, and said, "It was not her time. We will welcome her when she comes again. Tell me, Kamet, have you been to the kitchens?"

Surprised by the question, I said I had not.

"Do not leave it so long as my king did," said the queen. "You don't want your ear boxed."

It was a dismissal, so I returned to my feet and excused myself. As I withdrew, the attendants rose like a flock of attentive birds and adjusted the queen's pillows, offered her a tray of delectables, cast the woolen cloth over her legs and tucked it around her, and then settled again, some to stools, some to the ground, with their peaceable activities, embroidery, handweaving, sewing, back in their hands as silent accord returned to the grove.

Once out of sight of the queen, I continued walking along the garden paths. There was nowhere else I needed to be, the heavy schedule of meetings had finally begun to thin, and so I wandered, the flowers and leafy branches nodding at me as I passed. The palace gardens were extensive, with interlocking paths and long alleys of plantings linking open spaces with green lawns and often a fountain or a statue or both. I came eventually to the high wall that surrounded the garden and separated it from the sacred grounds beyond. That land belonged to the temple precinct on the hillside above the palace. Guards pacing the wall looked down at me, and I had no doubt they'd been watching me for some time. Their queen had chosen to leave her private garden, and I was probably the only person nearby except for her attendants and guards. I wondered if they could tell that I was delaying. I looked over my shoulder at the scuff marks in the gravel walk, clear evidence that I had in absolute truth been dragging my feet.

Attolia's extensive gardens fed her palace. There were fruit trees as well as herbs and other edible plants. Every morning the gardeners moved through it, filling baskets to be carried to the kitchen yard to join the wagonloads of provisions arriving there. Throughout the day the cooks sent the youngest workers out to fetch another handful of tarragon or one more perfect bunch of grapes to adorn a dish for the royal table, and whenever I had seen them in the distance, I had headed off in a different direction. In my recent rediscovery of the palace I had visited every part of it but had never crossed through the kitchens, sometimes taking long detours to avoid doing so. I had been one among them once when I was a slave. They had been kind to me, but full of my own self-regard, I hadn't appreciated the community they'd offered. Since my return they had sent trays of food up to my room carried by well-behaved servants I didn't recognize, who never looked me in the eye. Did they remember me? Would they remember me and even so bow politely and shoo me back out of some place I no longer belonged? I didn't want to find out but took the queen's directive to heart. There was nothing to be gained by delay. Screwing up my courage, I crossed over my reluctant footprints and headed back toward the palace.

The closer I got to the kitchens, the less ornamental and more practical the plantings became. I walked between lemon trees, standing like soldiers at attention on either side of the path, to a door into the orangerie, where the trees were planted in circles around an open grassy lawn. On the other side of the orangerie was another enclosed garden where the vegetables grew in tidy rows, and waist-high stacks of clay tubes held hives of honeybees. The insects hummed in and out of them as I passed.

Beyond the walled garden was a gate into the paved yard with multiple open doors leading into the soot kitchen, where the roasting was done. I made it as far as one doorway and stopped on the threshold, directly in the way of anyone trying to get in or out—a behavior I despised in others, and yet there I stood, rooted like an inconvenient pillar of salt. At long tables, men and women worked, chopping vegetables, plucking feathers, boning fish, grinding ingredients in mortars. Some of the mortars were stone, but the ones for spices were metal, with a metal pestle that made a constant soft ringing in the background. There were quiet moments in every day, but I had not arrived at one. Woodchoppers and spit boys, roasters and carvers, dishwashers—all were busy. Beyond the bank of roasting ovens, doorways led to passageways that led to more kitchens. There was an entire room for the sauce makers, the boiling kitchen. There was a pastry room and a room where the bread rose and was baked in special ovens. Attolia's palace was nowhere near the size of the emperor's, but more than a hundred were employed in its kitchens—and that didn't include the servants who carried the food up to the tables in the main hall and out to various smaller dining rooms and to me on a tray in my apartments. It was no surprise that one extra boy-at-all-jobs and sandal polisher had not seemed out of place.

No one looked up at me, and at first all the faces were unfamiliar. Some of the ones near to me I began to recognize. Tarra was chopping herbs—I could smell the rosemary. Semiux was boning a lamb, but the ones farther away were indistinct. Someone bumped into me from behind, Zerchus, pushing past with an enormous bowl filled with honeycomb that he thumped down on a table. The honey reminded me of the nutcakes Costis and I had longed for during our days of eating only caggi.

A young woman I didn't recognize bustled up to me, wiping her hands on her apron. "Did you want something?" she asked briskly.

I opened my mouth to ask if they had nutcakes, but in Attolia's kitchens the cooks were notorious for denying sweets to those not in their favor. Straight-faced, they would claim that such treats were unavailable and send petitioners on their way while the kitchen staff laughed behind their hands. I would ask for coffee. There was always coffee—they would grind it and prepare a tray for me, and I would take it back to my room and be done with this unpleasant moment.

"It's Kamet," I heard someone say.

"Kamet!" said Tarra, looking up from her chopping, and then I heard my name repeating across the room. The chatter died down—the only person seated in the kitchen stood up. At one time this would have been Onarkus, head of all the kitchens, but the king had sent Onarkus away, and in his seat was Driumix, promoted to be head of the soot kitchen. With a wave of his hand, Driumix permitted a lull in activity, though of course those stirring pots or turning spits kept at their work.

The woman now in charge of all the kitchens was Brinna from the bakery. I remembered her as every bit as dictatorial as Onarkus had been, and even more likely to fly off the handle, but she leavened her shouting with affection and was much better liked. My name had reached her ear far away by the baking ovens, and she came through the crowd gathering around me like the royal barge displacing smaller, less significant vessels.

"Kamet!" she cried, and opened her arms, but instead of a more enveloping embrace she seized my cheeks between her hands. "A month!" she scolded. "A month you have been here and not come to see us."

"Not a month!" I protested, trying to shake my head, held fast in her grip.

She eyed me sideways.

"I've been busy," I said apologetically.

"Hmpf," she said. "We are not so neglected as we have been by someone else." She spoke like the queen she was. "And we will not treat you as harshly."

"I heard you boxed his ear," I said.

"Ah," she said, unhanding my cheeks and wrapping me in her arms, squeezing hard enough to make my ribs protest. "I would never box the king's ear. I gave it the merest tweak." Then she laughed, her bosom heaving, as she released me.

Brinna's "tweaks" could leave a large man in tears, and her accuracy was unerring. In fact, this would not have been the first time she'd hung the king up by his ear. She'd caught him often enough helping himself to one of the rolls cooling on racks in her kitchen.

"He should have come to talk to us sooner. He wouldn't have eaten so much sand." She nudged me with her elbow and laughed at my amazement. Then she sent everyone back to work and me on my way, after assembling a tray of pastries for me to take. She told me to come back and visit when they were not so busy. "Stop eating alone," she said. "I don't have enough boys to send one up with your dinner every day."

I did try to take the advice hidden behind her complaint. I had a standing invitation to the king's public dinners, and I went to a few. Once I did, I was invited to private dinners by people who thought I might be useful to them. Many of those people were good company. I dined with Relius occasionally, and when he suggested I open a correspondence with Sounis's magus, I did that. I made the acquaintance of various members of the indentured, but my heart wasn't in it.

I poked through the collections in the king's library. The king had offered again to have a copy made of anything I particularly liked, and as good as his word, he had already set a scribe to preparing a copy of the Enoclitus scroll. I put aside a few other scrolls to be copied, but my heart wasn't in that, either. As each day passed, I grew more uncomfortable—I had more and more hours to fill and nothing to do. I hadn't seen Costis since the day we'd arrived. I wouldn't ask about him if he did not wish to contact me first, but my new life had an aching void in it and I was out of the habit of being lonely. Finally, I told Relius I was leaving. I intended to take what coin the king would give me and head north. I asked him for his help to get out of the city without being seen by Melheret's spies.

"Kamet."

The king spoke from behind me, and I dropped my pen. I made a blotch on this account, the one in my description of the cargo on the deck of the *Anet's Dream*, and that is why I had to recopy that entire paragraph.

I stood to face him, apologizing as I did. "I'm sorry," I said. I meant to forgo his hospitality, and I knew that was why he'd come, appearing alone again at twilight in my room. This time I was awake and had the lamps lit, but I still hadn't seen him arrive. He was already seated in Nahuseresh's favorite chair before he said my name.

He waved my apology away. "You wish to leave Attolia. Has someone made you uncomfortable here?"

"Oh, no," I said. "I've been very comfortable, but . . . I cannot make a place for myself because I cannot leave the palace." Not without worrying that one of the emperor's agents, or my master's, might find me.

"You can take the guards outside your door with you."

"That's not . . ." It wasn't what I wanted. What I wanted was to not be cooped up like a chicken, but I could hardly say that to the man who was both responsible for my predicament and far more closely caged himself.

"It's a nice coop," he said. "But it's up to you, of course." Looking down, he toed the carpet with his boot. The silence stretched between us.

"Your Majesty," I said suspiciously, speaking not to His Majesty at all, but to the sandal polisher I knew better.

"Yes?" he said, looking up with his inviting smile, and I knew he had maneuvered me again.

I crossed my arms. "Why don't you tell me your devious plan?" I might have glowered. It was no way to treat the king of the Attolians, but I had not yet made those two images of him align, the work-dodging sandal polisher and the king. I seemed to toggle between one and the other, flipping from deference to overfamiliarity. "You do have one," I said.

"I have a suggestion. That's all," he said. "I did mean it when I apologized for bringing you here. I didn't imagine that you would be comfortable in Attolia, even if as it turns out, most of the court *can* read and write."

I refused to be embarrassed. It was true—the preference for oral recitation did not preclude most of the court from being literate. I had misjudged them. I plead special circumstances.

The king said, "There is a temple in Roa in Magyar where they have discovered a collection of scrolls in their treasury, quite rare ones. They wish to have them recopied. I wonder if you would be willing to take up the task. The Duke of Ferria is already sending scholars, so you would not be the only foreigner in town, and your arrival would be unremarkable."

"And?"

"The temple is on the heights, of course. It overlooks the Ellid Sea. With a good glass, you could see any ships sailing toward Attolia. We have lost many of our observers of late, and we need people we can trust outside our borders. There would be danger. I can't tell you how much or how little. Perhaps you would be safer in Mûr. Perhaps safer in Roa as an unremarkable temple worker."

"It's the least—"

"No." The king was so firm, I stopped.

"You owe me nothing, Kamet. You are a free man. It is I who owe you, and I would only be more indebted if you chose to help Attolia further." He looked at his toes again. "Think about it, will you?" He got up to leave, headed toward the door like any man, but he turned back as he opened it.

"Nahuseresh has retreated again to his family estate. He won't be returning to the capital soon, if at all, and he sold off his possessions before he went. Our agent was able to purchase the dancing girls and Laela together without raising any suspicion. He'll take them to the delta, and they will be freed there."

I swallowed and nodded. I had worried over Laela's fate, fearing for the harm that would come to her when my master learned how he had been betrayed. It may seem foolish to my reader, but I could not entirely forgive her for what she had done. She had meant it for the best, though, and I hated to think she would suffer for it.

"It might not have worked out so well," said the king, and added unnecessarily, "I would have pursued this course anyway."

His plan might have sent Laela to a gruesome death, or me, or Costis, who was his favorite. "Why send Costis?" I asked, still puzzled by that.

"He's honest, not stupid," the king pointed out.

"No, of course not. That's not what I meant."

"You would have eluded a man with twice his cunning," said the king, and that was probably true. "He is in the Gede Valley these last few weeks. I sent him home to his family." He was admitting that he'd left me lonely on purpose. What a piece of work he was. I don't know why I like him as much as I do.

"Your Majesty," I called, and he looked back as he was leaving. "Your youngest attendant needs a better tutor."

"Thank you, Kamet," said the king. "I'll look into it." And then he was gone.

A week later I was on a ship in the harbor, waiting for it to sail. I was headed west, though Roa lay to the east. I would take a long and circular route as far north as Rince in the Gulf of Brael, then south again on the River Naden and over the mountains to Magyar and Roa. We hoped to throw off any pursuit by my master or by the enraged emperor of the Mede. Melheret would have relayed my extraordinary contributions to the Attolian state, and I could count on the emperor to be vengeful indeed.

For the sake of caution, if nothing else, I would not be traveling in style. On the other hand, I had money for the journey and I was quite confident I could manage. I needn't impersonate a free man—I was a free man—and no one was expecting me to be a caravan guard.

I would miss the Attolians. I had taken my leave from various people over the previous days with real regret. Setra had no hold on me, nor did I feel I owed anything to the Medes, but to Attolia I felt a growing attachment. I did not know if I would ever return, but I knew I would feel a tie to Attolia for as long as I lived. I would go to Roa and I would copy scrolls and I would be glad to work in her interest for so long as Eugenides could keep her free. I could have been—almost—grateful for the sense of purpose he had given me.

I missed Costis. I was beginning to believe that what I had thought of as pride all my life was no more than a kind of self-deception, and I wished that I could have apologized to him again for my abuse of his better nature. Almost as if wishing made him seem to appear, I noticed that a man on the dock with a duffel on one shoulder was very like Costis in poise and in gait. The man turned onto the gangplank to board the ship, and my heart lifted, though I tried to squash what I thought was a ridiculous hope. He was almost standing right in front of me before I could be certain it was him.

"Come to see me off?" I asked.

"Come to point out that you are far from plying your trade on a dusty street corner," said Costis.

"So," I conceded. "You were right and I was wrong."

It was so very good to see him again. He asked seriously, "Are you worried by the journey?"

"I am sure I will manage, though I am not used to traveling alone," I admitted.

"Would you like company?"

I didn't think I had heard him correctly. "What of your king? Your position here?"

"It was his suggestion."

Eugenides and his "suggestions."

"He sent me to visit with my family for a few weeks and to say good-bye. I took my sister a wedding present. I am going to look a fool if you say you don't want me along with you, Kamet."

"Gods forbid you should look like a fool, Costis."

"Is that a so then?"

"So it is," I said.

"Immakuk and Ennikar," he said.

"Where?" I snapped my head around to scan the dock, and he nudged me with his elbow.

"Idiot. Us," he said.

"Oh, of course." I was squinting down at the dock nonetheless, but I saw nothing out of the ordinary there.

Dear Relius,

Forgive the briefness of this note. We have arrived as expected and are settling in. Costis acquires a reputation as a naturalist hiking the surrounding hills all day, bringing home grubby specimens to fill the house. I think he's beginning to like them. He has mapped most of the observation points he was looking for.

There are a number of scrolls by Enoclitus here that I have never seen before. I cannot help suspecting the king of knowing about them all along.

To your new student, who I have no doubt opened this private message, my greetings, and you should not have done so. It was very wrong. Be sure you use the smaller brass straightedge—the one that hangs next to the armillary sphere—and press the seams in the paper when you refold it so that they are crisp and Relius will not know right away what you have done.

Kamet e dai Annux

✦ ✦ ✦

ENVOY

Melheret stood at the rail and watched the capital of Attolia disappear behind the bulk of the offshore island that sheltered it. The emperor had recalled his diplomats from Attolia and Melheret was not looking forward to his homecoming.

The imperial fleet should have been moved, no matter how adamantly the emperor's nephew had insisted that his slave could not know its location. Melheret had said as much, as delicately as he could, knowing he risked offending people far more powerful than he was. Ignorant, narrow-minded counselors had disagreed, arguing that the allied navy was too small to be a threat, and the Emperor was nearing the end of any need for secrecy. Melheret had been right, and they had been wrong, and that was far more dangerous to Melheret than the reverse.

His sense of foreboding only increased as his secretary

approached and he held up a hand to caution the man, but it was a hopeless gesture. Ansel blurted out his news for all the sailors around them to hear.

"The figurine of Prokip by Sudesh is gone. Forgive me, Ambassador."

"How?" asked Melheret, surprised by his own calm.

"I did just as you instructed, sir. I checked its case this morning, I locked it, sir, I know I did. I did not take my eyes off it today, I swear, not once did I look away."

"And yet you tell me it is gone."

"I do not know how it could have happened. I just opened the case and found this." He handed over a message with the ambassador's name written on it in the king's hand, familiar to them both.

The ambassador didn't have to open it to know what it held, but he did anyway. It was a thoroughly civil note wishing him a safe journey home and a reminder that he was always welcome to return. An invitation so warm and so damning it would mean his death if the emperor ever heard of it. It wasn't on paper. The king had written on thick parchment, deliberately, the ambassador was sure. It didn't tear easily. He had to wrench it to pieces, growing angrier and angrier with every effort, until he could feel his face suffused with blood and hear himself snarling as he finally gave up and threw all of the pieces over the ship's rail.

Ansel had backed away in alarm. "Forgive me," he said again and again from a safe distance.

"Oh, shut up," said the ambassador wearily. "You're a free man, I can't throw you over the side, too." There was no point in blaming the secretary for the theft. Melheret would have sworn on his life that the figurine had been impossible to steal—locked in a case and the case guarded every minute, but the king of Attolia was still the thief of Eddis.

"You could have waited until I came belowdecks to tell me," said the ambassador. He looked around at the crowded deck where sailors hastily went back to their work and the other passengers went on pretending to watch the slowly receding shore.

It was Melheret's unfortunate task to persuade his emperor that the king of Attolia was a threat. The sinking of the Imperial fleet should have been evidence enough, but Melheret knew that men far more powerful than he were scrambling to convince the emperor that the catastrophe had been an accident, a fluke, entirely unpredictable and no fault of theirs. Certainly it could not be the result of Eugenides's careful plans. The Attolian king's intelligence, his ruthlessness, his cunning were going to be obscured by distance and no matter how much the ambassador tried to convince them that the new king of Attolia was dangerous, the Imperial Court was only going to hear that he was an irresponsible fool who stole the ambassador's statue.

"Never mind," sighed Melheret. "Never mind. Go away."

The servant retired belowdecks to the Ambassador's cabin where he locked the door and opened the case that held the statue of Prokip. It was a lovely thing, the god at once graceful and strong, stern but kind. Even the ragged edge where the hand had been broken off to appease the gods did not really mar its beauty. Ansel opened the porthole. It was a shame, really, but the Attolian king paid well and he was a dangerous man to cross. Ansel dropped the statue into the sea.

A replica of Kamet's map, in his hand, found in the Royal Archives.

SOUNIS

EDDIS

ATTOLIA

LITTLE PENINSULA

MAGYAR

SHALLOW SEA

KIMMER

ELLID SEA

Sukir

Zabrisa

N

HEMS

MIDDLE SEA

MEDE

He

The Three Cities

ANAN

P—

I have received your letter of last month. Your
handwriting has greatly improved. I am sorry
that the archivist would not let you look at the
map of the Empire. I am sure that when your
tutor returns he will allow it. I have made this
map in haste to give to the messenger who leaves
today. I will hope you have already seen a better
one by the time it reaches you.

Yours in Friendship,
—K

BRAEL

EPIDI

PENTS BRAE

GANTS

TERRIAT

SOUTHERN
GANTS

Greater Peninsula

M
E
D
E
S

M
i
d
d
l

This map
of Eddis, Attolia,
and Sounis was
prepared for Her
Highness Gitta
Kingsdaughter by her
tutor, Tykus Namikus,
for her reference while
reading the books of
the Queen's Thief.

Hylas

A N A N

Ananite
Highlands